What people are sayⁱ

The Narrow Wi_{nd}

The shocking rape of a Peace Corps volunteer shatters the precarious balance of American idealism and hypocrisy in 1969 Swaziland, a newly independent country dealing with its own equally fraught postcolonial issues. Full of fascinating characters in exquisitely described exotic locations, where everyone has their own agenda, the new modernity mixes with native customs and spirits, and expats only think they know what's really going on. Above all, Wilson's heartbreaking novel exposes the irony of the USA's continuing desire to benevolently remake the world in one part of the globe while waging war in another and what happens to those trying to make it all work. A tale of identity and the meaning of belonging. The scars we leave behind and the scars we take with us.

Rita Dragonette, author of *The Fourteenth of September*

There is the poetry of quiet to Gary Wilson's storytelling, always there beneath the surface of narration. Quiet masking horror, pain, some manner of fury, longing, the mystery of being. Here, in *The Narrow Window*, that still solitude of a story's telling seems more looming shadow than mask. Quiet frames the most jarring din of a collision in this intersection. This is still the contemporary term for the realm in which the bearers of cultures meet and, if not outright clash, then attempt to take from the other, yes? Quiet before the intersection of characters arriving from disparate realities to a shared land, surrounded by still another country. Humans bearing intents and notions in purposed conflict between themselves. All mutually seeking to take some unspeakable advantage to get somewhere, something, before they indeed collide and all that is left for them is the quiet lingering afterwards.

Bayo Ojikutu, author of *47th Street Black* and *Free Burning*

Wilson's writing is thoughtful, patient, and above all, illuminating. Setting and character converge in highly concentrated light, but it isn't a light by which Wilson forces us to see. Rather, Wilson invites us to consider, in brand-new light, the ways in which humans deal with guilt, integrity, fear, duty. The gaps between these elements widen as we read each sentence and fill themselves in with increasing tension. *The Narrow Window* is a moving work.

Paul Luikart, author of *The Museum of Heartache*

The Narrow Window

A Novel

The Narrow Window

A Novel

Gary D. Wilson

ROUNDFIRE
BOOKS

Winchester, UK
Washington, USA

JOHN HUNT PUBLISHING

First published by Roundfire Books, 2024
Roundfire Books is an imprint of John Hunt Publishing Ltd., No. 3 East St., Alresford,
Hampshire SO24 9EE, UK
office@jhpbooks.com
www.johnhuntpublishing.com
www.roundfire-books.com

For distributor details and how to order please visit the 'Ordering' section on our website.

Text copyright: Gary D. Wilson 2023

ISBN: 978 1 80341 462 1
978 1 80341 463 8 (ebook)
Library of Congress Control Number: 2022923179

A CIP catalogue record for this book is available from the British Library.

Design: Lapiz Digital Services

UK: Printed and bound by CPI Group (UK) Ltd, Croydon, CR0 4YY
Printed in North America by CPI GPS partners

We operate a distinctive and ethical publishing philosophy in
all areas of our business, from our global network of authors to
production and worldwide distribution.

For Modena

1

She had no idea how much time had passed, if any, since they'd gone to sleep, hands held across the hump between the twin beds they'd pushed together to make a double. It was what the government had given them, standard issue for teachers. Not as intimate as they might have liked, but they'd tried to make the best of it. Had earlier that night, in fact, and then drifted off, Brian first, breathing steadily, rhythmically, just short of a snore, like wind playing through the tops of eucalyptus trees; and she had followed quickly behind.

She didn't see or hear anything, only sensed a weight descending on her. *Again?* she wondered. *So soon?* Pinning her down now, rough fingers prying at her legs. Tried to say wait, she wasn't ready yet. Tried to twist free. A lunging, piercing pain. She grabbed his face, no beard.

"BRIAN!"

He sat bolt upright in bed, lunged before he could possibly have seen the figure crouching in the window. Yet he never once seemed to question whether it was the right thing to do or the right direction to move. Never once did he falter or hesitate or turn to seek assurance from her but took one leaping step from the end of the bed, rammed his head into the man's side and wrestled him to the floor, the tang of wood smoke and unwashed flesh, the stench of native beer filling the room.

He forced the man onto his stomach and cocked his arm behind his back. "Light!" he called out, yanking the arm like a pump handle as he stood, the man rising with him, fairly dancing on tiptoe to the wall just inside the bedroom door.

She lit a match. The candle flame flickered, held.

"You know what the fuck's good for you, mister, you'll stay exactly where you are," he said, reaching for the bed behind him.

The man, dressed in a dingy undershirt and baggy blue boxer shorts, flattened himself like a roach against the wall, a single wary eye peering toward the door.

"Don't try it." Brian rested naked against the mattress, reached down for his shoes and socks and said over his shoulder, "He does have balls, you gotta hand him that. I mean, it's one thing to break into a house when nobody's home, but—"

He glanced back at her. She was trembling, tears running down her face. "Hey, it's all right. I don't think he took anything."

Her face quivered.

"Meg?"

His neck bowed as he shot up from the bed.

"Sonuvabitch."

The man ran for the door. Brian caught him, slammed him into the wall. "Sonuvabitch." Pulled him away, slammed him into it again. A hard, brittle crack. The man's eyes rolled up, his knees buckled, he hit the bare cement floor with a smack, a shiny dark trickle of blood on his right temple.

Brian backed stiffly toward Meg, sat, pulled the sheet she was holding like a shield from under her chin and put his arms around her. "I'm sorry. God, I'm sorry."

She laid her head against him and listened to him breathe, closed her eyes and burrowed deep inside him, until the man groaned and Brian stood, slipped on his shorts and dragged him into the hallway. Another moan, a scuffling sound, what must have been Brian going into the spare bedroom, back out, he and the man shuffling, sliding past into the living room.

"Kneel." Brian said. "On your knees. Don't play dumb with me, goddamnit, get down."

They didn't own a gun, but the image of Brian holding one to the man's head execution-style wouldn't go away. She swung her legs over the edge of the bed to go see what was happening, felt her feet touch the cool floor. But that was it. That was as far as she got. When he came back into the room, she was still sitting there, staring first at one foot, then the other, as if trying to decide for certain whose they were.

"All right, that should take care of him for now," he said.

Her head swung in his direction, light, hollow as a dried gourd. "Where is he?"

"Tied up in the living room. Why? You didn't think I'd—"

"No."

"That would be easier, though. I could claim self-defense. Nobody'd argue. And he'd be out of the way then."

"Don't say that."

He walked to the hallway, glanced into the living room, turned back. "What the hell are we going to do with him? How can we get him to the police or get them here? I mean, there's not even a fucking phone around here, nothing."

"What about Joseph?"

"What about him?"

"He has a car."

"It's the middle of the night."

"But didn't he tell us just the other day if we ever needed anything...? Remember? Anything anytime?"

"Okay, maybe so, but that still means one of us'll have to go over there."

"That would be you then."

"I'm not about to leave you here alone."

"I'll be all right, no longer than it'll take you."

He stared past her toward the corner of the room.

"Please, Brian. Somebody has to and there's no way I can talk to them, explain what happened."

"All right. On one condition."

"What?"

He darted out of the room, came back with a butcher knife.

"No," she said.

"Either take it or I don't go."

3

Every house in the compound looked alike, mirror image two-bedroom, salmon-colored stuccos, pale under the full moon. Untreated asbestos roofs, god help them, because exports had fallen and the government had to figure out something to do with the excess supply. A pair of casement windows per room, four rooms total. Five including the bath, she remembered, with panels that swung out like wings on either side.

Joseph and Sarah's house was at the end of the cul-de-sac, not over a hundred feet away, facing west toward them instead of north or south, a turquoise Cortina parked in front. But the car was the only way you could tell it was their house and not someone else's. No numbers or names showed who lived where. The thought snagged her breath. So how had he—?

"Madam?"

She spun toward the door, the knife gripped in both hands.

"You can hear, Madam?"

She tried not to make a sound. No breathing. No swallowing. She would have stopped her heart if she could.

"I thank you too much, Madam. That man kill me. My head it is throbbing and full of noise."

She glared at a speck of food on the knife blade. She couldn't remember what she'd last cut with it. But she would. She had to. If she didn't, she would scream. And she couldn't do that, no.

"I am too sorry, Madam, for what I do. It is a terrible thing. A bad thing. But the spirit... Take off the rope so I must go there. My mother, she is old."

Probably cheese or meat that hadn't washed off. And they'd told her you could never be too careful here. With the water. With food. Everything. Keep it clean. Keep it cool. Keep it locked.

"How! How! I do a bad thing and I am sorry. But I do nothing. The spirit tell me to come here. He tell me that to come here to the Madam and do what I do. So I come and see the Madam and say no, this too bad. This thing too bad. But I am being too frightened by the spirit and he make me to go in the window and look in and see the Madam there. Sleeping. Waiting."

She could no longer feel the knife handle.

"He tell me I must go in. The spirit say she say she wants me to go in and be with her. So I do and I am feeling sorry when Madam open her eyes. She is being a pretty lady. I am too sorry I see her that way. Oh, Madam, please. I beg you."

A rustling now in the living room.

She backed to the wall.

A sliding, hissing sound. "Please."

She braced herself against the rough plaster, held the knife at arm's length like a sword, and turned to glance once more out the window, Brian now at Joseph and Sarah's front door, his bare back a brilliant white spot she was wishing home with all her might.

She heard Brian drag the man back into the living room. Heard him come in and take the knife from her and tell her again how sorry he was, how he should never have left her alone and how terrible Joseph and Sarah felt. She felt nothing. She couldn't speak or scream or cry. She could barely stand.

"Here." He motioned toward the bed and took her elbow to guide her there.

She pulled her arm away.

"Okay," he said, stepping back and going to the bed himself. He sat and patted the space next to him.

They sat in silence, until he said, "They'll probably be here before long. The police. You need to get ready. Do you need any help?"

"No."

"Are you sure?"

"Yes," she said, trying to smile.

He reached toward her face, lowered his hand. "I'll be in the living room. If that's all right. I think somebody—"

5

She nodded and he left. Just like that. Walked to the doorway and was gone. Like a normal person.

She stood. Her knees bent, but she willed herself not to fall. If she did, she would collapse onto the bed like a rag doll and never get up.

One step. Another. She was doing it. A third. A fourth.

She rested against the wall. It was cool, and she stayed close by it for support as she made her way along, careful to avoid the bloodstain where the man's head had hit, a short, dark line with legs. She had taken great pleasure in that, the sound of it, the look of pain on his face.

At the doorway she gathered her robe about her and leaned around to peek into the living room. Brian was at the table, his head outlined against the window, the man tied on the floor beside him. Other than that, it could have been like any other Saturday morning he'd gotten up early to listen to the shortwave or read or split kindling for a breakfast fire.

She lurched across the hall into the bathroom. The door was warped and didn't really latch, so she leaned against it, bumping it, jamming it as tightly closed as she could. The match she struck flared a reflection from the window. She lit the candle on the sill, recoiling from a huge praying mantis that had perched beside a can of Right Guard, its front legs drawn up like hands beneath its elegant, skeletal head. Neither of them moved, she from surprise, the mantis as a way of not calling attention to itself. She'd once watched one take up a position near a propane reading lamp and hold its pose nearly an hour before a large moth flew too close, was singed, and dropped directly in front of the mantis. Like an elegant diner, it carefully inspected its meal, head cocking side to side, before finally dipping to its task, leaving nothing but a set of wings to mark the spot.

The mantis shifted slightly as she soaped a cloth to wash herself. The water was cold—their only choice—the material rough and scratchy. She scrubbed until the insides of her legs stung. She rinsed and scrubbed more. But she knew already it would never be enough. She could scrub down to the bone and still not feel clean. That was one thing he'd taken. That was one thing she could report missing.

The mantis shifted again, almost facing her directly now, and she was suddenly seized with fear.

She yanked on the door. She'd done too good a job jamming it closed, and now it wouldn't open.

That stare, that long uncouth stare, like fingers on her back.

She yanked harder. The door wiggled in its frame but wouldn't budge. She heaved on it with all her might. Still it wouldn't give. She fell sobbing to the floor.

"What's wrong? What's going on in there?"

The door bounced, but she couldn't rouse herself.

"Let me in, Meg."

She scooted away. The door clattered open.

She waved him away as he tried to help her to her feet, and clawed her way up the wall, crying and apologizing for being such a mess. He told her for chrissake not to be ridiculous and led her slowly back to the bedroom, where she asked him to stay while she dressed, but to hold up her robe as a screen and keep his head turned. Which he did, and she again burst into tears. She'd always been proud of how she looked naked—how Brian had smiled at her, eyes dancing in appreciation the first time he'd seen her without clothes—and she had never once felt the need to keep herself covered in his presence, to be worried about what he might think.

Underwear. Blue skirt. Blue blouse. Shoes.

He tossed the robe onto the bed and left, returning with a chair and a book, looking at her the way she imagined he might at a dear old neighbor whose husband had died. He told her she should sit down and try to read a while to take her mind off things. He'd stay if she wanted him to. If not, he was going back to the living room to keep watch and she wasn't to hesitate calling him for any reason at all.

She told him no, to go on, she was okay now, and she picked up the book from the chair but didn't sit or read, staring instead out the open window, a red-and-black *emahiya* cloth curtain hanging motionless on either side, as though it had never been filled by anything but the wind.

Dawn had broken behind Mdzimba Mountain, its mossy, wrinkled hump silhouetted against the sky, its facing slope still cloaked in deep purple shadow, a thin band of fog at its base sliding slowly north ahead of the rising sun, parallel to the asphalt highway that ran between Manzini and Mbabane. There were other roads, of course, connecting to the fertile valleys of the east and the forests and mines of the west and north. But this was the main one that mattered.

At last it came, the high whine of Joseph's Cortina. Almost like a mosquito buzzing at first, followed by the more and more distinct roar of a Land Rover now riding in under it. The sounds dropped as the vehicles slowed for the curve above the river a mile away and accelerated across the bridge and up the short hill on this side. They cruised past the parliament building and the national stadium, and downshifted for the turn onto the market road.

They came bouncing into view, lights jiggling. Up to the top of the road, left a bit, and down into the housing compound, motors unwinding the length of the drive.

Joseph pulled ahead to his usual parking place while the Land Rover, brakes screeching, came to a halt directly in front of their house.

Red dust drifted lazily up and over the constables as they got out, one stocky and round-faced, another tall and boyish-looking in knee socks that were too short, and the driver, older, with bandy legs and a paunch, but clearly in charge.

Brian stepped out to meet them. The driver snapped to attention.

"Sir. Mr.—"

"Bernard."

"Yes. Forgive me, please, Sir, Mr. Bernard. I am Sergeant Gama. And this is Constable Bhembe. Constable Zwane."

Brian bowed slightly to each of them. "Did Mr. Lukhele tell you—"

The sergeant's heels clicked. "Yes, Sir. The man, where is he?"

"Inside."

Motioning to the constables, the sergeant started toward the house. Brian fell in behind them.

"That is the man?" she heard the sergeant ask in the living room.

"Yes."

"Untie him. Take him outside and put him in irons. Wait for me there."

Sergeant Gama then asked Brian to show him the bedroom, where, after tipping his hat to Meg, he spent some time at the window, pulling the curtain back, looking out, looking in, scribbling in a small spiral pad—perhaps noting what looked like a foot scuff on the sill. He stepped off the distance from the window to their bed, gathered up the sheets and Meg's nightshirt—"I am sorry, but it is necessary for the investigation"—tagged them and put them into a canvas bag. He touched the scuff marks on the floor, the bloodstain on the wall.

"There was a struggle?"

Brian nodded.

"With this?" touching his pen to the knife on the bureau.

"No. I gave that to my wife when I went to the neighbors' for help."

She trailed after them and watched from the hallway while the sergeant examined the ropes in the living room, the chair where Brian had sat, the table, the floor. He walked through the kitchen, the bathroom, the spare bedroom. When he had finished, he took one last look around, folded his notebook shut and said they could close up the house now if they wanted to.

Brian asked why, and the sergeant said they could suit themselves, of course, but he always locked his house when he left it.

"We're going somewhere?" Brian said.

The sergeant smiled, confused, as if he hadn't caught a joke. "You must come with me. And the others. To the station in Mbabane."

"Why?"

"For the statement. Each one must write and sign." He smiled again, as if more confident that he'd cleared up the matter.

"Can't we do that here?"

"Oh, no, you must be at the station."

Brian shook his head.

"I am sorry," the sergeant shrugged, "but those are my instructions."

They stood by their front door at the top of the small red-clay apron she and Brian called a yard as they waited for the sergeant to tell them to get into the Land Rover. A small crowd had gathered, as it always did, always does no matter where, when there's police activity. A couple of herd boys looked on with wide eyes and bloated bellies as they drove their cattle toward the mountains to graze. An old woman stopped en route to the market, a massive red mesh bag of oranges balanced on her head. Other teachers from the compound lined the far side of the drive, dressed in bathrobes and pajamas, children's round little faces in the windows behind them, like drawings on paper plates, only black, each framed behind a single pane of glass. Joseph and Sarah watched from in front of their house, Joseph as elegant as ever with his perfectly creased trousers, perfectly rolled shirt sleeves, perfectly held cigarette, Sarah beside him, one hand to her mouth, the other clutching closed the top of her robe. As soon as she saw Meg, she came and stood shoulder to shoulder with her but said nothing. The prisoner, shackled hand and foot, slumped between Bhembe and Zwane. He was still wearing only his underwear and seemed so small and forlorn, so miserable, Meg might actually have felt a twinge of pity had he not raised his head, glared at her and spat on the ground at her feet.

"Put him in the van," Sergeant Gama said, "and this," pointing with the bundle he'd made of the man's clothes, which he must have found somewhere outside the house.

Bhembe and Zwane each took an arm. The man shook them off and thrust his head at Meg.

"Who are you that a man must believe what you say?"

"Take him," the sergeant said.

"No one can believe you. I am Kunene. I am a man." His eyes narrowed. He sneered. "You, you are a whore. A thieving whore who brought me here."

Bhembe and Zwane wrestled him to the back door of the Land Rover and shoved him inside.

"I am Kunene!" the man yelled. "I know the king. I—"

"The gag," Sergeant Gama said. "We must hear no more."

Scuffling sounds, the Land Rover rocking and bouncing. Muffled, incoherent grunts, Sarah squeezing Meg's hand now, saying, "Do not listen. He is a madman."

When the ruckus had quieted, Sergeant Gama approached them. "Aieee! Such a business. But we must go that side now, to the station. Madam and Mr. Bernard may ride in front, if you wish."

"Bu—" Brian began.

"No," Meg said. "Let's just go and get this over with."

The sergeant opened the door of the Land Rover. A heavy metal grate, through which they could talk but nothing could pass, separated the front seat from the passenger compartment, where the two constables and the man named Kunene were seated on benches across from each other. Before getting in, she and Brian said goodbye and thank you again to Joseph and Sarah.

Tears stood in Sarah's eyes as she touched Meg's arm. "Do not forget that we are here."

"It is broken," she heard Sergeant Gama tell Brian from under the raised hood. Bhembe and Zwane were there, too, which had left her alone with the prisoner, so she'd gotten out to stand at the side of the road while they decided what to do.

"But it was not broken when we came to the mountain," the sergeant was saying. "Then pugh, pugh. And it would not go more."

Zwane and Bhembe bent under the hood, flailing their arms in the steam.

"It wishes to have the water," Bhembe said, stepping away.

"What do you know of such things?" Zwane asked.

"My brother drives the bus. It always breaks in the mountains. They must give it the water to go to the top," he said, crossing his arms to lock in his explanation.

"Can't we get a different van?" Brian asked Sergeant Gama, who stood in front of the open door of the Land Rover, POLICE half-obscured behind him.

"Not until the next duty patrol comes to the station house with a new driver."

"How long will that be?"

The sergeant shrugged. "Two hours. Maybe more."

"Can't you radio the station and have them send one before that?"

"Not everyone can drive, Mr. Bernard."

Zwane withdrew from the mouth of the van, shirt soaked, hat cocked to the side of his head. "Bhembe is right. It wishes to have the water."

Sergeant Gama straddled the white stripe at the side of the road, arms locked behind his back, his paunch bulging even further. "They are right. It wants water. I am the driver and I knew always it was so." He held a finger in the air. "We must go back there to the bridge and the water. Zwane, close the bonnet."

It slammed like a gunshot in the still morning air.

"When I give the signal, push. Bhembe there, Zwane there. Mrs. Bernard," stepping back and opening the door for her. "Mr. Bernard."

"I'd like to help," Brian said.

The sergeant thought a moment, nodded, then got in behind the wheel and released the brake. "Now."

The van rocked, hung on the lip of the tarmac, and slipped slowly backward down the mountain, the sergeant staring imperiously forward as the Land Rover weaved across the median line. He finally jerked his arm on the wheel, and the van curled in toward the guardrail.

"The speed!" he yelled. "I must make the speed. Push harder."

They did, and the Land Rover moved off again like a boat being launched onto a quiet lake. Brian stepped up on the front bumper and lay across the hood, staring in at Meg. Gama squinted toward the road, his foot riding the brake pedal, knuckles white from gripping the steering wheel. He drove much more carefully than when the motor was running, she thought, backwards now down the mountain, trees, rocks, ravines, spots of huts, bare red patches of plowed fields slipping silently forward. She closed her eyes until she felt the Land Rover come to rest against the bridge abutment.

Gama set the brake, leaning back and blowing. "So we are here, but the water is still in the river."

Bhembe and Zwane leaned over the bridge railing, clicking their tongues and shaking their heads.

"We need a can or a bottle or something," Brian said, looking toward the roadside.

"There will be nothing," Gama said, head out the window. "People take everything to carry water to the hut."

"Don't you have a cup or bottle in the van?"

"No," Gama said, getting out to join the others.

"A bucket?"

He shook his head.

"Damn."

No one said anything, the constables twisting and turning, looking all around and at each other, perhaps expecting something to appear miraculously in front of them.

Behind her, the prisoner laughed through the gag. She couldn't imagine how, but she'd almost forgotten about him and wondered whether the others had as well. He laughed again and muttered something she didn't understand. Chills ran across her shoulders, her skin prickled.

"Our hats," she heard Bhembe say as she tumbled from the van. "We must use our hats."

She felt like crying. Kissing him and crying, telling him that was the most brilliant thing she'd ever heard.

Bhembe grabbed his hat, flipped it over. "You see. They even have this," tapping the bill, "for pouring the water."

The sergeant held his hand on top of his head. "It is part of the uniform. We may not use them. The captain, he—"

"He'll give you a medal for being so wise," Brian said. "It's a great idea, Constable Bhembe."

"But, Sir," Zwane said to Brian. "What must you give?"

She knew the plan was in jeopardy if he didn't offer something. But it had to be from him and not her, and all she could do was think shoes as hard as she could: Shoes. Shoes.

Which he evidently heard or concluded himself, because when she looked up again, he had them off and was waiting for the sergeant to give orders.

"Zwane will get the water. Bhembe next." They scrambled to the end of the bridge but waited before going down to hear who would pour. "And the teacher," his hand on Brian's shoulder, "will give the van to drink."

"But, Sergeant, you must show me how."

Gama raised the hood, shifting his eyes to the bridge to be certain Zwane and Bhembe were watching, and removed the radiator cap. "This is the place where the water can go. When it is filled, you put the plug in the mouth just so. It is too simple." The sergeant looked at Bhembe and Zwane and walked proudly around to the driver's side. "I must first start the van so the water will go to the stomach."

The motor ground, barely turning over, but soon roared to life. The sergeant bounced to his position in line next to Brian, yelling at Zwane to dip faster and for Bhembe not to spill. He carefully handed the hats and shoes to Brian, calling for more and more. "Hurry. Hurry. The machine has a great thirst."

She heard the sergeant tell Brian that there was a crack in the top radiator hose, but he thought they'd put enough water in they could at least start out. They might even make it up the mountain, for all he knew. It was at least worth a try.

Everyone piled in quickly. Kunene laughed again, and she heard someone smack him and tell him to shut up.

The engine growled and they were off, everyone staying quiet, as if to stave off another breakdown.

The higher they rose, the darker the land grew, pine forests and scrub-filled gullies beside egg-colored outcroppings of

15

granite where the mountain range curved to intersect the highway.

"I think we're going to make it," Brian said, hand squeezing her knee.

As the van topped the last rise, her stomach swelled. In the saucer-shaped valley ahead, it was still dark enough that studs of light formed spokes from the hills to the center of the city, which appeared larger than it was, for it had only fifteen thousand people and a single stoplight and a single police station she had never had reason to visit before.

Hissing like an old steam engine, the Land Rover rolled to a stop in front of a building that looked more like a post office than a police station. Colonial white stucco, with a long veranda bordered by well-trimmed bushes, a few nicely spaced red and yellow flowers, a sidewalk that must have been swept a dozen times a day. In the middle of the veranda a strip of drab green carpeting led to a pair of oak doors, one of which was marked ENTER PLEASE THIS SIDE.

The sergeant pulled the door open and ordered Zwane and Bhembe to take the prisoner in but held his hand up to stop Meg and Brian from entering. After a moment, he bowed slightly toward them and said, "Now you may go."

The station was hot and stuffy and smelled of wax eddies on the floor where a buffer had passed, swirling sunlight so you couldn't see the color beneath.

"For you," the sergeant said to Meg, gesturing toward a nearby row of red plastic chairs held in place by a rod welded to their back legs. When she sat, the whole row shifted, quieted. He next escorted Brian to a counter behind which an officer hunched over a desk, writing, on the wall behind him a photograph of the king posed in a black police uniform with white commander's braid. Similar pictures decorated almost any public place. Same face, same intense gaze and cryptic smile. Only the costume changed. Sergeant Gama spoke to the officer, who at first looked distractedly in their direction, then back at the pad he was writing on. Meg heard her name mentioned, Brian's, Lobamba.

"Sir." The chair snapping backward, the officer catapulting to his feet. He was a giant of a man, barrel-chested, with thick muscular arms and hands, face round and dark, rough from old acne, an upper incisor broken off on the diagonal. "Sergeant Khumalo at your service, Sir."

"Mr. Bernard and Mrs. Bernard are here for the statement," Sergeant Gama said.

"Of course," Khumalo nodded, glancing at Meg.

"Now if you may excuse me," Gama said, with a stiff bow, "I must go. The prisoner is waiting."

"What will you do with him?" Brian asked.

"We must—how do you say?—question him and—"

"I mean will he be locked up?"

Gama turned toward Meg, as if waiting for her to interpret. She raised her brows at Brian.

"Will he be, uh, you know, put away? Behind bars? In jail?"

"Oh, yes, in jail. Just there," pointing down a long corridor.

"Good. As long as he won't be out running around."

"Not to worry, Mr. Bernard. We will keep an eye to him."

"On him."

"As you wish," Gama said, clicking his heels and turning to go.

"Sergeant?" Brian said.

"Yes, Sir."

"I'm sorry. That was rude. Thank you for all you've done."

A brief smile, a salute before he marched off down the hall.

"So," Brian sighed, arms braced against the service counter as he gazed across it at Khumalo. "What about this statement?"

"Yes," the sergeant said. "You must write and sign." He ducked behind the counter and came up with two sets of forms.

Slipping carbon paper under the first and second pages of each, he tapped them lengthwise and on end until everything was aligned. Satisfied, he paperclipped the corners and carried them gingerly, folded bottom to top, around the end of the counter.

"Please to come with me."

"Meg?" Brian said, holding his arm out to her.

She rose, balancing herself.

"If Mrs. Bernard would rather—"

"I'm all right," she said.

He led them to a hall where the doorways of four small evenly spaced rooms faced each other. He ushered Brian into the first one on the right, which contained a single chair, a table, and a bare bulb hanging from a cord above it. The sergeant laid a form and a ballpoint pen on the table.

"Remember to sign and put the date. I will return when you have finished."

He took Meg to the last room on the left, identical to Brian's, except for a window.

"Remember to sign and put—"

"I will."

The sergeant backed away, reaching for the door knob.

"Look," she said. "I don't mean to—It's just—"

"Not to worry." Khumalo smiled and shook his head. "Not to worry."

As soon as he left, she sat down, stood. Her back was to the window. That would never do. She moved the chair to the end of the table, listened to African jazz on a faraway transistor radio, the squeal of a saxophone weaving between drums and voices. Someone switched the radio off, and it seemed suddenly too quiet. A constable hurried down the hall. Zwane, maybe, Bhembe, she couldn't be sure. A Land Rover started, drove past the window.

The form. The pen beside it on the table. It was like a test. She'd always been good at tests. Only this was different. A test you could fail and it wouldn't matter. Not in the long run anyway. But this she needed to get right. And in her head it was, where she could let it float around as amorphous as it needed to be. To write it, though, meant she had to bring it out, make it make sense, put it together one piece at a time, like a puzzle without a picture to go by. Would her story in any way resemble Brian's? There were things she needed to ask him about, to make sure she was remembering them the way they were—or was that even possible? What was he writing now, this very moment? Was it about her? What was he thinking, even if he wasn't writing it?

She had to start. The sergeant was waiting.

She leaned forward: "At approximately four o'clock the morning of March 20th, I was awakened by…" She scratched that out, started over: "About four o'clock this morning (March 20th), I woke up to the sound…" No. Sight? Sensation? What? "Sometime this morning (March 20th)—it was still dark so I didn't know the exact hour and only later figured out it must have been around four—I felt a man on me and screamed my husband's name. I sat up in bed and…"

"Bloody awful business, this," a doctor named Martin said, releasing the bulb that hung above the table where she lay, the same one where she'd written her statement. Dated it. Signed it. Turned it in. The bulb swung in a slow, steady arc. Back and forth, back and forth. "Just bloody awful."

He had decided to perform the medical examination at the station instead of the hospital, as was customary. She'd been through enough already, she'd heard him tell the sergeant in the hall. No need to heighten her anxiety.

"If I had anything to do with it," he'd gone on, a bit too loudly, perhaps for her benefit, "we could dispense with this nonsense right now and hang the bloody bastard on her word alone. But that would never do, would it? This is a free country now, isn't it, and we have to at least go through the motions. Innocent until proven guilty and all that rubbish. So we might as well get on with it."

Linens had been brought, the table swabbed with alcohol, a sheet spread over it, another left on top for her to cover up with.

"What about the window?" she'd asked.

"Of course," the doctor had said. "How thoughtless of me." He'd fetched a blanket, draped it over the opening and gone back out. She'd undressed and gotten situated. When he'd returned, he asked if she wanted someone else in the room. The only person she could think of was Brian, but there didn't seem to be any reason to put him through that too, so she'd said no, just go ahead.

Under closed eyelids, the white chalk line of light from the bulb faded slowly away, and she could hear the doctor scuffling about, his bag opening, things clinking.

He folded the sheet back to mid-thigh, moved the chair around to the end of the table and sat. "Can we scoot down this way a bit? That's right, very good. Time to see what we have here. Lift your knees now and spread."

She dug her fingernails into the underside of the table, caught the tarnished flash of an instrument across the ceiling, felt the probe going inside, moving vaguely around, tugging, twisting. Sweat ran down the side of her face. Her neck and arms ached. The doctor held up a long cotton swab, as if sighting her over the end of it, inserted it, smeared the tip on a culture dish, which he immediately covered and put into his bag. He then took what appeared to be a small spatula, slid it in, turned it, removed it and scraped whatever he'd found onto a microscope slide, which he again covered and put into his bag.

"That's about it," he said, pulling the sheet down and patting her shin like a horse's neck. "Except I would like to ask what happened to your legs."

"My legs?"

"The marks. The redness on the insides of the thighs. Was that from—?"

"No. I did that."

"May I ask how?"

"With a washcloth. Scrubbing."

"I see." He rummaged through his bag. "In that case, you might want to try this salve. I carry it as a matter of course, since you can never predict what someone's going to come down with here. Which reminds me, it's too soon for me to administer a pregnancy test. As a young married woman, I assume you practice some form of birth control."

"I'm on the pill."

"Wonderful. Perfect. But remember they aren't—what I mean is that there are cases—"

"I know."

"So keep track, and if you miss your period, we can do a test and go from there." He paused, gloved hand to his cheek. "For the rest, I suggest you take these," reaching into his bag. "Valium. No need to be frightened of them. Particularly if you use them only as necessary. And I guarantee you'll know quite well when that is. I also want you to take one of these three times a day for the next week or so, until you run out. It's a general antibiotic, purely precautionary, you understand. But better to be safe than sorry. So." He packed his bag and walked to the door. "I'll be in touch soon with the results of the tests, but if you have any questions before that, feel free to ring me up, for any reason. My number's on the bottle." He turned the door handle. "Oh, and it's okay to have sex again, whenever you feel like it."

A reflected wafer of light from a ceiling lamp rippled over the uneven tiles of the hallway in front of them, staying just ahead of their feet until they stepped through it and into the stifling heat of the lobby.

21

Sergeant Khumalo slumped against the counter, fingernails white against the pencil he held above the form he was filling out.

"Aiee!" shoving himself back from the desk. "So many papers. I can never finish. They are here when I go to my home, here when I return. Will you have tea, Mr. Bernard?"

He glanced at Meg, who nodded. "Yes, that would be nice."

The sergeant served them from a tray on the countertop. The tea was strong and dark, a trail of steam rising from each cup.

"How many lumps?"

"None," Brian said. "For either of us."

"Cream then?"

"No thank you."

"Nothing?"

"That's right."

"I have heard this about Americans. Is it so for everyone there?"

"No, not everyone. But many," Brian said.

"I have heard you have many strange customs there."

"I'm sure it seems that way."

"Your tea, Madam, Mr. Bernard. A biscuit perhaps?"

"Please."

The sergeant passed the plate. They each took one. He seemed relieved. They took another. He smiled.

They drank and ate, and when they'd finished, they thanked the sergeant and said if there was nothing more, they'd be on their way.

He set down his cup. "I am sorry to say so, but two last things before you go. The first," one meaty index finger pressing his palm, "a person from the Ministry of Justice will come to you to talk about... what has happened. It is for the trial. They said I must tell you. They gave me this telephone number." He slid an index card toward Brian. "And two, the prisoner. You must identify him."

"We already did," Brian said.

"But it must be done here as well. Each one who signs the statement." He fingered a gouge in the countertop. "I am sorry, but those are my instructions."

"Well, I'm sorry, too," Brian said. "Because there's no way that's going to happen. Goodbye."

The sergeant spread his hands and shook his head.

"Look, damnit. Look at her and tell me you can make her go see him."

"I am sorry for what has happened and do not wish to make more trouble, but my instructions are set." He wiped his face with a wrinkled handkerchief and glanced to each side. "Perhaps there is something. Once in a strange place my mother was in need of help and someone came. I will never forget that man. Perhaps I can do for you what he did for my mother and you will not forget. You were there, you saw him?"

"Of course I did."

"Then perhaps you can do for both."

"And that'd be all?" Brian said. "Nothing else?"

"No, nothing."

"All right. Show me where he is."

A thin cloud of smoke hung over the hillside below the police station. Through the open window, she could faintly hear people up and about, washing, cooking, laughing, calling to each other, dogs barking, children crying, fires snapping against a backdrop of bright swatches of African cloth coming together like runs of color through the deep green trees.

The scene was so peaceful and reassuring she could have stayed there forever had Brian not told her he was finished, they could leave now.

Sergeant Khumalo, back behind his counter, raised his hand in farewell.

They walked down the hill, across the stream at the bottom, up toward the main street of the city, pausing at the intersection with the lone stoplight, which cycled red, amber, green before they moved on past a row of shops, all stucco and painted white, green, salmon or beige. She gazed into each window as they went by—glimmering pyramids of canned goods in the grocer's, racks of brown-crusted bread at the bakery, a half-dressed manikin standing amid arms and legs and faceless heads in the dry goods store, transparent images of her and Brian against the drawn shades of the chemist's.

"Something to eat?" he asked.

"I don't care."

"Probably be good for you. Us."

"Fine."

"The Londoner all right?"

She screwed up her face.

"I know it's dirty, but it's likely the only place open except for the market, and I don't think you're up for a bunch of gawking right now."

They walked a half-block back in the direction they'd come, turned down a short mall, across an alley and through the open sliding glass doors of the restaurant. A handful of African laborers and shop assistants chatted quietly at tables in the rear. Two men who might have been bank clerks or government workers read newspapers in a booth near the entrance. The owner, hips and legs overlapping a plastic chair at the end of the serving counter, blue dress streaked with sweat, held a lace handkerchief to her head as she took aim at a swarm of flies that had flown within reach. A quick snap of the swatter and they fell dead on the floor at her feet, among dozens of others. Meg's stomach turned. The woman smiled benignly and asked what they would like. Brian ordered eggs and toast, Meg milk from a carton.

They ate and drank in silence, until the two men in the next booth folded their newspapers and left. She watched them walk back through the mall and out of sight.

"Tomorrow," she said.

He tipped his head, as if waiting for her to continue.

"They'll be in here tomorrow, those two men. It'll be in the papers by then, and they'll be reading about it."

"Maybe."

"And it'll be on the radio."

"I seriously doubt it," he said. "But even if it is, it'll probably be something really obscure about a breaking and entering. They might mention an assault. But I don't think they'd say anything about... I don't think they'd use the actual word."

"Why?

"For one thing, it doesn't seem customary here to name names or the details of a crime. And if it's not customary, well... And besides that, we're in a sort of special situation. The country's been independent less than a year, and they've invited us to come and help beef up the education system. The government won't want the embarrassment if something like this gets broadcast, and Peace Corps doesn't want the bad PR. They don't even want us to say we're volunteers, remember, because they're afraid people will think we're spies like they do in other countries. So I think you're more worried than you need to be."

"But people will find out anyway, Brian. People at Lobamba already know, and they talk. They'll hear about it from each other. They don't have to read about it or hear it on the radio."

She sipped her milk. He poked at his eggs.

"Okay, let's say you're right," Brian said, "and you probably are—what do you think people are going to think or say?"

"That I made it all up. That nothing really happened."

25

"For god's sake, Meg."

"And that it was my fault."

WHAP. Another half-dozen flies dropped to the floor.

"People are already embarrassed, Meg. Don't you see that? Sarah, Sergeant Khumalo? Embarrassed as hell. I can guarantee you that they're a lot more afraid of what you're thinking about them."

"I want to go home."

He smiled, as though relieved that was all she'd been leading up to. "Great. We can catch a bus just as soon as we're finished here."

"No, I mean home."

"To the States?"

WHAP. The flyswatter smacked the side of the glass display case. Flies looped away from the blow, resettled as the old woman eased back in her chair with a sigh.

"I don't see how we can do that," Brian said. "For one thing we just got here."

"Not really." She blinked furiously, not wanting to let him see her cry. "It's been a year."

"We have an obligation."

"To hell with that."

He stood to scoot around beside her.

She raised her hand to stop him.

"I know you're upset, but we at least need to fight fair."

"Fair?" She almost laughed, glancing from him to the old woman, swatter twitching on her lap like a cat's tail. "Tell me what's been fair about any of this."

In the silence, the morning sun glared from the white wall across the alley.

"Okay," he said finally. "Maybe nothing has been, or ever will be, but the thing is, the point I'm trying to make is... Maybe point's a bad word, I don't know, because I'm not really trying to make a point. I'm trying to express a... concern maybe. And it's not just about our obligation. It's about you. And me. Us. Because I don't think it would be the healthiest thing to do—to up and leave right now. Before we've had a chance to try to work through this thing first. Otherwise it's just running away. And there might not be any end to that once we start. Okay? And the second thing is this: a man's in jail because of something we said he did. And he did do it, all right. But if he's going to get the punishment he has coming, I think we have to stay at least long enough to see this through a trial."

"And if we don't?"

"I'm not sure, but maybe Kunene could just walk away then. Like in traffic court if the cop who stopped you doesn't show up? And I for one don't want to take that chance. And don't forget the other thing if we go back to the States now."

She studied the black fleck pattern in the floor tiles. "You mean the draft?"

They both turned toward the old woman, who shifted in her chair and flipped the swatter: WHAP. Quickly again: WHAPWHAP. Grinning first at him, then at Meg, then down at what must have been a record kill.

2

"Mr. Philips? MR. PHILIPS?"

"Elizabeth?"

"Yes," her face peeking around the doorway to his room.

"What is it?"

"There is someone—"

"Come closer. I can't hear you."

"But, Sir—"

"Sorry," pulling the sheet over himself. He rarely slept in more than an old pair of gym shorts and often not even that.

She walked toward him, head bowed, hands folded in front of her. He should be happy, he supposed, that she wasn't crawling on hands and knees. But he was going to have to remind her again the differences between courtesy and submissiveness and that he didn't expect her to act like a servant or his daughter. She was a guest in his house who in turn worked for her keep. That was their agreement. Nothing more.

"Now," he said, "tell me what you want."

"It is not me. It is someone else. Wanting you, Sir."

He smiled at the irony of what she'd said as he squinted at the window. Daylight, but it hadn't been for long.

"On the telephone," she said.

"Who is it?"

"He did not say, Sir."

"What time is it?"

She pursed her lips. "I cannot say that either, Sir."

"What can you say, Elizabeth?"

"I can say good morning, Sir," eyes still to the floor, but at least a hint of playfulness in her voice.

"All right, all right. I surrender. Good morning to you, too, Elizabeth. Tell the caller I'll be right there."

She scurried out as he threw back the sheet.

"And Elizabeth—"

"Yes, Sir?" her voice echoing from the hallway.

"Some coffee, please. With toast."

"And jam, Sir?"

"And jam."

She had appeared on his doorstep six weeks ago, dressed in a traditional female student's long-sleeved white blouse, straight black knee-length skirt, and in her case, shoes—black rubber-soled, boxy oxfords that probably stood up well to all the walking she did. She'd carried a small suitcase in one hand and a letter in the other from Phineas Nkhosi, chief of a village east of Mbabane, reminding him that he had once successfully helped Nkhosi with a legal matter, for which the chief was eternally grateful, and going on to say that he hoped he wouldn't be imposing too much on their friendship by taking the opportunity to introduce the young woman before him as Elizabeth Shongwe, daughter of Elias Shongwe, a village shop owner. She had come to the city to finish secondary school and prepare for her A-level exams. As she had no relatives here, Chief Nkhosi wanted to know whether Harry Philips might not take Elizabeth on as a house girl. She came from a good family, the letter said. She was energetic and well-behaved, and was a good worker who could clean, cook, shop and do laundry. In return, he could provide her room and board, books, a clothing allowance and a small amount of walk around money. Did he think such an arrangement might be possible? If so, the chief would be even more indebted to him and would hope to return the favor soon. And since, in such cases, there was no room for refusal without being rude, he'd had little choice but to ask her in.

After initial unease on both their parts, they'd soon begun talking about what she would do and the manner in which she would go about it and how they would relate to each other, since he'd never been involved in such an arrangement and wasn't sure he was going to like it. But she was so responsive and good-humored that before long he found himself thinking *what the hell*, with Carolyn gone eight months now and him living alone in a large though not opulent house in a country where solitary existence was considered antisocial at best, it would not only give a better appearance but might actually be nice personally for him to have some company, especially company as becoming as Elizabeth—tall and slender, with delicate hands, tea-colored skin and a bright, open face—so he showed her to the back bedroom, which still had several boxes of Carolyn's odds and ends stacked against one wall. He told her to use what she wanted from them and to put the rest in the hallway, and he left her to unpack and settle in.

That evening she'd cooked mealie-meal porridge. The next chicken curry. The third some rice dish he couldn't identify, which was probably just as well. The following day he bought the ingredients for meatloaf and boiled potatoes and showed her how to use a recipe. Then they planned menus for the rest of the week and went over what she would need from the market each day to keep dinner on the table and the house tidied, and soon the relationship was going far more smoothly than he had imagined it would.

Except for coffee. She could measure grounds perfectly, have the water just the right temperature, and still produce coffee strong and bitter enough it was undrinkable. All because of brewing time. How long five minutes seemed, even with a timer, and why it made a difference. Regardless, he still liked the smell of fresh coffee as he walked down the hallway to the kitchen, liked holding a warm cup between his hands in the morning. The ritual of it. The sense of necessity and continuity. Carolyn had made perfect coffee.

He took the cup Elizabeth offered him, thanked her, and picked up the telephone receiver from the counter.

"Harry Philips here."

"Good day, Mr. Philips."

Gideon Dlamini. He glanced at the kitchen clock. Ten to seven. What the hell.

"Sorry to be a bother, Mr. Philips, but there is something of concern I need to discuss with you."

"Right now?"

"Oh, no, not on the telephone. In private. At my office."

"It's Saturday, Gideon." He smiled at the wince he knew had just swept Dlamini's face upon hearing a subordinate use his given name.

"Yes, of course, but I believe you will not mind making an exception in this case. When may I expect you?"

A half-hour later he backed his battered VW bus out of his driveway and drove down the hill toward town, a rust-colored plume of dust drifting slowly over roadside trees and grass behind him. He should have walked. It was just over a mile to the office and would have worked off the irritation he felt at being called in on a weekend. One of the real perks that came with his job was that at 4:30 Friday afternoon, the week was finished, period, one of the rare attitudes carried over from colonial days that he thought worth maintaining. Besides, walking would also mean he would get there later and Dlamini would have to wait longer, although he couldn't afford to annoy the man indiscriminately. If he wanted to keep his job, which for the time being he did. It was what he'd opted for, after all, the night Carolyn had said she was leaving. Her father's heart condition was getting worse and she couldn't ignore it any longer. She hoped he was coming with her—or would join her soon after. He told her a problem like her father's could go on forever, and he couldn't afford to be away that long. Afford in what way, she wanted to know? Was he willing to afford losing her instead? At which point she had wept so bitterly that tears streamed down her face, her neck, into the cleft between her breasts. He'd felt helpless and vaguely guilty at having upset her and finally found a box of tissues which he slid toward her and said "here" but nothing more. No, something else had driven her to leave. Her father was only an excuse. Had she gradually come to suffer from sickness of place after all? Or homesickness, sickness of heart, of soul, sickness of him? He honestly hadn't seen it coming, but probably should have. When they'd first come here, he'd said they would stay five years, she'd reminded him, and now they were approaching twice that. With his most recent promotion in the Public Prosecutor's Office, she wondered aloud if he had any intention of ever going back, an idea that she found completely unacceptable.

He drove past several women with baskets or bundles on their heads, a boy rolling an iron rim with a stick, an old man pulling a wagon with wattle sides—all on their way to market. Normally, that's where he would be, zigzagging between cars parked wherever there was space, empty buses next to them still leaning from their loads, trucks lumbering in and out, emptying their beds of hitchhikers to join the streams of people flowing up and down among rows of bread, fruit and vegetable vendors, mat makers spinning sisal, sculptors carving wood and soapstone, old women squatting beside pots of mealie-meal porridge and *tjwala*, or tending spits with young pigs, goats or chickens roasting over low fires to be sold one slice at a time. Roughly half the crowd flowed down on one side of a middle aisle, half up on the other, like countercurrents, someone occasionally stopping to buy something, the pressure building behind until bodies broke around the obstacle, momentarily intertwining with those from the opposite direction, regrouping, moving on, a single cacophonous but friendly voice greeting, laughing, bargaining over every purchase, down to a single orange worth a few pennies, anyone paying full price being branded a tourist or *mungulu*, stupid. He knew of no other place remotely like it. Carolyn had loved it as well and had spent full days there, drawing, chatting, basking in the scene. She had called it her muse.

The Ministry of Justice, a beige frame and stucco building with a terracotta tile roof, had once housed the Hotel Blanchard. The façade, lobby and gardens had been retained during the conversion, along with a bank of creaking, grinding elevators, one of which Harry Philips rode to the third floor. The heavy mahogany door to Dlamini's office stood slightly ajar and he pushed it open into a space that occupied at least three former rooms and had a private bath. Dlamini sat behind a massive, carved desk, the windows to either side offering commanding views of the city and the mountains beyond.

"Ah, yes, Mr. Philips," Dlamini said, rising, taking in the sockless tennis shoes, khakis, T-shirt and unshaved face. "I trust this hasn't been too much of an imposition." He gestured toward a chair. "Tea?"

"Sure, I guess so."

Dlamini was at least a half-foot shorter than Harry Philips, more slender and handsome, almost to the point of prettiness, with graceful nose and mouth, a pianist's hands, and the same confident air and enigmatic smile the king, his father, had in the photograph hanging to the right of the country's flag in the corner behind him. He was one of many children from many wives but, according to what Harry Philips had heard, he had been earmarked early on as brighter than most so had attended university and studied law in Great Britain. He returned home to work as an assistant to his father's chief adviser prior to independence and in the Ministry of Justice afterward. Within the past year, he had been appointed to the position of Minister of Justice, and, as Harry Philips' immediate superior, was responsible for his promotion or firing, consequently becoming, in Carolyn's mind, the person largely to blame for their separation. She called him The Weasel, but Harry Philips thought of him more as a royal peacock willing to do anything necessary to preserve the monarchy.

Dlamini handed a cup of tea across the desk. "I am sure you are curious, Mr. Philips, as to why I asked you here."

"You could say that."

Dlamini drummed his fingers a moment before raising his eyes to Harry Philips. "Early this morning, I received a telephone call from the Mbabane Police Station. They were reporting an incident that occurred last night at Lobamba which they thought I should be aware of. Immediately, of course."

"Well, Lobamba is Lobamba," Harry Philips said.

Dlamini nodded. "The incident occurred at the school— the secondary school—which, as you know, is not considered ordinary."

Lobamba National Junior Secondary School, as it was formally called, was founded as a pet project of the king's. He intended it to be a symbol of national pride, a prime example of what post-colonial Swaziland could achieve. He directed that a new building be erected, outfitted with a library and toilet blocks with running water. Classes were to be filled with handpicked students, including many members of the royal family. Everything seemed in place for the king's dream to be realized.

Harry Philips had never heard exactly what had happened, but from the beginning students at the school didn't perform as expected. With the new teachers' college at the national university unable to train enough Swazi nationals as teachers to fill the demand, the situation at Lobamba became bad enough, he'd heard, that the king swallowed his pride, fired the headmaster and teaching staff, and brought in outsiders, including teachers from the Republic—Zulus, no less—and two young white Americans who were among the first cohort of Peace Corps volunteers in the country.

An uproar ensued. People picketed the Ministry of Education. A man was jailed for calling the king a baboon. But eventually calm returned and with it higher morale and enthusiasm among the school's students and staff. Within a year and a half exam scores had risen dramatically and everyone, from the king and the Minister of Education on down, was ecstatic.

"What kind of incident?" Harry Philips asked.

"I have not read the full police report and am relating to you only what I was told, but as I understand it, last night—deep into the night—a man crept into the Americans' home on the teachers' compound and attacked the woman as she slept."

"What do you mean 'attacked'?"

The prince picked up his teacup, set it back down.

"Did he rape her?"

"Yes."

"Shit."

"Fortunately, the woman's husband caught the attacker before he could escape."

"Where is he now?"

"In jail," Dlamini said. "At the Mbabane Station."

"And the woman? Is she all right?"

"I believe she is, or I would have been informed."

"That's good. And her husband?"

"I believe he was unharmed as well."

"Also good."

"Yes." Dlamini held his cup in both hands. "I was wondering, Mr. Philips, if you happen to know either of them."

"No. I've only heard about them."

"I see. So you have no idea how they might—"

"React?"

"Yes."

"Not really, but I'm sure they're plenty pissed."

Dlamini's eyebrows pinched.

"Angry."

"And justifiably so." The prince laid his right index finger to his lips, tapped twice and folded it back into his palm. "I doubt as well that you would care to speculate how this might affect their work or their feeling toward the country—toward Swaziland."

The chair creaked as Harry Philips shifted his weight. "I have no idea, but at least the case itself seems fairly straightforward, which should help."

"If that were only the case, Mr. Philips. First, the teachers are Americans."

"In case you're worried the embassy will get involved, don't be. They'll see this as coming under Swazi jurisdiction."

"And they are volunteers."

"But I'm guessing Peace Corps'll stay out of things, too, as long as everybody's okay. They're pretty strict about not messing around in a country's internal affairs."

"There is one other complication," Dlamini said, "and that is that the woman is white, and the assailant is African. Even though I have not made a thorough search of the matter, just now I cannot recall a single other case like this. Can you?"

"Not since I've been here anyway. Nothing that got talked or written about anyway."

Dlamini rose. "I find the whole situation rather strange. Troubling." He walked to the bookshelves, ran his fingers over several dark volumes, like a blind man browsing. "For instance, if the assailant were only seeking sexual satisfaction—"

"He could have gone somewhere else?" Harry Philips said.

"Exactly."

"And maybe found an African woman to rape?"

"I see no reason for sarcasm, Mr. Philips. The issue is that, as distasteful as what you suggest is, it would have been far more predictable, would it not, more unfortunately common? But he did not seek out an African woman. Instead he ended up at Lobamba with someone who is not only white and American but—What was he doing there, Mr. Philips? What was he thinking?"

"Maybe nothing. I mean, maybe he was just a dumb son of a bitch who couldn't keep his pants on."

"Perhaps. But do you believe that there was nothing more to it than that?" Dlamini returned to his chair and reached for the teapot. "I can only speculate, of course. Raise questions. For instance, I am curious to know whether this Kunene fellow— Solomon Kunene, according to the police report—whether he acted on his own or was under the direction of someone else."

"Like who?"

"Piet Giesen, or someone else in that apartheid-loving crowd."

Harry Philips sat up straighter, leaned forward.

"They could wreak all manner of havoc with a story like this," Dlamini went on.

"You mean use it to wreck the Multiracial State conference this fall? Something like that?"

"Yes."

"Wow. I don't know. What you're telling me is that they plotted this—a crime against an innocent person—to smear the king."

"Perhaps, yes, particularly since the king is such a strong supporter of multiracialism."

"That just blows my fucking mind."

Dlamini's face twitched.

"Sorry."

"No, I agree that it does, if I understand the phrase correctly." Dlamini took a sip of warm tea. "Neither the king nor I wish to appear paranoid, but as you are aware, he reigns through a rather delicate balance of power between him and his people, him and the queen mother, him and the ancestors. It is the way we have followed from the beginning of our time as a people, and the king takes quite seriously his role as their leader.

He is a monarch and all decisions made come from him. All decrees and directives are his. His people believe in him and his strength. It is he, after all, who brings the rains, eh? Any hint of weakness from him—politically, spiritually, economically—and things could get out of hand. I don't have to tell you, I am sure, Mr. Philips, that there are forces afoot who would love to see him stumble—even to fall. Not only your Mr. Giesen, but liberals, conservatives, communists, unionists, and perhaps even some within the royal clan itself. He feels that he cannot be too watchful." The prince smiled, leaned back and spread his arms, palms up, as though measuring the immeasurable. "I am sorry for rambling, but I wanted to be certain you grasped what could be at stake."

"Oh I do. I get it."

"Good, because I spoke with the king before you arrived, and he—and I—would like to know if anything beyond the obvious is involved in this case. And we—the king and I—would like for you to be in charge of finding that out for us."

"Why me?"

Dlamini glanced at the portrait of his father across the room. "We thought that you might be able to bring a unique, what should we call it, perspective to the matter?"

"Meaning I'm white and American?"

"That played a role in our decision, yes. We felt that you might perhaps be able to speak with Mr. and Mrs. Bernard more effectively—as one of their own—about the nature of the case as it proceeds and what they might expect within our judicial system. Without knowing for certain, I suspect it is substantially different from what they might encounter in America."

"Different enough," Harry Philips said. "And I understand that. The interpretation thing. But why put me in charge of the overall investigation, when you have a whole department of more experienced people to handle that?"

Dlamini stood and stretched himself to his fullest height, chest out, which still left him looking boyish. "Because, as odd as it may sound, Mr. Philips, we trust you."

The muffled clatter of a passing diesel truck ran through the room. In the silence that followed, Harry Philips looked up and said, "I see."

"I believe you do." Dlamini walked to the window, hands folded behind his back, and stared out at the low mountains to the west. "And I believe you also understand that your investigation must include the American couple. And once you finish with them, we will expect the same diligence elsewhere. You must look under every rock, every blade of grass. Because I would vastly prefer, if we do err, that it be on the side of thoroughness rather than negligence."

Dlamini's pep talk made him smile, which he quickly checked with the swipe of a hand over his mouth. "So am I supposed to report back to you?"

"I would think so, yes. That way if anything of interest comes up, I can pass it along to the king." Dlamini rose on tiptoe, lowered himself and cleared his throat. "I should add that I will see to it that officials at the embassy and the Peace Corps office here are informed of what has happened. I believe they will be relieved as well that one of their own will be working with the victims of this egregious crime."

Harry Philips slid to the front of his chair, as if to stand, but froze in place when he saw a frown flicker across Dlamini's face. It was the height of rudeness for him to presume that he could even think of leaving the presence of a superior before he was dismissed. "So, if you think it's a good idea, I can get started on this by dropping by the stationhouse on my way home."

"Yes," Dlamini said, "an excellent place to begin. But there is one other small favor I would ask of you before you leave, Mr. Philips."

"Sure, what's that?"

"The king would appreciate your using the utmost discretion as you proceed. I trust that you will."

As he backed out of the parking space, he could see Dlamini at the window, chin up, chest out, hands behind his back. The last thing he needed was more work to do, especially something as unsure as this, which could turn out to be nothing more than it seemed or could end up all over the place. But what choice did he have? Saying no to his boss was one thing—he'd done that often enough—but this was the king asking, for all intents and purposes. You don't say no to the king, or you might find yourself at the airport buying a ticket for the next flight out of the country. And besides, he kind of liked the old guy. He'd seen him several times at state occasions and had once had a private audience with him to explain a legal matter. He was gracious, handsome in an elfin way, and articulate—even more so than his son, in whom he must have seen a younger version of himself—and he was revered as the man who had more or less single-handedly led his people to independence. Since then, he had stabilized the country politically and economically. He had won back much of the African native land occupied by whites after ill-advised concessions one of his ancestors had granted three-quarters of a century earlier. And he truly had thumbed his nose at the Republic of South Africa by establishing a multiracial state on its very doorstep.

Even given all that, however, one prickly issue remained, an issue he was sure the prince shared with his father, and that was the establishment of a constitutional monarchy patterned on Great Britain's. The king and his counselors had agreed to the idea as a critical step toward independence, but Harry Philips wasn't convinced that everyone in power truly believed in the arrangement. Lip service was paid, yes, but commitment? What he saw instead in subtle and not so subtle ways was that the power of the monarchy was far more important than the constitution. Nothing, as the prince said earlier, should interfere with the king's authority.

So what the hell, he goes to the station, reads what reports and statements he can, relays any pertinent information to Dlamini and still has the afternoon to himself. Not so bad and lots less trouble than not doing it.

As for investigating the Americans, that was almost too easy, unless there was something off about them, some psychological malfunction with either or both that had eluded attention. But he doubted that was the case. The Peace Corps thoroughly vetted anyone applying to serve—and he could have told Dlamini as much in his office but didn't dare on the chance of sounding like he wasn't taking the assignment seriously enough. What he assumed was that they were youngish—probably mid-twenties, give or take—childless, since he hadn't heard anything about kids. Chances were, they had found themselves between degrees or jobs and had decided that this was their chance to get out and see the world—not on a lark like some of their friends, going off to Europe to camp and hike or to the Himalayas to smoke up and seek wisdom—but to go somewhere and live and work there and learn something about the place and maybe even themselves. Unfortunately, what they were going through now might be more of a test than they'd bargained for. Would have been for him and Carolyn. It hadn't taken anything nearly as traumatic to send her packing.

He pulled out of the parking lot and onto the main road, turned left by the market, and started down the hill toward the police station.

And of course there was that godforsaken war, nobody could forget that. Everybody seemed edgy about it and what it meant. From what he'd heard and read, most current Peace Corps volunteers—men especially—considered the Peace Corps as exactly that, a peaceful alternative to near certain death. And the rest of the US was a mess, too, with protests and shootings. John

Kennedy, Robert Kennedy, Martin Luther King Jr., Malcolm X. Hell, even George Lincoln Rockwell. All assassinated. It was enough to make anybody want to run away. He probably would have too. Did, he supposed, when he was honest about it. Only he'd done it ten years earlier.

It wasn't even noon and he could already feel the heat settling like a brooding hen, and it was fall, for god's sake, although they were coming off a punishingly hot summer. He pulled into the police station parking lot, drove toward a row of plane trees bordering it, and glided under a shade curtain he calculated would last as long as he would be inside. He left his car windows down and made his way slowly toward the entrance of the station, where one of the dark double doors had been blocked open for ventilation.

"Mr. Philips," Jacob Khumalo said, flashing a broken-toothed smile from behind the reception counter. "A pleasure to see you."

He took Khumalo's hand in both of his and squeezed more than shook it. He and the sergeant had known each other for years, and he had come to value not only Khumalo's friendship but also his cooperation and good humor.

"How is your family?" Harry Philips asked.

"Well, thank you, and—" Khumalo said, as if, according to custom, he was about to ask after Harry Philips' family but remembered that he no longer had one. "What must make you come here so... how do you say—?"

"Bright and early?"

"Yes."

"I wanted to make sure I got to talk with you, if you were on duty."

"Ah," Khumalo said, a wary look in his eye. "You honor me too much. Tea, Mr. Philips?"

"No, thank you, I just had some."

Khumalo poured himself a cup.

"I believe you took a man into custody this morning," Harry Philips said.

The sergeant lifted the spoon from the cup and cradled it along the edge of the saucer. "It is a shame, Mr. Philips. A terrible shame, this thing that happened."

"Did you see the Americans?" Harry Philips said.

"Yes."

"How were they?"

"Mrs. Bernard, she is too pretty and too kind, but she has much sadness."

"And Mr. Bernard? Is that his name?"

"Yes. He is big, with a—" rubbing his chin.

"Beard?"

"Yes. He has the sadness, too."

"The man who attacked Mrs. Bernard—"

"Solomon Kunene."

"Do you know anything about him? Ever heard of him, ever seen him before?"

Khumalo shook his head.

"Does he have a record?"

"I do not know, Mr. Philips. I am not allowed—"

"Of course you aren't. Did anybody else seem to recognize him?"

"Not that I—" Khumalo glanced outside. "He is a foolish, shameful man."

"Did everyone make a statement, including Mr. Kunene?"

"Yes."

"In writing?"

"Yes."

"May I see them?"

Khumalo's shoulders slumped.

"I'm on official business, remember?"

Khumalo stared at him a moment longer, sighed, and retrieved the file folders.

"There are only two files here," Harry Philips said.

"That is because this Kunene fellow said many words which have to be translated into English for the court. Perhaps by the time you have read these two, the other statement will be ready for you. Now please go there so no one may see you," tipping his head in the direction of the interrogation rooms.

Both Bernard statements were more or less what he'd expected, describing how late the night before, Solomon Kunene had entered their house and attacked Mrs. Bernard, how her husband had subdued him and gone to a neighbor's house for help, how the police had arrived and they'd all returned to Mbabane in the Land Rover. More or less routine, except for the attack itself.

According to Kunene's translated statement, he didn't hold a gun to Mrs. Bernard's head or a knife to her throat and force himself on her. He didn't punch her or choke her or beat her with a knobkerrie. He didn't jump out of the bushes and drag her kicking and screaming into his lair. No. What he apparently did was to undress outside their bedroom window, climb through it, and get into bed—with both of them in it.

But the attack wasn't his fault, he said. Some force had taken over him and, although it was night when spirits roamed the earth according to his mother, who kept the ways of the ancestors, he had been drawn like a dream-walker over Mdzimba Mountain, not only to the teacher's compound at Lobamba School but to a specific window of a specific home. Inside, he saw a man and a woman sleeping on a bed. A white man and a white woman. The woman was on her side, he said, her bare leg over the man's lower half, which was covered with a sheet. The man's upper body was naked and the woman was only wearing what looked like a shirt, light in color as well. For some reason he didn't understand, at that very moment the woman stirred in her sleep and rolled to her back, the unbuttoned shirt falling open to expose her.

He wasn't a bad man, he said, he would never have done such a thing on his own. But she had brought him to her, and before he knew it, he was inside the room, approaching the bed, naked now himself but for his boxers, even though he didn't remember undressing.

So neat, so obvious, so full of shit, Harry Philips thought, closing the folder. To say his victim had through some mumbo-jumbo compelled him to come to her bed was too easy an answer. Blaming your actions on spirit-possession was like pleading insanity in the States. Everybody did it. So he couldn't buy Kunene's story for a minute. There had to have been another motivation that no one had figured out yet, because nothing occurred in a vacuum, which, as always, was the problem.

.

3

Dear Mother and Dad,

I might as well get right to the point. One thing first, though: we're okay, as okay as we can be.

Three nights ago—it was really more like early morning but before dawn—a man climbed through our bedroom window and raped me in my bed. Again, I want you to know that I'm okay—well, you know what I mean. I was asleep and at first thought it was Brian touching me, but it wasn't. I shoved the man away and yelled for Brian who woke up immediately and was able to grab the man before he escaped and tied him up in the living room. It took me a while to realize what had happened, but when I did, I felt so awful. I thought it was somehow my fault. I still ache when I think about it, like some part deep inside me has been bruised and may never heal. I shouldn't be saying this. I mean, here we are 10,000 miles apart and there's no way to just hug.

Brian took care of everything. He got our neighbor to drive to Mbabane for the police and came back to help me get ready to do whatever we would need to. And everybody has been nice—more than nice. So nice that it gets in the way at times. Like the sergeant at the police station. I don't know if he was embarrassed or what, but the whole time we were there he couldn't—or maybe wouldn't—look at us. And the doctor who examined me—all the tests he did were negative, by the way—was angry about what had happened and said bad things about the country and the people here, which didn't help anything. Right after we got back to Lobamba, a man at the US embassy came to tell us they had been notified of the situation because the crime involved a US citizen, was there anything they could do? Our Peace Corps Director was told, too, and stopped by to check on us. We even heard that the king knows about it and he's not at all pleased.

We've had more attention than we ever wanted, but you don't need to worry that we're being ignored. The thing is, though, I wonder how they'd have acted if I'd been an African woman. I try not to think about that because it makes me feel even more guilty.

I can't say don't worry. I know you will. When you do, just remember things could be a lot worse. I'm not dead, and I have Brian. I just needed to talk.

All my love,

Meg

PS: Share with Trina and Max as you see fit.

Holding the blue aerogram in both hands, she reread what she'd written, folded and sealed it, addressed it and printed CONFIDENTIAL across the bottom. She gathered her books and papers, tucking the letter into her math text, and walked to school, where she dropped the letter into the battered postbag hanging on a coat rack in Mr. Dube's outer office. She listened for its soft plop in the bottom and walked away safe in the knowledge that in a week or so her parents would find it with their other mail in the black box with the creaky lid beside their front door. They would sort through bills and flyers on their way into the house and stack everything, her blue aerogram on top, beside the napkin holder on the kitchen table, waiting to read it until they'd put their things away and changed clothes. Her mother would sit then and slice open the letter with a sharp paring knife, careful not to leave a ragged edge that might obscure an important word. She would unfold it, smooth it against the tabletop, and begin reading, her father following along from where he stood behind her mother, his hand on her shoulder. She might or might not cry, but she would sigh several times and shake her head and reach for her husband's hand. She would sit back when she'd finished, and they would say how terrible it was, how very sad, and wonder aloud whether what happened meant she and Brian might be coming home sooner now. Her mother would refold the letter and lay it in a desk drawer on a stack of other aerograms, resting her hand there a moment, as if that might somehow draw Meg closer to her.

She took a deep breath and wiped her eyes as she made her way to opening exercises. She could just as easily have turned left and gone home out the front door. No one would have said a word about it. Sarah had, in fact, suggested she might want to take a day or two off to rest and regain some balance. But she'd said no, she had to go back sooner or later and sitting at home alone wasn't going to help.

Teachers and staff had lined up as usual in the shade of the veranda that ran the length of the building in the rear. Students stood in rows facing her on the bare ground between the veranda and two beige-colored stucco outdoor toilets, rectangular 20-by-8-foot buildings 40 feet apart, vents at the peak of the roof on each end and a single door to each. Girls wore gray dresses over white blouses and black shoes, boys khaki slacks with white shirts and black shoes, their faces bright and speckled with sweat from the heat.

Meg felt everyone's eyes on her when she slipped in next to Sarah to listen to the students sing the Swazi national anthem, directed by Percy Mavuso. He was tall and lean with close-cropped hair, his arms graceful as a swimmer's bringing forth such beautiful harmony it made her want to cry. At the end of the song, Mr. Dube, the headmaster, read announcements that amounted to a pep talk about staying prepared and always doing one's best. He turned slightly at that point and seemed to look directly at her, and she immediately fixed her gaze on the mountains rising in the near distance behind the students and squeezed Sarah's hand that had found hers, hoping against hope that Mr. Dube didn't welcome her back and wish her well, as if she had some terrible condition everyone was aware of and understood to be terminal.

But all she heard was, "Dismissed."

During her third-period math class, Sisi Banda raised a hand.

"Yes, Sisi."

"Madam, I can be too happy if you can explain again which is the numerator and which is the denominator."

Meg braced her arm against the desk in front of her and stared at the hand pressed against the rough wood. How odd it looked compared to the ones around it. The hand wasn't white, exactly, any more than the others were black. *More pink*, she thought, *pale pink*.

"Madam?"

"Sisi?"

"The question, Madam."

She raised her head, lifted her hand from the desk, slowly, carefully, as though it were a piece of heirloom china a fussy old aunt had given her for safekeeping.

"All right, then, let's see." She drifted toward the blackboard, and the hand wrote 3/7. "Who can tell me what this is?"

"A number," Sisi said.

"But what kind of number? It has a special name."

No response.

"We've talked about it. Does anyone remember?"

"A whole number?" Luke said.

"No. This is a whole number." The hand wrote 3 by itself. "And this is a whole number." The hand wrote 7 by itself. "But when I put them together with this line between them, what is it called?"

"Three-slash-seven," Prudence said.

"And that is a...?" Please. Someone. Anyone. Pale pink hand, chalk between thumb and forefinger raised at the edge of her vision.

"Fraction," a voice called out. One of the boys.

"Who said that?"

A timid hand went up.

"Yes, Philemon. Yes. You are absolutely right."

"But why, Madam?" Sisi said.

"Please let me finish."

"Why do we need them?" Sisi asked.

"Who can answer?" Meg said.

"Because it is written three slash seven," Reginald said.

"No, she asked why we need them. Please pay attention to the question."

Vonya: "We need them so that we may... so that we may be able to..."

Elena: "Count."

"How do they help you count?" Meg asked.

"By making the number smaller?" someone said.

"No, no, that cannot be the answer the Madam seeks," Amos said, standing, drawing himself to full height, as if about to deliver an address. "We need them to do the problem."

"What problem?"

"Why, the one that you must give to us, Madam, on the examination."

She turned toward the sound of boys practicing soccer on the field in front of the school, calling out instructions to each other.

"Who can tell me the number of days in a week?" she began again, chalk tapping beside the fraction.

Hands everywhere. Russet, mahogany, ebony, dark and shiny as a raven's wing, light as creamed coffee.

"Val."

"Seven, Madam."

"Correct. Now who can write them here, across the chalkboard? Okay, Moses."

He was a tall, gangly boy of 15 or 16—although she had never been good at determining her students' ages—with dark bushy hair and an unusually large mouth that had broken into a huge grin. He took the chalk from her and rubbed the heels of his palms on his khaki trousers.

"Start here," she pointed. "What day will come first?"

"Sunday?" Moses said.

"Anyone knows better," Absalom boomed from the back of the room. "He is not a Christian. Ask one who is."

"Are you a Christian, Absalom?"

He took a deep breath, held it.

"All right, then, if not Sunday, what day should come first?"

"Monday," he burst. "Now everyone can say that Absalom has spoken the truth."

"Good," she said. "With that taken care of, let's begin with Monday, Moses. Right here."

He printed carefully, intensely, until he reached the end of the week and the board.

"Wonderful. Thank you. Who can tell me what day of the week it is now?" she asked as Moses took his seat.

"Friday," Domezile said, then dropped her head, as if embarrassed.

"And how many days of this week have already passed? Paul?"

"Five."

"How can it be so?" Absalom said. "We are still in this one."

"What about by the end of today? Would you agree that five will have passed then?"

He nodded, but seriously, as though the question and his response were equally weighty matters.

"So let's draw lines through these five days. Now once again, how many days all together in a week?"

"Seven."

"And how many days have already been taken?"

"Five."

"Good. Now that same idea can be expressed—stated, said—in this way: Seven shows the number of equal parts the week is divided into. Seven days, seven equal parts. Five shows how many parts of the week have been taken or used. So if we look at the list, there are seven days total. The number seven then goes down here. It is that which names the whole—a week, seven days—and it is called the denominator. This number—five—goes above the line. It tells how many parts of the whole have already been taken. It numbers and is called the numerator. Denominator names the total number of parts, numerator numbers the parts already taken. So now we can say that five-sevenths of the week is past. How many sevenths remain?"

No hands of any color.

"Think about it, now. Five-sevenths are gone. How many are left?"

"None," Vonya said.

"But five-sevenths isn't a whole. What about Saturday and Sunday? Aren't they part of the week?"

As she looked at the boy, she knew the answer to her question: they weren't. Not in his reckoning. His week—his real week—went from Monday to Friday, the week the school made for him. The rest of time sank into a more African concept Meg hadn't even begun to comprehend. Vonya was right and she hadn't been able to get her point across—at least to many of her students, from the looks on their faces. She should have been working in fifths. Everybody could have grasped that. Maybe even Sisi. They could have talked about how many days until the soccer match, what fraction of the school week that was. Now there was nothing and she had wasted another day and probably even backtracked, since she was sure she'd done more to confuse than enlighten anyone, and she left the room at the end of the period feeling even more inept and stupid.

Normally she would have gone straight to the teacher's lounge to spend her only break of the day, other than lunch. She might work on lesson plans, read, write a letter or chat with Sarah, who had the same free period. They often talked about their classes—Sarah taught history and siZulu, Meg math and science—or about sewing or knitting or a new recipe. And they always talked about Jabalile and what she was now doing or saying. Sarah was as close a friend as Meg had here, and she always enjoyed her company.

But that day she hesitated when she thought she heard voices coming from the lounge through the doorway in the far-right corner of the foyer—scratchy and tinny, as if from a transistor radio, but voices nonetheless, meaning Sarah was not alone. She stood still in the stifling heat, gazing at the faint path of red dust that tracked from one set of glass double doors to the other across the bare cement. The space was larger than it needed to be and empty, save for two worn benches shoved against cinder-block walls, themselves barren of pictures, posters, even a bulletin board that might have held news of school events and activities. The voices swarmed again in the prickly heat, laughter now mixed with them, around and around her head, until she slumped against the wall, a trickle of sweat along her right jaw, and closed her eyes against the familiar dizziness that she'd felt at times when they'd first arrived here, on the other side of the earth, where water swirled counterclockwise down a drain, where Easter came in fall and Christmas in summer and everything had seemed so inside out and upside down that she had wondered then, as now, why they didn't fall off weightless into space, hanging as they were like bats from the ceiling of a cave.

"Are you all right?"

She blinked, saw Sarah, then Grace Mtetwa standing above where she now sat on the floor, back against the wall, legs splayed, her yellow dress pooled between them, with no memory of how she'd gotten there.

"Are you injured?" Sarah knelt, fanning her with her handkerchief.

She shook her head.

"Come. Try to stand. You must take some air," Grace said in the sing-song Afrikaans-cum-Xhosa accent that made her seem even more exotic and beautiful. She was Cape Coloured, tall and lithe, with long legs and arms, and fingers that seemed almost too delicate. Her skin was khaki-toned, and curly black hair coiled carelessly over her forehead. Jade green eyes locked on Meg as she and Sarah each wedged a hand in an armpit to help her stand and walk slowly to the lounge.

She slid into a chair close to the windows, 6-foot-high curtainless casement wings that caught what breeze there was and wafted it up and over her shoulders; and they all sat silently, Grace to her right at the end of the table, Sarah across from her in a straight knee-length dark skirt, a light-blue sweater, despite the heat, and a knit tam pulled squarely over her head.

She took a deep breath, smiled as much as she could and said, "Thank you. I don't know what would have happened if you hadn't been here. But I'm feeling better now. Sorry to be such a bother."

"No, no," Sarah said.

"Not to mention it," Grace said.

"I feel so silly."

Sarah tisk-tisked and shook her head.

Grace pulled back in her chair, squaring her shoulders. "That is nonsense. We have all been saying that you have come back too soon. That you did not rest enough."

"I don't know about that. Besides, I'm fine. Really. I just—"

"Fainted," Grace said.

Sarah took her hand, held it.

"Granted the heat has been dreadful, but it is still too much. All of it," Grace said. "You should have gone on holiday. To the mountains or to the ocean. Some place with a hot spring and a massage every day."

Meg shuddered at the thought of some stranger touching her.

"It is what I would do. No question." Grace shifted her gaze to the schoolyard. "But it does not matter. They do not care what you or I think? They are the ones who decide. The men. And they won't hear of it. A holiday? Ha! They think you and any of us who might suffer the same misfortune—and there are many, far too many—have nothing more than a headache. You should lie down and rest and it will be gone in the morning. Bah! Such fools. Like that Maphalala, who came to my room just now."

Sarah released Meg's hand and clapped her own together. "Oh, yes, please. Go on with the story you were telling me about why you are not teaching."

"I was kind of wondering that myself," Meg said.

Grace's green eyes sparked, as though glad herself for something else to talk about. "Well, I was saying, this Maphalala fool—and I do not care how important he thinks he is, he is still a fool—he came to my room at the beginning of the last period and said he wanted to borrow my students. Now wouldn't you think that to borrow them must mean he has some work for them to do? But, no, he said he needed to lecture them about the toilets and told me I should leave. He said he would send someone for me when he is finished. But I stood outside the door to listen as long as I dared."

"What's wrong with the toilets?" Meg said.

"They are blogged."

"Blogged?"

Grace puffed out her chest and continued in her deepest Maphalala voice: "The students have been blogging them with stones."

Simeon Maphalala was assistant headmaster of the school and it was his duty to deal with students on issues like toilets, given that the headmaster would never address anything so mundane. Maphalala was a squat man with a doleful face and an unfortunate knack for mispronouncing even the simplest words, which often made him an object of ridicule, though discreetly, since it was said that his uncle was a local chief who had close ties to the king and could, if the story were true, make life uncomfortable for anyone too overtly critical of his nephew.

"He told them he had heard that some of them had been using stones in the toilets to clean themselves when they have nothing else. And stones do not flush down."

"You have to be kidding," Meg said.

"I am sorry to say I am not. He asked if anyone could explain how stones would get into the toilets otherwise. Would they sprout legs and walk? Would they jump in by themselves?"

Meg and Sarah smiled at each other.

"I swear it is true. He was even saying as I left that if they did not stop, the toilets would be locked and students would have to use the bushes again like animals. Since no one would want that, he was certain the blogging would cease immediately and that those who were guilty would confess."

"I'm sure that caused a stampede," Meg said.

"Like cattle?" Sarah asked. "When they become frightened?"

"Yes."

"I doubt it," Grace said, "since here I remain after so much time."

"Oh, but someone will step forward," Sarah said. "The students do fear him."

"It is true." Grace raised an eyebrow. "Remember the Mamba boy?"

"Yes," Meg said.

"And do you know why he was dismissed?"

"Not really."

"He sassed Mr. Maphalala."

"That was all?"

"Nothing more. But you may be certain his father beat him for embarrassing the family and sent him off to herd cattle in the mountains."

"That is why students listen when Maphalala speaks," Sarah said. "Even if it is nonsense, like stones in toilets."

The entryway door creaked then clunked, and all three of them glanced toward the foyer. When no one came, Grace continued: "And it is even worse for the girls."

Sarah glanced at Grace. "Perhaps it would be better if—"

"Have you seen the way he examines each new one. The way he starts with the—what do you call it?—flirting. If the girl does not smile and blush, it is clear she will not do other things he might want, either. So he is finished with her and moves on. But he remembers, and the first time something comes up with that girl—like Precious Simelane."

"It was gossip," Sarah said. "Nothing more."

"Perhaps, perhaps not. But she is gone, is she not? And she never sassed a soul."

"But why does Mr. Dube—?" Meg said.

"Because she is a girl and not a boy. A young girl who is frightened of men who threaten her with this and that. But say she is a brave one and she does go to Mr. Dube and tells him what has happened. Mr. Dube then calls Mr. Maphalala in and Mr. Maphalala says she is lying. What can she do? Who will Mr. Dube believe—a girl or his assistant, who is also a man? And then these other girls, they see immediately what has happened and that Maphalala means business and they should… cooperate or else."

"You find devils everywhere," Sarah said.

"Have you not seen the way they act with him?"

"They are girls," Sarah said, "and girls—"

"Yes, I would like to think so as well, but the way they are with him is not natural. It is not like when they are with boys or each other. And let us not, God help us, fool ourselves and think there is nothing wrong with that."

After a moment, Grace stood, collecting the maps and charts she carried from room to room for her geography lessons, and tucked them under her arm, picked up a tied bundle of books and papers in her free hand. "But that is enough of that. Surely they have finished by now. After all, how much can anyone say about toilets? Even Maphalala?"

The outside door thumped shut behind Grace and they sat in silence for their remaining minutes together, Sarah laying her free hand now over Meg's, rubbing gently, not *there-there* so much as *I understand*, while Meg stared at the empty soccer field, a dust devil caught in the middle. The scene looked painted on, the sky embarrassingly blue and cloudless, scrubby sage-green humps of mountains across the valley, trees lined in rows of emerald dots following the course of the river through the valley. But flat, two-dimensional, without depth or feeling. Without Grace or Sarah or Brian or Maphalala or the girls or herself, for that matter. No one to feel sad or angry or disappointed at. No one to hurt or be hurt by. No one to weep for.

"I am sorry," Sarah said at last, "but it is time. We must go now, too."

They stood, with their own books and papers.

"Will you be all right?" Sarah asked.

"I always am, you know."

Sarah dropped her head, like one of the girls who'd been scolded.

"I didn't mean it like that. Really. I'll be fine. Don't worry. Besides, it's Friday. I only have two more classes of fractions, and then I'm free as a bird."

"Such a pleasant thought," Sarah said, tilting her head and sailing her hand up and away from her. "But what if you really could be free as a bird? What would you do?"

Meg thought a moment, shook her head. "I'm not sure. What about you?"

"Oh, I would fly away, just like that," fingers snapping.

"To a spa to swim and have massages?"

"Oh, no, that is not for me."

"Where then? Where would you go?"

"Home, perhaps."

"Here, or there, in the Republic?"

"That would depend." She gazed at Meg a moment. "On many things."

4

Harry Philips had first met Bertie Magongo a year earlier at a party in Mbabane hosted by the US embassy. How Magongo came to be there—whether he had been invited or walked in off the street—was never clear and in the end didn't matter. The party was in celebration of the Apollo 11 lunar landing a week or so earlier, and Magongo was making the best of the situation, going around the room, person to person, congratulating each on the accomplishment of the astronauts and telling everyone that they should be damned proud. He was damned proud. The world should be damned proud. That Armstrong, man. One small step, one giant step, one small step, one giant step, swaying to an internal rhythm as he danced himself in a tight circle, red wine splashing over the rim of his glass onto Harry Philips' arm, Magongo pawing at the spill, still swaying, saying "Sorry, man, damned sorry, but that Armstrong, man, he's my brother, you're my brother, we're brothers, man, brothers," dancing Harry Philips around with him now, each connecting with someone else, on and on until they were all circling together, shouting "Brothers, we are brothers."

By his own admission, Magongo knew everything about everybody, and what he didn't know—wink, wink—he said he could find out. But he would also be the first to tell you he wasn't a gossip. He was a businessman who, as he called it, harvested information on people and passed it along—after proper "consideration," of course—to anyone who might be interested. He said he had adapted the idea from his hero, Tomasto Tomassino, a detective in an Italian crime novel series that he read and reread with a devotion most people reserve for sacred texts. Tomassino was the same character who informed Magongo's whole professional life, including not only how he talked, dressed and acted but also his keeping regular hours at his office, a table next to the front window of Lena's Pub in Mbabane, where he spent his days chatting and drinking and scribbling notes on a yellow legal pad—date, hour, name and subject reference—on all who stopped by or came up in conversation.

And Lena's was where Harry Philips found Magongo that Monday afternoon.

"Hello, Bertie. Mind if I join you?"

"Brother Philips. My old friend. Not at all, not at all. Please." He gestured toward the empty chair across from him, a short, lumpy man who looked for all the world like a baked potato in his brown wool suit, white shirt, and faint yellow tie that hung the length of his torso. "I am—how is it?—delighted to see you."

"Can I buy you a drink?" Harry Philips asked.

Magongo eyed his nearly empty beer bottle. "You are too kind."

Harry Philips signaled Noah, the barman and waiter, who came immediately. "A Castle lager here, please. You, Bertie?"

"The same." Magongo fished a crumpled Lucky Strike from a pack near the ashtray to his right and offered one to Harry Philips.

"No, thank you."

"Of course. Forgive me. I forgot you do not smoke. Did you in America?"

"No."

"Never?"

"No."

"Hmm."

Noah cleared Magongo's now empty bottle and wiped the table before setting down the fresh Castles.

"Then you do not believe smoking can be able to help you think?" Magongo asked.

"I don't see how it could."

"Not even a little? Because without the cigarette, Tomasto says he is, uh—" hand wiggling as he looked to Harry Philips for the right word.

"Dull? Worthless?"

"Worthless, yes. Only worse than worthless." He lit his cigarette, picked a piece of tobacco off his tongue, studied it a moment and wiped it on his pant leg before leaning forward with a sidelong glance to make sure no one was eavesdropping. "And do you know what else it is good for?"

"Not off hand, no."

His eyes looked this way and that: "Women think smoking men are for sex."

"Is that right?"

"Tomasto says that if you put the smoking man and the fucking woman and the beer together—"

"You mean wine, don't you?"

Magongo frowned.

"Your friend, he is Italian, after all. Wouldn't he have wine instead of beer?"

Wetting the tip of his finger, Magongo made a mark in the air between them. "You are right. He must drink only the wine. Wine, women, and—What is it, my friend? There is much trouble in your face."

"Sorry."

"Perhaps I may help?"

"I need some information."

Magongo threw up his hands. "Is that not why everyone comes to me?"

"Do you know a man named Kunene?"

Magongo laughed, which sent him into a smoker's coughing fit. "You make the joke, right? Because of course I know a man named Kunene. There are Kunenes here, Kunenes there. They are like cats on a rubbish heap. Only Dlaminis are more." He tapped a column of ashes into the tray. "You see, when Swazis were people who lived like monkeys in trees, as the Zulus said of them, the Dlaminis asked the Kunenes to join them against the Zulus. Then they asked another clan, and another. From that, a nation grew, and the Zulus came and fought a great battle with the Swazis, who drove them over the mountains to Zululand, and they return now only when Swazis say they may."

"Are you Swazi? I never asked."

"I am and I am not. I was not born here—only in the Republic—as a Zulu."

"Then that makes you—?"

"Both," Magongo said. "My blood is Zulu, but my heart is Swazi. I have been here so long. It is not who you are there but what you feel you are, here." He held a fist to his chest.

"Okay," Harry Philips said. "That makes sense, but back to whether you've heard of Solomon Kunene."

"Ah, the wisdom of Solomon—or do you not think this one is so wise?"

"That's what I want to find out."

"Whether he is half a wit or sly like a fox?"

"Exactly."

Magongo paused, then spoke to whatever it was outside that had caught his eye. "Where is the home of this Kunene who may or may not be wise?"

"Zombodze."

"Ah."

"So you have heard of him?"

"No. I was thinking only what a shame to have to live in that place where you would find nothing like this one," head tilting now toward the sidewalk where a young woman wearing a leopard skin pillbox hat was strolling past, heels clacking, thigh slashing through the slit in her dark skirt. At the corner she glanced back, with what appeared to be an expectant smile, and was gone. "Not to worry. She will be back exactly one hour from now."

"How do you know that?"

"She is my friend, and every day she goes there, and every day she returns in one hour. Same path," his index finger rocking to and fro like a metronome. "Just like that. She would be too happy if we asked her to join us."

"Maybe some other time."

"Suit yourself." Magongo leaned forward, lowering his voice and peering at Harry Philips from the tops of his eye sockets. "But Tomasto Tomassino would not think twice about having her."

"That's him, not me."

"He says if you think too much about anything it fucks the brain."

"Fucks it up, you mean?"

"Up down around, what does it matter?" Magongo smoothed out another cigarette, lit it, took a long drag. "So this Kunene—this Solomon Kunene—why do you ask about him?"

"Let's just say he has run into trouble with the police."

"This thing, it is something more than burglary?"

"Yes."

"Murder? No, I would have heard about that. At least anyone important." He ran his hand over his balding head. "Bank robbery? But that, too, would be talked about all over the country. You must say, so I have a place to start from."

Harry Philips now looked about the room himself, glanced out the window before he spoke. "All I can tell you is that a crime was committed recently at Lobamba that involved Solomon Kunene."

"Lobamba, is it? At the kraal, the palace, parliament?"

"The teachers' compound at the secondary school." Harry Philips held up both hands. "But that's all I'm going to say about what happened for now."

"No matter. At Lobamba everyone knows everything that happens. And if they do not themselves, they know how to find someone who does. And if there is anything interesting or strange about this Kunene fellow, they will know that too."

"Which is exactly the kind of thing I want to find out. Anything at all about him beyond the usual who what when where business. I want to know what skivvies he wears, what toothpaste he uses, what his mother had for breakfast the day he was born."

Magongo nodded.

"I want to know everything there is to know about him—who his family and friends are, who he talks to now or has talked to in the past twenty years, whether he's a member of any groups regardless how uninteresting they may seem. I want to know how he spends his time and his money, if he has any—and if he doesn't, why he doesn't. I want to know what he eats, what he drinks, what he smokes, who he fucks. I want to know if he's ever been sick and why, whether he owes money to anybody or is in debt in any other way—even if he just needs to repay a favor. I want to know whether people like him or think he's a jerk. What makes him happy, what pisses him off. What's he capable of doing whether he's happy or not? What's he capable of doing, period? What are his talents and his failings? What are his habits and obsessions? What does he want more than anything, what does he hate? What was he doing at Lobamba on that night and in the place where he was captured? What, if any, relationship did he have with the people there? I want to know everything."

Harry Philips rested back against his chair, drained the rest of his beer and ordered two more while Magongo wrote furiously on his legal pad, seemingly short one- or two-word notes, summarizing what Harry Philips had just said. Magongo finished, underlining the final entry, and laid his pen diagonally across the page.

"I can tell you, my friend, that you will be more than satisfied with Bertie Magongo on the case. Me and Brother Tomassino. A genius, I tell you, a true genius. A giant among men. You might even ask what would I be without him, and I can say I would be nobody, nothing, that's what." A column of ashes dropped from his cigarette onto the floor. "The problem is—"

"I'm listening."

"—he is an expensive genius. He likes to eat the good food and drink the good wine and fuck the fine women."

"All of which cost money, of course," Harry Philips said.

"I am too happy that you understand, my friend."

Harry Philips pulled his wallet from his hip pocket, took out three 20-rand notes and laid them next to Magongo's beer glass. "This should help for the time being."

Magongo covered the money with his hand but didn't pick it up.

"Something wrong?"

"Only that this Tomassino chap, being the genius of high times that he is, usually likes numbers that are more, um—what can I say?—round?"

"Closer to a hundred, you mean?"

Magongo smiled and Harry Philips tossed two more twenties on the table.

"For that much, I expect only the best, Bertie. Only the best. And if it's good enough, your buddy Tomassino might be even more pleased, if you get my meaning." Harry Philips slid him a business card. "Call me when you find out something."

He brooded in his car for a while, around the corner and out of sight of Lena's Pub. He should go back to the office, he supposed, but that would mean having to talk to Dlamini. Again. About nothing, because he had nothing more to report, except his meeting with Bertie, and he wasn't sure how his boss would feel about his hiring, if you could call it that, a person who referred to himself as a harvester of information. He supposed he could explain to Dlamini how apt the image was, really, when you looked at it more closely—cutting and gathering the stalks, winnowing out the grain. But Dlamini's mind didn't work metaphorically—or if it did, he didn't like to admit as much, preferring to project himself as less a Sherlock Holmes and more a Joe Friday.

He was also worried that he hadn't given Magongo enough information to go on, although he would find out for himself quickly enough what had happened. News of the crime would be widespread, though not much talked about under orders from the king's people. But, if Magongo was as good as he said, he would learn what he needed to know. As many details as he was willing to pay for, at least, with cash or *tjwala* or a small bag of *dagga*. An odd bottle of whiskey. But most of what he came up with would likely have to do with Kunene rather than the Americans. Prying into white lives might be too intimidating. In the end, Magongo probably had enough information to get started, and Harry Philips frankly didn't know the man well enough to judge how far, given more to go on, he could be trusted not to say too much to the wrong people. Which may have been exactly what the king meant when he'd requested that Harry Philips be as discreet as possible.

So he decided, as Magongo suggested, to stop thinking for the moment at least, and to follow the much more pleasant option of watching the woman in the pillbox hat as she waited on the opposite corner for a car to pass. She appeared taller, more stately than when he'd seen her from the pub window, lean yet voluptuous, angular face sculpted by the afternoon sun. As she stepped from the curb, that same display of bare leg he'd seen earlier peek-a-booed from her skirt with each stride. She stopped midway across the street, her head snapping in his direction, sunglasses glinting. She held the pose long enough that heat rose in his cheeks and ears, like a teenager caught peeping at the door of the girls' locker room. He had an urge to wave at her to say yeah, he knew, he was sorry, it wouldn't happen again, but instead he cleared his throat and glanced away. When he looked back, she had passed from view.

Carolyn would have shaken her head and called him a pathetic creep. She would have told him that he should keep his fantasies about fucking the woman to himself. How did he think it made her feel? She had nice legs, too, she was pretty, had a good figure, and he could have her most any time he asked. So why didn't he? Why didn't he right then start the car, drive her home and take her to bed?

Because she wasn't there. She was only a voice in his head.

And who was she to talk anyway? Who was she sleeping with now? That grad student she'd had a fling with at Cal— Chase or Chad or Fad? Or the professor she thought was so sexy? Fuck 'em! Fuck 'em all!

The van took off with a lurch that didn't smooth out until the corner, where he turned and coasted to the stop sign a block away. He glanced left and caught the woman crossing again a street away from him with that same steady, rocking gait and thought about asking if she wanted a ride, before Carolyn smacked him—he damn near felt the sting of her hand—and he sped away, turning right on Miller Street and right again on Pine Valley Road, following it north toward the mountains, away from town, the woman, Carolyn, because he wanted to and could and didn't have to explain it to anyone.

5

The Friday of Meg's first week back at Lobamba, Glory Khoza sat in her living room and said for the second time that she'd stopped by just to say hello on her way home from school. At one time she'd been a student there but now worked as secretary to Mr. Dube, typing, keeping attendance records, sorting mail, and generally minding everyone's business.

"And Mr. Bernard, he is not here?" Glory asked.

"No, he went into Manzini with Mr. Lukhele to pick up some supplies."

"Will he be along soon, or will they stay on a while?"

"I'm sure they'll be there as long as it takes to get what they need," Meg said, not about to play into Glory's need for gossipy tidbits, no matter how trivial.

"And all that time you must be here without anyone."

"It's only for a couple of hours."

Glory shifted in her chair, clutching the rolled top of the red canvas bag on her lap. "Are you not frightened?"

"No, why do you ask?"

"When I stay to finish up work for Mr. Dube after school, I can hear the noises sometimes. Like people walking or whispering."

"Probably students or teachers who haven't left yet."

"Oh, no. I have gone to look and found no one, but it truly is as if there is someone else." Glory looked side to side and tightened her grip on the top of her bag. "The wind can make strange sounds."

Glory was young—maybe 20—tall for a Swazi woman, and large-boned, but not at all overweight, with short, tightly curled hair that she sometimes braided into elaborate cornrows. "When it happens, I do not like it at all. It frightens me and makes me know that I am alone."

She wished she could get Glory off the subject she was on, whatever it was, but Glory was Glory and correcting her course once she'd set her mind on something was nearly impossible without insulting her.

"And you, Mrs. Bernard —"

"You can call me Meg."

"Oh, I may not do that."

"Why?"

"You are the teacher and I am not." Glory waited, as if letting such an obvious fact about the natural order of the world sink in before continuing. "Do you ever feel frightened and lonely?"

"I'm not sure whether you mean lonely or alone?" Meg asked.

Glory put her hand to her mouth as she thought. "Lonely."

"Then I can say, no, not really. I have Brian."

"Yes." Glory drew out the word as she inclined her head toward Meg and lowered her voice. "But tell me, if you do not mind — Mr. Bernard, he is your husband?"

"Of course he is."

"Some say he is your brother."

Meg glanced quickly out the window to keep from smiling. "Why would they think that?"

"Because you have no children."

"Some people wait until they're older to have a family."

"But how can it be if you and Mr. Bernard —?"

"There are ways," Meg said.

"Even Mrs. Lukhele — she has Jabalile."

"Yes."

"So when Mr. Lukhele is gone, she is not lonely."

"Like you think I am when Brian's away?"

Glory nodded. "How can it not be so? You have no children and now no husband. And in this house. It is so big."

"Four rooms isn't that big," Meg said.

"How! Not even one person for each? It is settled then."

"What?"

"You must take a house girl. Or boy," Glory said, again clinching the top of her bag. "Someone to cook and clean. Someone to wash your clothes. Someone to keep you company."

"I don't know, Glory. Americans usually don't like to have other people around all the time, especially doing work they think they should do themselves."

Glory seemed as perplexed as Sergeant Khumalo had been about their not taking milk and sugar in their tea at the police station.

"A few rich people have servants but that's about it," Meg said.

"So it is not like in England?"

"I don't think all English people have servants either."

"Ah, but many do. Have you not seen when the English come here, they always have—what did you call them?—servants? Even Mrs. Lukhele has a house girl."

How could she explain that Sarah had a small daughter, and a husband who taught and drove his car but did little else around the house? He never chopped wood or swept or went alone to the market or helped cook like Brian. He didn't touch the laundry, wet or dry. But he did play with Jabalile now and then.

"Mrs. Lukhele needs someone," Meg said. "I don't."

"Perhaps you may change your mind."

"I doubt it, but if I do, I'll be sure to let you know."

Glory raised her hands, as if in surrender. But Meg knew better. Glory rarely lost any argument she put her heart into. She lifted the bag from her lap. "You have said you will not take a house boy, or girl, and that is your decision. But I must not let you live here frightened and lonely a single day longer." She reached inside the bag to pull out a brown tabby kitten not much larger than her hand.

"Oh. Oh, my." Meg took the kitten from Glory, who nodded, beaming like a proud aunt. As well she might. She had played it perfectly, knowing from the outset that Meg could refuse one offer without being rude but not a second. Especially when it involved a gift, a kitten besides. "Where did you get him? If it is a him."

"My mother sent him."

"Does he have a name?"

"Ro-jer. It is what the soldiers say. When they understand something."

"Oh, you mean Roger."

She nodded, eyes sparkling. "Yes, 'ro-jer,' and 'over and out' when they have finished."

Glory gathered her things, still smiling, and Meg walked her to the kitchen door, holding Roger to her chest, his fuzzy head nuzzling her neck.

"Oh, I must not forget," Glory said, pausing on her way out, empty bag tucked under her arm. "There was a man. An African man. He was asking for you. I told him you were gone but I could give you a message. He said not to bother, but could he ask me some questions?"

"About what?"

"You and Mr. Bernard. Things such as how old you are, which I told him I did not know, and what you teach, whether the students and other teachers like you, and so on. I told him what I could and he said thank you, he was satisfied."

"That was all?"

"Yes, Madam."

"He didn't say anything else?"

"No, Madam."

"Did he leave a card or his name?"

"I am sorry, no card. But he did say his name was Magongo. Mr. Magongo."

"But nothing else?"

"No, Madam."

"How strange."

"If you say so, Madam, then strange it must be." Glory smiled again, squared her shoulders and gave Meg a little salute. "Rojer, over and out."

The next morning Meg got up early to make sure Roger hadn't run off or made messes everywhere. She found him napping on the window ledge in the living room, his tail dangling down the wall, and turned to the kitchen to see what she could find for him to eat. The evening before, she'd stirred water into powdered milk, which he'd walked away from at first but must have warmed to later, since she found the bowl empty when she went to bed. She now washed and dried the dish, cut small cheese squares to put in it, along with some leftover meat-substitute crumbs from the fridge, and set it on the floor under the table, beside another bowl filled with water.

The scraping sounds brought a mew and three thumps as she imagined Roger hopping down to the table, the chair, the floor on his way to the kitchen. She smiled, openly, for the first time since… She used to be known for her smile, her good humor and optimism. Not because she was the perky type. No one would dare call her that. Happy, yes, but peacefully so, content with who she was. And she wanted at least some of that confidence back.

She glanced up as Brian danced around the cat in the hallway, yawning and scratching his bare stomach, hair a wild ring around his head. He started to say something but got a startled look, held up a finger, and sidestepped into the bathroom, closing the door behind him.

She was surprised when he and Joseph hadn't gotten home until almost nine the night before—he'd hardly let her out of his sight the past week and a half—and was both amused and annoyed by his explanation that they'd stopped for a beer at a bar Joseph liked on the outskirts of Manzini and Joseph saw some people he knew and they started talking and one beer led to another until Brian checked his watch and said "holy shit," they needed to get out of there, spreading his arms in triumph until he saw what she was cradling to her chest.

It wasn't that he disliked cats. They'd had one in the States before they'd left, and he'd been quite attached to it. There, a pet cat was okay, he explained. But here, it was different because Africans, in general, didn't have pets. They kept animals around because they had some usefulness, he said. Dogs barked at strangers and helped herd cattle. Chickens laid eggs and occasionally ended up in soup or curry. Goats gave milk and were roasted for feasts. Cattle symbolized wealth. Even cats caught mice and rats and kept lizards in the roof thatch, where they belonged. The only people who had pets, he said, were Europeans, and he would just as soon not be associated with colonialist bastards like too many of the British expatriates who'd remained in the country after independence, not wanting to go home because they wouldn't be able to afford their servants and big houses and Mercedes Benzes if they did. And she was sadly mistaken if she didn't think Glory gave them the cat because they and the British seemed so similar to her—they all looked alike and spoke more or less the same language. So why wouldn't they have the same attitude toward animals as pets? Meg said that might all be well and good but the fact remained that they now had a cat and would most likely continue to have one unless he was willing to do whatever he'd have to to get rid of him.

She heard the toilet flush and the shower come on. She shivered thinking of him under the cold spray and wondered how he tolerated doing it as often as he did. Twice a week in winter, when they heated water on the wood stove and poured it over each other with a small pitcher, and three times a week in summer was all she could stand, with sponge bathing of critical areas in between and daily cold-water hair washing at the kitchen sink.

While he finished, she perked coffee on the propane burner and mixed powdered milk for breakfast, both of which she loaded onto a tray and carried to the living room.

She switched on the BBC as she offloaded things to the table and heard news about the continuing invasion of Cambodia by US and South Vietnamese military forces, an action, the newscaster said, that was provoking ever larger and more strident protests against the war across America.

Water pipes banged when Brian turned off the shower, as if in response to the report that another 50,000 US military personnel had been withdrawn from the conflict, which met the pledge President Nixon had made the fall before, but still left 420,000 troops in place, and it terrified her to think Brian had any chance of becoming one of them.

The Paris Peace talks were ongoing but had shown little observable progress.

She sat at the table and picked up the blue aerogram they'd received the day before from Louise Hicks, a graduate school friend who was now teaching history at a small college in the Chicago suburbs. Their family and friends wrote regularly with news from the US that they would read over and over, as if afraid they might otherwise miss some tidbit of information or subtly nuanced phrasing.

She unfolded Louise's descriptions of what she was doing at school and how it was going: she had one class on Colonial America that had enrolled so many students she'd had to change from teaching it as a seminar to holding it in a formal lecture hall where she used a lectern and a microphone. But she shouldn't complain. She had a job in her field, which was better than some of their friends had ended up with. Some of the men had been drafted, did they know that? Kevin Milowski, Brad Dominick and several others. She hoped they were okay. There were so many people dying for no good reason she could think of. She didn't know if Meg and Brian were aware that she'd begun counseling interested undergrad males on ways to avoid the draft, short of burning their cards, an act that could still land them in jail. She always mentioned Peace Corps to seniors as a way to get a two-year deferment and used her—and Brian in particular—as examples. She'd also gone to a couple of protests in Chicago and thought of the two of them and the "old" days. Did they miss the marching, the chanting, the anger? What a senseless mess. The war—and even the weather, for that matter. She wondered if it was ever going to be spring, although she had seen a few blue crocuses peeking through the ground. How was the weather in Swaziland? Life in general?

Meg glanced up at Brian flitting naked across the hall to the bedroom.

Life in general had lately been not so good. You might say it had been horrible, but would she say that to Louise and tell her why? So far, her parents were the only people at home who knew anything about what had happened. She drew a deep breath and decided that, no, she probably wouldn't tell Louise, or anyone else for that matter. Not for a while anyway. She most likely would continue as she had before that awful night, writing about Swazi dress and customs and food, the incredible scenery, thunder that sometimes boomed from clear skies, the hot springs near the river where they stripped and lay back in the soap-smelling water and got stoned by gazing at the endless wash of the Milky Way across the night sky. That life in general she could talk about. That life in general was what they'd bargained for here, not the more recent version.

"So where is he?" Brian asked, rounding the corner into the living room. "Ro-jer the Cat?"

"In the kitchen. Probably still eating."

"You must be a magician. We barely have any food ourselves."

"I found some stuff, but we'll need to get to the store. Did Joseph say anything about going to Mbabane today?"

"He said he'd see us around noon, like always."

"Great," she said. "I know they'll think we're nuts, but Roger's a lot better than the alternative."

"Which is?" He poured two cups of coffee and handed her one.

"A houseboy or girl."

"What?"

"Glory can't believe only two people live in a place this big, especially when we're not even married."

"Where'd she get that idea?"

"We don't have kids."

"So we must not sleep together?"

"I guess."

"But we know better than that, don't we?" he said, reaching under the table to squeeze her thigh.

She moved his hand and leaned up to retrieve an old white business envelope from the windowsill. "Here's a list I started of things I think we'll need for Roger."

He sat back, wrapping both hands around his coffee mug. "So are you still mad about last night?"

"No, I'm not mad. I never was. But I did think you might wonder if I'd be worried where you were, or if something had happened to you. I couldn't stand that."

"Like I told you, when I realized how late it was—"

"It's just harder to be alone now, especially after dark."

"I know, I know, and I'm sorry. I really am. Okay?"

"Help yourself to some cereal, if you want."

"Meg?"

"Eat," she said. "It's okay. Everything's okay."

As she watched Brian follow the dirt path to school to work on organizing books Barclays Bank had donated for the new library, she reminded herself that she wasn't the only person suffering, and she needed to back off and be kinder. It was that simple. They were in this together, and she wanted them to stay that way.

The library was a huge project, and Mr. Dube had asked Brian to be head of the library committee, which, of course, meant he was doing most of the work himself. Other teachers helped out occasionally, and Meg did as well, when she could. But most of the work had fallen to him.

In the beginning, the job wasn't at all burdensome. The government had built the additional room on the far end of the school, but it had stood empty until the British embassy bought itself new furniture and sent a truckload of used tables and chairs to the school. Mr. Dube called ten or so of the biggest boys from class and directed them, with Brian's help, in unloading the truck and arranging the furniture in the library. But the shelves remained empty until word spread about what the British had done. Nearly every week after that, another delivery had arrived—from the US embassy, the French embassy, the Russian, Chinese, Indian and Kenyan embassies. Mostly propaganda materials on the respective countries, musty pamphlets and economic reports, some books on agriculture and industry, education and social progress. But it was nothing anyone, except maybe Percy, would have an interest in reading. Certainly not younger people. But then the Swedes, Danes, Norwegians and Finns brought box after box of illustrated young adult books, with colorful covers, and all English-language editions. They also sent Dala horses, a Viking head mobile from Denmark, reindeer carvings from Finland, a large framed photograph of a fjord in Norway. And once the Scandinavians had upped the ante, another wave of books and artifacts from all over Africa and the rest of the world arrived, capped off by a generous shipment of reference books and more serious reading materials—histories, classic novels, and biographies of famous people from Barclays, the biggest bank in the country. Stationers, office supply companies, even the government, contributed paper and ink pads and stamps, a card catalogue, a book cart, pens, bookends, paperclips, and a rolling chalkboard.

Stacks of boxes loomed head-high along the perimeters of the room and on top of and under every available table and chair. Brian tried to keep it corralled into general categories, but the donations proved to be almost too much of a good thing. Mr. Dube had a cousin who reported for the *Times of Swaziland* and he asked her if she would be interested in writing a piece on the new library, in which she could mention that the school was grateful for everyone's generosity but that they had reached a limit for the time being on further offerings. The story ran, and the pipeline dried up.

But the issue remained about what to do with everything. Brian had told Meg that probably a third of what they had could be pitched — particularly the propaganda. Once that had been triaged and disposed of, the rest, although time-consuming, was more straightforward. Sort and assign — after relearning the Dewey Decimal System, of course. Fortunately, the basic outline for classifying books and other printed matter, which was mainly what they were dealing with, accompanied the new card catalogue. On his good days, Brian told her it was doable. It would take a while, but they could get it done. Bad days left him demoralized and irritated by the enormity of the task.

He told her he had already done the easy part by determining what they wanted to keep. But how to get rid of the rest in a country that didn't waste a scrap of anything was another matter. And he was right, she thought, glancing at the garbage pit he had dug halfway between their house and the fence. Each Saturday night they carried out their trash but waited to burn it until after the herd boys came by early Sunday, driving their cattle to pasture. Chatting and jousting for position, they lifted the sheet of plywood covering the pit and got down on hands and knees to scour the refuse she and Brian had dumped—any scrap of paper that seemed useable, glass or plastic bottles and jars, tin cans, broken electrical cords, you name it.

"So, yeah, it's a real problem," he said one evening after they'd eaten. "If there wasn't so damned much of it, we might be able to get by with burning it a little at a time. But can you imagine the shit we'd have to pay if even a single half-burned page of some god-awful five-year plan floated away and a kid found it and brought it back to school?"

"Could we maybe rent a truck and take it somewhere?" she asked.

"I thought about that. Even make two or three trips, if we had to. But the problem is, I'm not sure the dump in Manzini or Mbabane would work. They're too public. Too many eyes."

"Even if we did somehow get rid of the stuff," she said, "what happens if the embassy people come to see the results of their largesse—and they will, they always do." She tapped her finger rapidly against the table. "It sounds like we're stuck with the junk, like it or not, but how about this? What are we looking at volume-wise?"

His eyes roamed the walls. "I don't know, there's quite a bit."

"Too much to stow in that big closet?"

"Hard to say without trying. What are you thinking?" he said.

"Here's my hare-brained scheme: we put everything else—all the good books and art and so forth—we put that out nice and pretty—you know, make the place really inviting and appear to be full to the brim. But we leave a space—it has to be a prominent one, even if it isn't huge—and there we display some of the best material you can pull from the junk—anything bright, with flags on the covers, that kind of thing. On the wall just above it, we hand-print a sign in block letters that says REPRESENTATIVE WORKS FROM LOBAMBA NATIONAL JUNIOR SECONDARY

SCHOOL'S SPECIAL INTERNATIONAL COLLECTION. THE
REMAINDER IS HOUSED IN THE LIBRARY'S ADJOINING
ANNEX. What do you think?"

He stood, walked around to her chair, leaned down, and
kissed her. "I think you're brilliant. Just brilliant."

Any other day she would have gone to school with him, but
Saturdays, mornings especially, were hers to spend doing what
she wanted—sweeping, doing dishes, washing underwear
to dry in the spare bedroom. She called it puttering, because,
while she was doing necessary things, they didn't require her
complete attention, although enough so that her mind couldn't
stray to less pleasant thoughts, as it did too often when it wasn't
otherwise occupied. She envied Brian's ability to bluster and
fume about what bothered him, since once the irritant surfaced,
it seemed to disappear. She didn't have that knack and lived
with an uneasiness that dampened her mood more often than
she liked. It wasn't that she feared anything or anyone, and
she couldn't allow herself to believe the events of that night
could ever happen to her again. What she suffered instead was
a pervasive anxiety that no matter what she did, it wouldn't be
right. She had difficulty making simple decisions about what to
eat, what to wear, what to buy, how to get somewhere. She no
longer wanted to leave the house other than to teach, although
she still made herself do things, usually with Brian, like go to
the market. But to function at even such a modified level, she
had to busy herself with familiar routines and events she could
anticipate without trepidation, such as housework and Sarah
coming with Jabalile to tea at 10:30 sharp almost every Saturday
morning before they left for the market in Mbabane.

At 10:15, she put water on the gas burner and dropped three
Tetley bags into the pot of her blue tea service. As soon as she
heard Sarah and Jabalile chattering and laughing on their way
to her house, she filled the pot with steaming water, put the lid

on, and carried the set on its tray, along with a plate of chocolate chip cookies, to the living-room table.

"Yoo-hoo!" Sarah called after knocking at the kitchen door.

"*Kungena bangani,*" Meg said. "Come in, my friends."

Sarah ushered Jabalile into the living room. "You have been practicing."

"I try," Meg said.

"It was perfect."

"*Li bhisikiti?*" she asked Jabalile, holding the cookie plate toward her.

Jabalile took two. Sarah shook her head and held up one finger.

Jabalile peered at Meg, who smiled and nodded.

Sarah took her usual seat in the bentwood rocker and pulled the scarf she'd been knitting for her sister in the Republic out of a sisal bag. Jabalile played with jar lids on the floor at her feet and nibbled her cookies. Meg sat at the table, intending to mark quizzes she needed to hand back on Monday as they all listened off and on to the radio—"It's 10:30 Greenwich Meantime. Here is the news."

Sarah glanced up from her knitting to watch Roger's tail dangling down the wall. Her gaze switched to Meg, back to the cat.

"Glory gave him to us."

"Ah."

"Otherwise."

"Of course."

"Did you have pets?"

"Not really," Sarah said. "My father had a dog that stayed mostly at his shop."

"A watchdog?"

"Yes. I believe that was the idea, but he was more friendly than fierce. My brother and I played with him sometimes, trying to get him to—how do you say?—chase his tail?"

"Yes."

"He would run in a circle until he dropped."

"So you understand—at least a little."

Sarah smiled a bit.

"Brian says everybody will think we're nuts."

Sarah sucked in her right cheek and bit down on it softly. "Some might."

"Do you?"

"No. He will entertain you and make you laugh. That will be a good thing. See just now." Roger's tail twitched and flicked, once going into an extended spasmodic dance against the wall. "If it wasn't yellow and covered with fur, you might think it was a snake. Jabalile and I would be out of here just like that."

"And leave me alone?"

A shrug, a broader smile. "You would be welcome to go with us."

Fear of snakes was real. Nearly everyone they knew had been bitten by one or had almost been. There were mambas, cobras, adders, boomslangs—each of which could inflict a fatal bite. Spitting cobras were said to be able to hypnotize their victims before blinding them with a stream of venom to the eyes. In general, people seemed to think that the only good snake was a dead snake and that you had to be constantly on guard because they were everywhere.

"They sometimes do come into houses, you know," Sarah said, as if to explain her reaction to the cat's tail. "Why, I heard that a woman who works for some Europeans near Manzini just this past week shot a cobra in their kitchen."

"No."

"Glory told me. She is the woman's friend. She swears it is true."

"Right. And how many snakes have you killed in your kitchen?"

Sarah knitted a few stitches. "None. But my kitchen is clean. And I keep the ground swept around my house and the garbage burned, just like you. Snakes do not like it there or here."

"But even if the woman did see a snake in the kitchen, where would she get a gun to shoot it?"

"Oh, that is not so difficult. There are guns here, too, you know. It is not only in America."

"Do you have one?"

"Joseph does not care for them."

"Neither do we."

"But that does not mean Glory's friend has the same thoughts, and she would probably know if there was a gun in the house where she works."

"I suppose," Meg said. "And shooting the snake definitely makes a better story than smashing it with a skillet."

"Or a broom."

"Or a stone. Remember that day at school?"

"Oh, yes," Sarah said. "Who was it now? The Sithole boy. He shouted 'snake' and everyone came running and formed a circle around it and pitched their stones and when the snake was dead another boy brought a stick to toss it over the fence and everyone cheered like he had just scored a goal. It was quite exciting." She covered her mouth with the back of her hand as she smiled. "Do you think there might have been snakes in the toilets?"

Meg laughed. "Maybe that's why people were throwing stones down them."

"Someone should tell Mr. Maphalala."

"Do you think he would listen?"

"Oh, definitely," Sarah said. "Everyone listens about snakes."

A sharp, urgent knock at the front door brought Meg to her feet, and Sarah snatched Jabalile from the floor. A second knock followed, louder and more demanding.

Meg took a slow, deep breath as she glimpsed the van in front of their house, the thin young man at the door in black boots, high socks, khaki shorts, and a blue sweater vest over his long-sleeved khaki shirt. He was hatless and holding a brown paper bag with handles, his right hand raised to knock again. "It's the police."

Sarah tightened her hold on Jabalile.

Meg opened the door enough that she and the officer could see each other.

"Are you Mrs. Bernard?" he asked.

"I am."

"I have been instructed to give you this," raising the bag. He had a shadow of a moustache and goatee and an arrogant air that she feared would only grow more pronounced the older he got.

"What is it?"

"I do not know. The captain says you must look, then sign."

She opened the door wider but still did not take the bag. He set it on the floor at her feet. Inside she could make out a neatly tied and tagged white bundle, which had to have been their bedsheets, the shirt she'd worn, the washcloth, the knife, and other things the sergeant had taken folded on top of it.

"Where do I sign?"

"You may not until—"

"What?"

"Until you—I am sorry, I do not know the word."

"Identify?"

"Yes. Identify. That is what the captain said."

"But I already know what's in there."

"He said you must take each thing out and look at it and then sign."

"No," she heard herself say.

His eyes hardened.

"I'm not going to," she went on, willing herself to speak calmly, forcefully. "I won't now or ever, and if you won't leave it on those conditions, you can take it straight back to the station and tell the captain I refused to accept it."

The officer glanced at Sarah, as though appealing to her to intervene, to interpret, to explain the importance of following directions. But when she said nothing, he stiffened and thrust the clipboard toward Meg, a long finger jabbing "here, here, here."

When she'd finished signing, she handed the clipboard back to the officer and stepped away. "Please put the bag on the table."

The officer gazed at her, a quizzical look in his eye, and she gave him a single nod and a tight smile and showed him exactly where she wanted it. He grabbed the bag and swung it onto the corner of the table.

"No, I changed my mind." If the bag were there, she would have to look at it constantly and to move it. She would have to touch it, which she had no intention of doing, ever. "Put it there instead."

The officer dropped the bag onto the chair by the far wall.

"Thank you."

He bowed and clicked his heels.

"Is there anything else?" she said.

"No, Madam, that is all. Good day, Madam."

"Good day."

She closed the door after him, turning to brace her back against it. Neither she nor Sarah spoke—even Jabalile was quiet—all eyes on the bag.

"I hate this," she said finally.

"Yes," Sarah nodded. "Too bad it isn't a snake. We could stone it, kill it, and cut it into tiny pieces."

"And bury it?"

"Yes. Bury it."

"I only wish it was that easy."

She heard a low, steady voice and realized it was coming from the radio. Sarah seemed suddenly to hear it, too, and they both leaned their heads in its direction, as if what was being said was of vital importance. Meg turned the volume up slightly to announcements of a football union meeting Monday and a call for entries into an arts and crafts league competition, followed by the BBC news at the top of the hour, delivered by a man in a monotonic drone that she found strangely reassuring in its constancy and calm, no matter how dire the events it was describing. She wondered what he might say about her. Would she recognize herself and what had happened, reduced to a few words uttered by a stranger in a place she'd never seen and likely never would? Compared to war, disease, and famine, would her situation be deemed important enough to mention, even as a one-line story? Was it? She picked up Roger and held him, purring, against the hollow of her neck.

"Jeez, what's with you guys?" Brian said when he came in. "You look like somebody died."

Meg glanced at the bag. Brian opened it and peered inside.

"Is this what I think it is?"

She nodded.

"You don't want any of it, do you?"

"What do you think?"

He grabbed the bag and started for the kitchen. "I brought a box in case we need it for the cat. It's on the kitchen table."

She drifted along behind him, marveling at how decisive he seemed, how sure of what he was doing, the same as when he'd leapt from bed to slam Solomon Kunene into the wall. He took the paraffin oil from the corner by the stove and matches from the pantry and marched directly to the garbage pit. Sarah, with Jabalile on her hip, soon joined her, and they stood in the kitchen doorway, gazing on as Brian doused the bag with paraffin oil, lit it, and tossed it into the pit. He stepped back from the blaze and stirred the fire with a long, thin piece of wood they kept for that purpose, poking and spreading, ensuring that everything burnable eventually rose in a trail of smoke and ashes that floated up and over the school grounds, toward the valley and the mountains beyond.

6

Harry Philips nosed his creaky VW bus around the bend going south out of Mbabane, across the bridge, and along a dark granite wall carved into the mountainside. Beyond it, the vista broadened and the road dipped like a dog's tongue into the valley. To the right, plane trees and stone sills fell away to ravines of black wattle and knobwood trees, interspersed with tall grasses and scrub bushes he had no idea the names of. To the left, guava and fig and monkey rope trees bearding the lower reaches of the mountains gave way to holly and aloe, whose blossoms would soon burst into a brilliant yellow-orange display across the slope. The upper elevations of the mountains—Sheba's Breasts and Execution Rock to the west, the Mdzimba Mountain Ridge to the east—raised their bare, craggy peaks above either side of the valley that settled so gently below. Ezulwini Valley. The Valley of Heaven.

Aptly named, he thought, even from the first time he'd driven here. It was a place of such calm beauty and timelessness that he understood why the Swazi people considered it the spiritual center of the nation. The royal kraal at Lobamba lay slightly upslope from the bottom of the valley, and royal burial caves were said to dot Mdzimba Mountain opposite it, although he'd not seen one nor knew anyone else who had. But there was something even deeper and more profound that held sway over the land. Rocks here were three and a half billion years old— dating nearly to the beginning of the earth. Forty thousand years ago, people extracted and traded red ochre from a mine just to the west, near Ngwenya. The images he and Carolyn had seen on the rock overhangs were painted long before the area was permanently occupied by anyone. What he sensed there, when he allowed himself to, harkened to times so prehistoric they defied definition, so atavistic that chills crawled over his body, and hairs rose on the back of his neck and scalp. Once experienced, the feeling was impossible to forget, a bonding so complete that no matter where he ended up, no matter what he did, this place, this Africa, would always be a part of him. And that was something he didn't think Carolyn ever understood or felt.

He slowed to turn in to Mrs. Mabula's store to buy gas. Yes, gas. Not petrol, which seemed an unnatural term, as awkward on his tongue as living *in* rather than *on* Oxford Street, or pushing a trolley at the grocery store, or knocking someone up to awaken her—hoping, if she's in your bed, you haven't already.

As he pumped, he had a grand view of the crest of Mdzimba Mountain. He tried to imagine Solomon Kunene standing there in the middle of the night, a mere speck at that distance, having picked his way along a path up from Zombodze. Imagining him panting, sweating, parched was easy enough. But what the man saw was another matter. What was he looking at? What was he looking for? And why on that night, in that place? Harry Philips eyed what he guessed was the cattle path Kunene lumbered down to where it intersected the dirt road that led over the plank bridge across the Little Usutu River, past the hot springs and out to the highway. Across it, the road rose up and around a curve to the right toward the market and royal kraal, and Lobamba School and its teachers' compound spread in low stucco buildings across a lower knoll to the left. Did Kunene even hesitate at that point to decide in which direction to go, or was he, as he claimed, directed there, compelled by the mysterious force he said he felt?

Harry Philips finished fueling and went inside to pay Mrs. Mabula. She was sitting on the same stool behind the counter in the same spot just to the left of the cash drawer as she had been the whole time he'd been stopping in. And she looked like the same hungry black Buddha she had the first time he'd seen her. Maybe she, like his grandmother, another restaurateur, didn't eat her own cooking, which, if rumors were true, might have turned out to be wise in Mrs. Mabula's case. He greeted her, ordered a scone, coffee, and a tin of shortbread biscuits, paid up and wished her well—all with nothing but a nod from her—climbed back behind the wheel and drove on.

Toward the south end of the valley, another paved road led off to the right in the direction of Malkerns Valley and the college at Luyengo. To the left, just across from the junction, a large white roadside stand he occasionally stopped at sold pineapples for 10 cents, half-bushels of oranges for 50 cents, and small piles of tomatoes for 5 cents.

A half-mile later, he turned left onto a red dirt road that wound around the foot of Mdzimba Mountain and curled along its east side to Zombodze. The air in the car was stifling and his sweaty shirt stuck to the vinyl seat as he dodged potholes and rocks, halted for herd boys and their cattle, pulled off the road so a small bus could go by, and beeped his horn constantly at pedestrians, who to a person took their time getting out of the way and then stared at him as he passed, speculating, no doubt, on why he, a white man, was driving to Zombodze at all—not to mention alone.

He'd told himself he wanted to talk to Kunene's mother, which he realized from the beginning was a long shot, since he doubted he would find her at home; and even if he did, he suspected she wouldn't talk to him. Beyond just seeing her, he wasn't sure what he expected to learn. Certainly no magic answer to what had driven her son over the mountain to Lobamba. But he had nonetheless felt a need to go, to see with his own eyes the place Kunene called home. It wasn't that he believed where you came from dictated any more than the shape of your head who you were, or why you did or didn't do something. It was more a way to go to the source of things, so to speak, to begin at the beginning.

The road passed through a thicket of trees, curved sharply, and dipped down to the Mtilane River, where he found only a trickle of water flowing over the rocks below and no bridge. Instead, a concrete ramp led down to the stream and up the other side, serving in essence as a spillway. Which was fine for now, but during the rainy season the crossing would be largely unusable and anyone needing to get to Zombodze or out to the highway would have to detour many miles north or south to do so. The ramp looked relatively new, though, and he wondered why, when it was constructed, a bridge wasn't built in its place. Expense was the most obvious answer, but he imagined it had at least as much to do with the local chief thinking if a bridge were built, it would bring more traffic and more people—most of whom would be strangers, some speaking strange tongues and possibly spreading strange ideas—and he could eventually end up with problems on his hands he'd never dreamed of. So the matter would have been settled. A bridge was out of the question.

Harry Philips put his car in gear and inched his way across the river, quite handily as it happened, and he concluded, for the moment, that the chief might have been wiser than he'd first thought, since people without business to take care of on the other side most probably would have turned around and gone straight back to where they'd come from.

Zombodze was only a short distance to the north, a scattering of boxy cinder-block houses with rusted metal roofs amid traditional thatched huts appearing just past a copse of bush willow trees and leading to a general store. A thin man dressed in dark trousers and a white shirt—most likely the shop's owner—leaned, legs and arms crossed, against the doorframe, an old Swazi man sitting on a wooden bench beside him, shoeless and toothless, an *umbodze* ringing his head. The shop would be crammed, like every other one he'd seen, with bolts of African cloth; ready-made shirts, dresses and trousers; shoes and sandals; canned goods, cooking oil, loaves of bread, boxes of cereal, bags of rice, flour and mealie-meal; nails, nuts and bolts and a few tools; newspapers and magazines but no books; candles, matches and paraffin oil; skin creams, hair picks and lotions; toothpaste and brushes; hand mirrors; butcher knives but no cutlery or dishes; cases of warm Coke, Fanta and beer—everything infused with the piquant scent of incense.

To the right, a section of the room would be closed off, but for a barred opening arched like a church window, to serve as a post office, which would also hold what was probably the area's only telephone, where you could place a call—you had to book a time, perhaps a week or two in advance, and be sure to appear at the assigned hour and day or lose your chance. And even though the man at the door was present the whole time the shop was open, it would be his wife who ran it. Harry Philips imagined her as a short, going-on-plump woman, who still had a pronounced hip wag under her lemon sari and wore her dark, gray-wisped hair drawn back tightly into a bun, gold loop earrings, a vermilion bindi the size of a fingertip on her forehead above her nose, and eyeglasses that were slightly too large, causing her to look more interested than she probably was as she bantered with customers but refused to back down from anyone who questioned the cost of merchandise: "Fair prices. Always fair prices. You want? Yes or no."

Although his could easily have been the first car they'd seen that day, neither the owner nor the Swazi man waved or nodded or acknowledged his presence, remaining still as statues until he stopped and motioned for the shop owner to come closer.

Harry Philips asked where he could find Mrs. Kunene. After getting directions, he idled on up the dusty road, past barking dogs, chickens pecking the bare earth, women ambling to and fro, bundles of wood and laundry high on their heads, children with wide eyes and swollen bellies playing along the edge of the road.

The local school and a small mission church marked the end of the village, and farther on, across a sizeable mealies field near the mountain, the royal kraal nestled under a growth of eucalyptus trees, a cluster of gray-thatched hut roofs appearing like Chinese skullcaps above the top of the reed fence surrounding it. The current king had been born there, although people said he hardly ever returned now, preferring to spend his time near the queen mother's kraal at Lobamba.

Harry Philips stopped in front of a small hut so tattered and crumbling that it appeared abandoned, but for a 5-foot-wide snake guard of scraped red earth around it and a well-tended banana stand to the rear. He got out of his car and walked toward the low, arched doorway of the hut to look in but not to enter without invitation, which was unthinkable. The interior was dark and empty and the air heavy with the smell of wood smoke and the sweet scent of cow manure and mud plastered on the floor and walls. One sisal sleeping mat lay on the floor and a second had been rolled tightly and stowed beside it. The only thing that could be called furniture was a wooden box at the rear with a cooking pot on top.

He straightened and turned to see an old woman tramping toward him along the road he'd driven in on, one hand atop a bundle of firewood on her head, the other swinging like a pendulum, marking her pace. She passed a *tjwala* hut where men, old and young, already squatted in a circle and drank from the communal bowl given them by the woman who tended the pots. The men ceased their discussion until the wood gatherer, old enough to be their mother or grandmother, was out of earshot. Closer and closer she came until she drew even with him, their eyes meeting.

"*Sawubona, make,*" he said. I see you, my mother.

"*Sawubona, umlungu.*" I see you, white man.

She seemed older than old, bent yet straight, diminutive yet strong, time itself folding into the flesh of her face, as she rolled the bundle of wood from her head, cradled it in her arms, and leaned it against the wall of her hut. She sat on the bare ground to the right of her doorway, knees to one side, feet tucked toward her hips, hands crossed, palms down, on her leg.

Harry Philips squatted on his haunches to the left of the doorway, not knowing what to say. He would need to speak siSwati, having determined early on that, if he was going to live in Swaziland, he would need to learn the language as best he could.

Normally, he would have begun the conversation by inquiring about her health and her family's health, on and on until he'd run out of relatives. But in her case, her husband was dead and her children scattered. To have asked after them might have embarrassed her by her not knowing or, worse, having to lie and say they were fine when they weren't, particularly one who was under arrest in Mbabane. Instead, he offered her the tin of biscuits he'd brought, extending it in his right hand, left hand drawn back, fingertips atop his right wrist, and thanked her for receiving him.

Her mouth, puckered as a dried prune, twitched in a would-be smile as she accepted the tin with both hands, opened it, and offered him a shortbread. She then took one herself, resealed the tin, and cradled it in the crook of her arm.

When they had finished eating and dusted their hands, he asked if she had a son named Solomon Kunene, and she said her name was Kunene, Blessed Kunene, and, yes, she did have a son, Solomon. He asked if she knew where he was now, and she said they—pointing to the men at the *tjwala* pot—had told her he was in jail in Mbabane, was that true? Harry Philips said yes it was and did she know why he was there? She peered back down the road in the direction from which she'd come and said they—those same men—had told her he had slept with a woman. Harry Philips asked if that was all they'd said, and she nodded that it was.

He found two pebbles that he rattled in his palm and dropped over and over on the ground between his feet as he thought what to say next and how to say it but stopped when he felt the intensity of her dark eyes following his every move, as if he were an *inyanga* throwing bones to divine the future. The problem is, he said, if your son—if he had only slept with the woman the way a man usually sleeps with a woman—he would not be in the jail at Mbabane. She tilted her head a bit, blinked. But, Harry Philips went on, that was not what happened. That was not how he slept with the woman. Did she understand now? She asked if that meant the woman did not invite him to sleep with her, did not want him, and Harry Philips said yes, exactly, my mother, and she asked if the woman screamed or kicked or beat her son. Harry Philips said she did scream but he didn't know of anything else, and the old woman said then how can this be so and who said that it was? Harry Philips told her the woman's husband was in the bed with her and woke up and caught her son and held him for the police, and the old woman said so they were the ones who said he did it, and Harry Philips said yes, that was so. She asked if the man and woman were Europeans and Harry Philips said no, Americans, and she said but white? and he said yes, white, and she nodded and said nothing.

Harry Philips said there were other things as well from the police report—her son's clothes outside the bedroom window—and his own statement in which he—She snapped her head in his direction, eyes sharp as flint, and said what was paper? Paper was not truth. It could burn or get old and turn to dust. Harry Philips said that might be, but the fact was that her son, Solomon Kunene, had been arrested for the rape of the woman at Lobamba and he would be tried for that crime. She was looking now toward Mdzimba Mountain and all he could see was the side of her face, tears trickling from the corner of her one visible eye into the patchwork of creases on her cheek and chin, and she was repeating like a mantra: why Lobamba when his home was here with her in Zombodze? Why Lobamba? Which was exactly what Harry Philips wanted to know himself, so he asked her if she had any idea why her son would go there—did he have friends in Lobamba he might have been on his way to visit? Was he in any way associated with the school? Might he have known someone there? Maybe the white woman, a Peace Corps volunteer who taught there? Could she say anything to help him answer these questions?

She looked back at Harry Philips, cheeks wet with tears, and said that her son was a good man who did all he could to help her. He would never do what Harry Philips said he had. He could not, would not. Unless—she paused—unless someone had cursed him. The woman at Lobamba had to be a witch, an evil enchantress who preyed on young men to come to her for her pleasure. Used them. Ruined them. She wanted her son back. She wanted the woman to lift the curse from him. She should have been the one in jail, not her Solomon.

She stood, fitted the bundle of firewood onto her head, and started toward a narrow, rutted path that led toward Mdzimba Mountain, the biscuit tin gleaming on the ground where she had left it.

7

One evening as she and Brian were marking essays and quizzes by the light of the propane lantern, she put down her pen, pushed the stack of papers toward the center of the table, and said, "Can we talk for a minute?"

"Sure. What's up?"

"I'm serious," she said, glancing at the open essay he was still reading.

He slipped a bookmark into place, one of the two or three hundred Barclays had provided with their gift to the library, all of them printed to look like folded banknotes.

"The radio, too, if you don't mind."

He switched off Voice of Kenya and sat back in his chair. "I'm all ears."

"I can't stop thinking about the trial. What it's going to be like. What's going to happen. If it's even going to happen."

"It will," Brian said.

"Do you think I'll have to testify?"

"I don't know," Brian said, "but I can't imagine you won't be called on."

She watched a rhinoceros beetle drone around the lamp and tried to steady her voice. "But I'm not sure I can."

He stood and went to the kitchen, returning with a bottle of beer in each hand.

"We've talked about this before. Push comes to shove, you may not have a choice."

"Why?"

"Isn't that pretty obvious?"

"Don't use that tone with me. I'm not a child. I'm not stupid."

"No, you're not."

"Then don't treat me like I am." She gulped a mouthful of beer and nearly choked on the foam.

He stared at her and kept staring, as if to keep himself from shaking his head. "I'm not trying to be a jerk. I just—"

"Want me to be realistic, right? Well I am. I know I need to be ready to do it—psychologically, emotionally." Another, smaller swallow of beer. "But I don't have to like it."

"No, you don't."

"And I also need to be able to be mad and yell about it. You're the only person I can do that with who I think will still love me." She rotated her beer bottle several times before adding, "On a totally different subject, I wanted to tell you something that should be a relief: my period started today."

He did smile and nod and say yes as he reached for her hand, but she couldn't be certain, judging from his otherwise quizzical expression, whether the possibility that she even could have been pregnant from the rape had ever crossed his mind.

That night she dreamed she was standing at a bus stop that wasn't really there, near the junction of the market road and the main highway between Mbabane and Manzini. She could make out Mdzimba Mountain in front of her, which meant she was on the same side of the road as the school and the bus would eventually take her south, and that seemed wrong to get where she wanted to go. But no matter. She knew, somehow, that she was exactly where she needed to be. The sign behind her said it was, in plain English, and she had suitcases on the ground on either side of her, their ends squared neatly with the road so the bus driver could make no mistake about whether she wanted to get on board. Other people were there as well, despite the darkness and the fact that they never spoke nor had any more substance than the shadows they moved in and out of. The night was pleasant enough, even refreshing, a soft breeze rippling the hem of the gingham house dress she wore. How odd? She hadn't worn anything like that in her life. Her hair was shorter, as well, and more curled. And she was wearing black pumps with low heels. She never wore heels. She couldn't think for the life of her where she got those clothes or when she had put them on. So she wondered where this other woman had come from, this mockery of herself, who, without the suitcases, looked for all the world like a fifties housewife waiting for her husband to drive the Chevy by and pick her up. She glanced around but no one else seemed to notice how strange she looked. And maybe that was the idea. Maybe she was traveling incognito and just hadn't realized it. She smiled at the cleverness of her disguise, how unlike her it made her seem; and even though she hated the image she projected, she was willing to go along with it—to foster it, in fact—if it got her where she wanted to be. She squared her shoulders and arched her back, primly smoothing the dress along her hips and thighs before folding her hands in front of her and watching the first blink of lights in the distance. Within seconds, she heard the rush of the bus's engine and rose on her toes as if to see better, lowered herself lest she show too much eagerness. She was, after all, a housewife on a journey to see a grandparent or an elderly aunt, which would seem more a family obligation than something to be looked forward to with enthusiasm. The closer the bus got to her, the slower it appeared to move, shimmering lines spreading before it and around the windshield, above which she could see the destination blind with USA displayed dimly within it. The bus was large, like a Greyhound, although it didn't say as much anywhere on it and wouldn't, of course, since Greyhound didn't operate in that part of the world. There was no lettering at all that she could see, the sleek metal sides glimmering ever so faintly as the bus glided to a stop, brakes hissing. The door swung open to a dimly lighted interior, the driver's eyes catching hers and holding her in place as others brushed past her to board. Or seemed to. She didn't see them so much as feel their presence. Once everyone else had taken their places, the driver nodded at her and she leaned down to lift her bags. They were heavier than she remembered, and she could hardly budge them. The driver did nothing to help. She wrestled one on board, then the other and stood panting on the first step, saying, the US please. The driver shook his head no, that wasn't where they were going. And she said but, and he said the truth was they had no destination, she could look again, but she knew she didn't dare because he would drive off without her. She asked when the right bus would come, and he said never, as far as he knew. The next bus wouldn't be by for a year, if then, and who knew where it would be going? She said she didn't want to wait, that she would go where he took her, and she lugged her suitcases to an empty seat halfway back and sat down. The driver stood then and walked to the rear of the bus, which sprouted wings with propeller motors, and the printed card in the seat pocket in front of her read DC-3. She looked out the window and thought, but that's too old, too old to fly, and the driver, now pilot, strode back up the aisle toward his seat, now the cockpit, and turned before entering. He cleared his throat, twirled the ends of his long red moustache, fingered the brass buttons on his navy-blue Pan Am uniform jacket, as if to be sure it was properly closed, and announced through gapped front incisors that he was ready to see if he could get this bucket of bolts off the ground. He closed the plywood cockpit door behind him and started the engines, which coughed and belched smoke and finally sputtered to life. The plane taxied along the runway and turned onto the circular area at the end of it from which every plane took off. The fuselage shuddered as the engines revved, and she turned to glance at her fellow passengers, all of whom now appeared deathly pale and lay sprawled in their seats like corpses. No, she shook her head, no, please, no, as the plane hurtled down the runway, engines building to a throaty roar, before suddenly shutting down, the nose of the plane settling back onto the tarmac, the pilot's—or someone's—voice sputtering that they were too goddamn heavy to take off; there was one person too many on the aircraft. If that person didn't get off, no one would be going anywhere. There was no question that he was referring to her, and she knew the matter was not debatable, so she carted her luggage to the fuselage door, opened it, balanced herself with a suitcase in each hand and stepped back into the night.

After school the next Friday Brian bribed Joseph with a case of beer to take him to the hardware store in Manzini where he bought rebars, a hammer, a chisel, a brush, a tape measure, a carpenter's pencil, a hack saw with several extra blades, a trowel, two small bags of cement and a tray to mix it in.

She watched as he arranged everything in their room Saturday morning and covered the bed and dresser with their extra sheets. She'd wanted him to put bars in the window when they'd first come back to Lobamba, but he'd said no, he didn't think it was a good idea. And he'd continued to resist, regardless of what she'd said. Until now. She was curious about his change of mind but knew better than to interrupt him to ask.

He began working as soon as their duplex neighbor, Percy Mavuso, strode past in the direction of the local market. Percy was another Zulu expatriate from the Republic who had come to Swaziland looking for a job and ended up teaching history, although he was formally trained in music education. Apparently recognizing a good thing when he saw it, Mr. Dube put Percy in charge of school music, which included a student *a cappella* chorus that sang using a do-re-mi notation system Meg had never seen and turned out a delightful, almost professional sound.

Percy was a tall, gangly, Ichabod Crane of a man who outside of sporadic trips to Mbabane and Manzini spent the rest of his free time at home, much of it reading, she assumed, since she rarely saw him without a book in hand. Once, Meg had found him firing an air rifle at birds in flight behind their duplex. She finally asked what he was doing, and he said he was practicing how to shoot at airplanes for when the revolution came in the

Republic. That and nothing more, as though anyone who had thought about it would have come to the same conclusion. But he wasn't being rude or arrogant, she thought, as much as displaying a shyness born out of living alone. He had no wife and, as far as they could tell, no steady girlfriend, although he did on occasion host an overnight visitor. Otherwise, he seemed to prefer his own company.

The clink-clink, clink-clink of hammer on chisel carried on the morning air, turning heads even as far away as the market road, but no one stopped to pinpoint the source of the sound. Brian had measured and marked three equal spaces at the top of the window frame above the left- and right-hand casement openings and made three matching marks on the sill, left and right. At each mark, top and bottom, he drew a line from the inside of the frame to a point at exactly half its width, then stepped back to check that all the lines seemed parallel and in order. Picking up the hammer and chisel, he positioned himself at the upper left-hand line and etched a groove a half-inch left of it, outside in, and a second an equal distance from the line on the other side but with the chisel aimed at a 45-degree angle to it. The top layer of stucco chipped away more easily than she'd imagined it would, leaving a more or less uniform inch-deep groove where the line had been. He ran his finger along the space, nodded and began on the second line, then the third, all the way across the top of the frame, bits of paint and cement flying here and there, a grayish mist settling over the bed, the dresser, him, sweat soon streaking his face, arms, back, falling in dust blooms on the floor by his feet. She didn't care. She would happily clean it up.

After he finished the final groove, he dusted all of them out with the brush and began measuring, again left to right, as you would read a page, extending the tape measure bottom to top, bending it so that it fit into the groove for an accurate reading. He recorded each measurement on a piece of paper, redoing them all a second time to be sure, before carrying the hack saw and reinforcing rods to the turnstile in the school fence.

He marked the first measurement on a rod, laid it over two crosspieces and braced it against an upright post. The saw screeched and caught. Brian's face turned red and she knew he was swearing, even though she couldn't hear him. He rotated the rod slightly for a fresh spot to begin on, the saw blade settling into a steady, metallic grind that made her rub her tongue over her fillings. He numbered the first piece and each one after it, until he finished all six, gathered them and toted them back to the bedroom.

He fitted the first bar into the top and bottom grooves, tapping it in the last half-inch or so with the hammer. The second, likewise, the third and so on until a rusty grin spread across the spaces in front of the windows, through which she could see Percy rounding the upper bend in the market road, his canvas shopping bag bulging at his side. Even at a leisurely pace, his long legs covered the distance rapidly, and he soon arrived at the path that cut across the upper dam of tandem ponds that lay between the teachers' compound and the road. He topped the near rise of the ravine and crossed the drive that separated their duplex from the facing one. As he approached his door, he halted, cocking his head in the direction of their window, studied it a moment and went inside. He must have passed straight through, taking time only to drop off his bag, on his way out his back door and over to theirs.

"Hello?" he called.

She turned toward the kitchen, not really wanting anyone else around just then, but not knowing how to avoid the situation. "Come in, Percy."

"Thank you. I don't mind if I do."

He joined her at the bedroom doorway. Brian was mixing mortar in the flat pan, its rich, wet smell penetrating even the dust.

"Ah, a project I see," Percy said.

"Yep," Brian said, without looking up.

"Bars, is it?"

"Bars." Brian stood, lifting the pan, scooping mortar onto the trowel.

"An excellent idea and an understandable one." He lowered his head, as though embarrassed by having thought about the reason for the bars.

"They should be pretty secure once I get them cemented in."

"Oh, yes, I believe they should be. I worked as a mason, you know."

"Fantastic," Brian said. "Do you mind looking to see this is mixed right?"

"My pleasure." Percy took the trowel and stabbed the mound of mortar a few times. "Yes, that should do nicely. Only here, at the top," pointing a long, thin finger, "apply a small amount along the edges. When it sets, apply a small amount more. And so on, until the channel is filled. Otherwise—"

"It'll fall out and I'll have a mess on my hands."

Percy smiled, Adam's apple bobbing. "Yes. A mess indeed."

"Thanks."

"Not to mention it."

"Would you care for tea?" Meg asked as she walked him to the bedroom door.

"Oh, please, don't bother."

"I was going to make some for myself."

"No, I truly must be getting on. There is my market bag to unpack and then I go to meet someone at Manzini. But before I go…" He glanced once more toward the window, finger to his lips. "I was, yes, um, I was just wondering…"

"What?" Brian said.

"I was wondering if perhaps, um, well, if you were going to bar the rest of the windows, you might want to make only a small hole in the top, with a channel at the bottom, so that you might insert the bar in the hole and slide it into place. That way—"

"It's only half the work."

"Indeed."

"Thanks. I'll keep that in mind, but at this point I don't think we're going to do the others."

"Ah, I see," he said, nodding but hardly able to contain his puzzlement over barring only one set of windows. "Is that wise, do you think?"

"We do," Brian said.

"Well, um." He straightened, hands making a dry, raspy sound as he rubbed his palms together. "I'll just be off then."

"See you later," Brian said.

Meg walked him outside and a few steps toward his house, but not more than halfway, so he would feel welcomed to come back.

"I'm sure this all seems silly to you," she said.

"Not in the least." Percy bowed, shook her hand. "After what you have experienced—well, let me say that it is not unexpected. Window protection of one sort or another is quite common in my country, as you may know. And if you accomplish nothing else by it, you can again be able to feel the night breeze."

"Yes," she smiled, "I'm looking forward to that."

"Which reminds me," finger back to his lips, "do you think it would be too bold of me to ask Mr. Bernard—"

"Brian," she said.

"To ask, um, Brian if he would be so generous as to lend me his tools when he has finished with them?"

"I'm sure he'd be happy to. I'll ask him, if you want."

"Oh, that would be too kind, Madam," he said, bowing again. "Thank you, and goodbye."

"*Hamba kahle.*" Go well.

She picked up the broom and dustpan on her way through the kitchen and stood with them in front of her as she watched Brian fill the last groove on the windowsill.

"Looks great," she said, although she knew it didn't other than structurally. "You're becoming quite the revolutionary, you know."

"How so?"

"Percy asked me to ask you if he could borrow your tools when you're done."

"Really? That is funny. Hell, I'll probably get us all kicked out of here for defacing government property. You think he'll do all his windows?"

"What difference does it make?"

"None, but I'll bet he does. I'm sure it drove him nuts that we weren't."

"Maybe, I don't know. He was actually very nice about everything."

"It was Percy, after all." Brian walked back to the window frame, fingered the mortar along the top grooves.

She leaned on the broom, watching the slow, steady drag of the trowel, and said: "So why'd you decide to do it after you said so many times you wouldn't?"

He smoothed the last bit of mortar into the groove he was working on, dropped the trowel into the pan and turned to face her. "Because I knew I was going to lose you if I didn't."

She smiled, sort of, and he smiled back, sort of, but neither said anything more.

8

A crowd had gathered at the railing on the bridge over the Mbabane River, people peering down at the water, hands to their mouths. Throngs lined both banks below.

Harry Philips parked in the lot in front of the market and walked toward the river, as if into a painting or a surreal diorama where no one moved and all attention focused on a flat outcropping of rocks at the water's edge often used by younger girls to wash clothes. Skirts hiked and tied around their legs, they would wade into the river, dipping their laundry in a quiet pool behind an outcropping of rocks, while their younger sisters or cousins thrashed the water with branches to keep crocodiles away. They would lug the wet clothes to a specified rock on the bank, chosen for smoothness and height, lather each piece with a bar of green lye soap, carry them all back into the pool to rinse, wringing them, spreading them on bushes and rocks to dry, the whole time bantering and laughing with their friends. But not now. Now the girls stood holding hands, heads bowed in a semicircle behind the outcropping. All was silent—no talking, no laughing, no tinny jazz from a cheap radio, nothing. The wind itself had ceased, trees motionless.

He came to a halt when he heard the scrunch of his shoes in the gravel and stood in quiet acknowledgment of what he was almost certain had happened without having to be told. Someone—by the looks of it, most likely a washer girl from the group by the rocks—had been attacked and dragged away by a crocodile. It didn't happen often but often enough that people were watchful, and a sinister lore had grown up around crocodiles. The animal lies in the water, at times for hours, impossible to see but for two hooded eyes and nostrils at the end of a snout that might be visible above the surface. When a prey approaches the water's edge, the crocodile submerges completely and glides forward, eyes appearing briefly, re-submerging, gliding forward, until, within striking distance, it launches itself out of the water with incredible power and speed and clamps its jaws on whatever part of its prey is closest, dragging its victim underwater to drown. Once crocodiles have attacked, there is little anyone can do. They can be over 15 feet long, weigh more than 500 pounds and easily outrun the average person. Quick, efficient, grisly, which is exactly what makes them seem monstrous, Harry Philips thought. Something to be wary of and to guard against. He wondered what had gone wrong.

Sound seeped back to his attention when the girl in the middle of the semicircle raised her arms and began a rhythmic moan the other girls gradually joined as they began a swaying, slow-clapping procession up from the riverbank toward the market. Many from the crowd followed in what, if it were slightly more upbeat and accompanied by a brass band, could have passed for a New Orleans funeral march.

He waited until the area had cleared and glanced one last time at the riverbanks, where a few men still held vigil over a hopeless scene, before ducking into the market to buy the few things he knew they needed at home.

He could see Elizabeth talking with another girl in the backyard as he drove to the end of the driveway beside his house. They were huddled, as if trying to keep their voices from carrying. The sound of the car door closing snapped them apart, and they both turned in his direction. The other girl was shorter and thinner than Elizabeth and more casually dressed in an untucked yellow blouse and loose gray knee-length skirt. She wore round wire-rimmed glasses much like his own that she pushed up her nose, either out of habit or to bring him into better focus.

By the time he'd unloaded two bags from the trunk of the car, Elizabeth had appeared around the corner of the house. Even though it wasn't a school day, she was dressed in her usual black skirt, white blouse and blocky black shoes but now wore a red swatch of *emahiya* cloth knotted over her hair, a long canvas apron she must have found in the garage and a pair of blue and white cotton work gloves stained red with dirt. As she came closer, he could also make out a red smudge on her cheek that matched the red patches on her knees.

"What are you doing?"

"I have been working, Sir. There."

"Where?"

"Just there," she said, pointing a soiled glove finger toward round flowerbeds on either side of the walkway leading to the gazebo. Several years ago, Carolyn had cleared two 4-foot circles there and had bordered each with bricks angled so that sharp corners pointed up in a serrated row. The beds held an array of daisies, birds of paradise, gladioli and a single aloe in the center. Clematis climbed the gazebo and shaded the benches inside. He had to admit that the garden had been beautiful in its prime, but without her it had grown back to a more natural state.

"I was weeding, Sir."

"But this is your day off. Why spend it working?"

"Because I like the flowers when they—" Palms up, she opened the fingers of each hand. "Bloom?"

"Yes. I like them when they bloom."

"So do I."

She smiled and dropped her gaze. "May I help you with the bags, Sir?"

"That would be nice, thank you."

They carried two bags each to the kitchen. Elizabeth began unpacking, but he stopped her and said he would take care of it, she should go on doing what she wanted.

"Well then, I must go back and finish my work."

"Great," he said. "That'll be fine, if that's really what you want to do. But first, come with me."

He led her to her room, which still had boxes of Carolyn's things stacked in one corner even though he'd promised himself again and again to store them elsewhere.

She hesitated at the door.

"No, it's all right. You can come in. I just want to show you something."

She stood by the bed, hands crossed in front of her while he opened several boxes and reclosed them, until he found the gray sweatpants and T-shirt of Carolyn's he was sure he'd packed.

"I thought you might like to wear these so you don't stain your school clothes. They were my wife's, but I think you're about the same size."

"Oh, no, Sir, I must not."

"It's all right, she isn't going to be using them."

"But—"

He dropped the clothes on the bed. "Is it the pants?"

"My mother would not like it."

"But your mother isn't here. And it's not like you'll be parading up and down the street in them."

She reached down and trailed her fingers over the material.

"Besides, I see girls—and women—all Swazis—wearing pants now."

She picked up the clothes, held them to her chest.

"Oh, and you can have these, too," he said, taking a pair of sneakers from the box.

She dangled the shoes in front of her, as though unsure she should be touching them.

"But it's up to you. They're yours if you want."

He unpacked groceries and folded the bags to stow in the pantry. As he closed the door, he smiled at the squeak of rubber-soled shoes from the hallway. Elizabeth stopped at the kitchen, tossing her gloves on the counter and reaching up to retie the *emahiya* cloth at the back of her head, the hem of her T-shirt lifting at the same time to reveal a swath of smooth brown skin above her sweatpants.

"Are the shoes okay?"

"Oh, yes, Sir. Very fine." The hem rode even higher and held a moment before her arms fell back to her sides and the gap vanished. "The shoes, the shirt, the trousers, everything is fine."

He watched her a moment as she rubbed her hands and stared down at the floor. "But something is still troubling you."

"Oh, no, Sir. It is nothing." She glanced at the doorway behind her, through which she had entered the kitchen. "But if I may ask, Sir."

"Yes."

"About the girl." She now looked directly at him. "The one the croc took."

"How did you find out about that?"

"A friend. There," pointing to the backyard, "just as you came."

"Here, have a seat," he said, pulling a chair from under the small blue table beneath the window. It was one of Carolyn's favorite places. She used to start every morning there, sipping coffee and peering down the slope at Mbabane. "Would you care for tea?"

"Oh no, Sir, please not for me."

"I was about to make some for myself, so it wouldn't be any trouble."

She pushed herself back and stood. "Then I must do it, Sir, not you."

"Nonsense." He stood behind her, hands over the tops of her shoulders, and eased her back down, holding her there until he felt her relax.

"But, Sir."

"So about the girl," he said as he drew water and set it, hissing and popping, on the burner. "Your friend saw what happened?"

"No. She was not there. But another friend was and told my friend." She glanced toward the stove. "The water, Sir."

He turned off the burner and could feel her watching him measure leaves into a ceramic tea server, fill it with boiling water, and set it covered on a sisal tray, along with cups, saucers, spoons, and milk and sugar.

"Serviettes, Sir. You must not forget them."

"Thanks," he said, pulling two napkins from the holder and carrying everything to the table. "Biscuits? I think we have some in the pantry."

"No, Sir, I am satisfied."

He lifted the lid of the teapot and stirred, replaced it to let the tea steep longer.

"So your friend's friend, what did she see?"

"She is a friend of both of us, Sir."

"Then you can trust her."

"Oh, yes, Sir. No doubt about it."

"What did she say happened?"

Elizabeth sat back as he poured tea. "The friend who told the friend who told me, her name is Cebile, Cebile Zwane. She lives that side with her parents near Pine Valley. Her father is a headman and has a big mealies patch and a big vegetable patch and many cattle in his kraal. He is an important man, a rich man. Cebile's mother tends the vegetables and takes those she does not cook to the market in Mbabane to sell and have even more money. Cebile helps her when she is not studying to become a nurse. I want to become a teacher."

"Yes, you told me. You will be a good one."

"Thank you, Sir. I am trying my best." She added milk and sugar to her tea and took a sip. "About those biscuits, Sir, I believe I have changed my mind."

"Right away," Harry Philips said.

He rummaged in the pantry and stacked a small plate with an assortment of biscuits.

"These are too many, Sir."

"Take what you want."

She licked the icing of a Marie before eating it, followed bites of shortbread with sips of tea, and slowed to savor a lemon cream and a chockit before dusting her mouth and hands with her napkin.

"You should always feel free to help yourself to any of the food we have," Harry Philips said.

"You are too kind, Sir. But I must not do so without permission."

"Well, you have mine. Anything any time, okay?"

"Thank you, Sir," she said, peering once more toward town. "It is too sad, what happened there."

"Yes, it is."

She turned back toward him, sitting straight in the chair, hands folded at the edge of the table. "Another Friday Cebile would not be in Mbabane. She would be in school. I would be in school. The girls washing the clothes by the river would be in school. But today is Good Friday, the day the *umfundisi* says Jesus Christ died for our sins. There is no school." She paused, chewing her bottom lip as she glanced down at her hands and up again at Harry Philips. "But how can it be that such a day is called good when something so bad happened? Not only to Jesus our Savior. How can it be that on this special day such a bad thing must happen to anyone? Why can we not go on feeling safe and — what is the word?"

"Secure?"

"Yes. Everyone thinks it can be so, do they not? Otherwise no one would leave their hut. But, no, they go on doing this and that. Cebile's mother tells her come to the market and help sell vegetables. She does. She is happy and glad to be of assistance to her mother. The washing girls are happy, too. They have each other and are also helping their mothers. Everything is happy and normal until that girl forgets her duty and—"

"Her duty?"

"Oh, yes, Sir. She was the watcher, was she not, and she stopped watching. That is what Cebile told Happy Mota, who told me. Even before the other girls had finished spreading their last cloths to dry, this silly girl stopped smacking the water with her branch and turned her back to the river. But she did not leave. She stayed there, and—bam—just like that she was gone."

Elizabeth pressed the tips of her fingers to her mouth and shook her head.

"And your friend—Cebile?—she saw this?"

"Yes, Sir, she did. All of it. Her mother had told her to stop working and to go outside for the air. She did and watched the girls finish their washing. She saw them leave and the other girl stay. And she saw the croc leap from the river and take the girl. My friend was too sad and started crying and screaming and pulling her hair. That was when Happy Mota came from up the street and asked what was the matter and Cebile told her. Then they both cried and hugged each other."

Tears trickled down Elizabeth's cheeks. Harry Philips handed her a box of tissues from the counter.

"She knew better," Elizabeth said, dabbing her nose. "Every child knows better. Their mothers teach them from when they are this big—" hand hovering 2 feet above the floor. "Why to fear the river, how to fear it. And never ever to show your back to the water. But Cebile said this girl did. Showed her back and did not move away. Why, Sir, when we all have been told not to do so? What was she thinking?"

He shook his head.

"Cebile told Happy Mota that the girl looked odd, not herself, like she had been drinking *tjwala* or smoking *dagga*. Her eyes, she said they were—what do you call it?"

"I don't know, glassy?"

"Yes. Like they were not her own."

He hoped he had glanced away soon enough that she wouldn't see his reaction to what he knew she was about to say.

"Cebile says that the girl was cursed."

"Do you think she was?" Harry Philips asked.

"A boy near my home once, he was taken the same way."

"Standing alone at the river, with his back to the water?"

"Yes."

"And that somehow proves he was cursed?"

"But, Sir, it must be so. They would not have done those things if they were not." Her face hardened, as he imagined her mother's might have during a similar discussion. "My *umfundisi*, he says curses are the work of the devil, not the way of God. But they are there, they are real. The king makes rain, wizards bring curses and spells. They cause people to get sick and die or to become cracked in the head." She cradled her cup in both hands, peering at him over its rim. "They are too powerful, these wizards. They can even bring the lightning down on your enemy if you pay them enough. Have you not seen how people run inside when the storm comes? Who knows if the next —" her finger drawing a jagged line in the air.

"Lightning bolt?" Harry Philips said.

"Yes, who knows if the next bolt is for you?" She clutched her napkin in her left hand like a baton. "These same wizards, they can talk to the crocs that rule the river and say to them, take this one or this one, they will not run away because I have put a spell on them."

"And you're telling me they'd even do that to a child?"

"Oh, yes, Sir." She paused, as though to be sure he was listening. "If someone has wronged you and you hate them too much for it, what better way to punish them than to take one of their children? Then you have wounded their heart forever."

He shook his head but knew any objection he might make was as useless as trying to persuade someone who thought otherwise it was okay to walk under a ladder. The curses Elizabeth was talking about affected everyday life, from being killed by a crocodile to having a cold or being psychotic, from suffering a stroke to receiving a bad test score. They explained theft, divorces, miscarriages, diarrhea and car wrecks.

There were even people who would claim Solomon Kunene was cursed. Like his mother, for instance, and her belief that Meg Bernard had cast a spell on her son or had hired a wizard to do so.

"Are you well, Sir?" Elizabeth said, leaning toward him.

"I'm fine."

She tipped her head, brow raised.

"Really. I am. But it's nice of you to ask," he said, and, without realizing what he was doing, reached over to clasp her extended hand in thanks. But he moved too fast, gripped too hard, and she snatched the hand away, as if he'd burned her.

"I'm sorry."

She said nothing.

"I didn't mean—"

She glanced up, just beyond his left ear. "It is what men do."

"No. Not normally anyway. Normally I—I want you to feel good here, Elizabeth. I want you to feel safe."

"Oh, I do, Sir. It is only that when you did that—"

"I know, and I'm sorry. Really. I am sorry."

Her smile crept back but with more wariness. "Thank you for the tea and biscuits. Now I must go back and finish what I started in the garden."

The back screen door framed her perfectly, the walk a straight line to the gazebo, passing between the two bordered flowerbeds, her on her knees in front of the one to the right, bending forward, straightening, bending forward, the *emahiya* cloth on her head marking a red streak in the afternoon air. Every few minutes she put down her trowel and sat upright as she swiped a T-shirt sleeve over one eye, the other, and lifted the hem to swab her face. She rested a moment then, slowly stretching her neck by rotating her head full circle and back again before tending once more to her weeding.

Maybe it was the clothes or how she kneeled rather than squatted or bent straight-legged from the waist or even the way she paced herself that reminded him of Carolyn in the days before she stopped weeding. Before she stopped painting and making love, even though she said she still loved him. Before she stopped talking and started packing and making arrangements to go back to the States without him.

It could be he'd frightened her, too, only in her case by not being able to tell her he could and would go back home sooner rather than later. By not being able to give her some firm timeline. Maybe that was the fear she withdrew from, eventually ran from.

And he'd not been able to protect her from her fears, to make her feel safe enough to find at least some comfort in her life here. He'd failed her in the same way he'd failed Elizabeth, the same way somebody had failed the girl at the market, the same way someone else had failed Meg Bernard at Lobamba. Maybe we all failed all the time and nobody was ever truly safe anywhere.

He turned away and wandered toward his study, as he often did when he could think of nothing else to do. He slumped into his desk chair and swiveled sideways, eyes resting on the loose brass handle on the middle drawer to his left. He slid it open and fished through paperclips, a hole puncher, a stapler, pens and pencils and various yellow pads until he found the unframed photo he kept face-down at the bottom. He slipped it behind the first row of keys of the typewriter on his desk and leaned closer to it.

A passing hiker had taken the shot on a sightseeing trip they'd taken west of Lobamba near Sheba's Breasts not long after they had arrived in the country. He and Carolyn posed arm in arm beside a rusty slab of sandstone, on which, if you looked closely, you could make out faded human figures San Bushmen had painted thousands of years ago, an idea that caused her, a fellow artist, to tremble with what he thought was excitement, and after the picture, to turn and kiss him and whisper thankyouthankyou in his ear. He had a vision of her beside him, tanned and glowing, her hair caught by the wind on the drive back to Mbabane, past Montenga Falls, their late lunch at the market, freshening up at their house, making love. Later grilling steaks and drinking good wine, laughing and talking about what they would do next and making love again, falling asleep finally, curled together listening to the sounds of the African night.

He shook his head at how romantic that sounded, even to him, and thought that maybe it hadn't happened exactly like that. Maybe he'd added a few things or had forgotten others. But that didn't matter because the feeling was the same, the looking forward and not back, the wanting to make something new, like the artist she was, a new life, a home. Which was what she said she wanted to go back to, wasn't it? Home. Except there wasn't one to return to. They'd never really had a home. Not in the way most people thought about it. They'd both been in school here and there and had never settled and sunk roots as many of their friends had. Then they'd come here. Even as kids they'd not had a home as such. His father had been in the Army and had dragged his family from Kansas to South Carolina to Texas to California to Washington State and back to California. Carolyn's parents divorced when she was 5 and she lived back and forth, back and forth, mother to father to mother, week after dull and numbing week. So when they had the opportunity to move to Africa, they jumped at it. They came and bought a house and made what he believed was a home, what he felt was a home. Maybe she did for a while as well. He thought she had, for several years, in fact, before she began talking with more frequency about going back to the other home. And now with her father, to whom she was never that close, said to be seriously ailing, the issue became more acute. As his daughter, she came to think it was her responsibility to go to him and attend to him, no matter how long it took. So to his mind the home she talked about seemed to have become a place more emotional, more metaphorical, than physical, where she felt she belonged.

He often wondered whether their separation would have been easier, more fixable, if one or both of them had had an affair or been impossible to live with—he aloof and controlling, she a harpy for whom nothing was ever quite right. But they'd been so compatible on everything save one issue that their friends were shocked mute when it became clear that Carolyn was going to leave the country without him.

The first few months, he'd waited for some word, in a long soulful letter of regret explaining how she'd come to realize her mistake, her father wasn't that sick after all, and she hoped he could forgive her and welcome her back. Or that even though she wasn't ready to return to Swaziland, she didn't want to give up everything they'd built together and she would wait until he decided he was ready to join her. Or that, despite the fact he was stubborn and insensitive beyond belief, she was willing to concede he might have some reason for his inflexibility and she would be amenable to discussing the matter with him.

But now after eight months of silence, he had begun to wonder if there wasn't more going on than he'd imagined, that maybe she had left him for someone else, someone who Elizabeth might say had put a curse on her and kidnapped her emotionally, taken her away to live happily ever after in some la-la land he would never be allowed to enter even as a second thought.

He returned the picture face-down to the bottom of the drawer, straightened a stack of papers for no reason, straightened it again, pushed himself back from the desk but just sat, watching

Elizabeth through the far window bend down and up, down and up, like a dippy bird, and thinking how he needed to get his butt in gear and do something useful that wouldn't harm anyone.

9

Her watch on the nightstand said ten past seven. She threw off the sheet and stepped into the hall, where she was met by the smell of fresh coffee and something baking that would normally have levitated her toward it, as amorphous as a cartoon ghost. But she was halted by the voice of a woman on the radio reporting in a familiar British accent about ever larger and louder anti-war protests in the US and the increasingly violent opposition to them. She worried about what was eventually going to happen at home and whether they had made the right decision in coming here rather than staying there and... what? Chanting and yelling as they waited for Brian to be drafted?

She moved on, the cement floor cool beneath her feet, finished in the bathroom and found Brian at the kitchen sink.

"You're looking chipper," he said.

"Never felt better."

"Some coffee should help that." He poured two cups.

"What's in the oven?" she asked.

"Irish soda bread."

"Sounds wonderful."

"We'll have to see if it is. I had to play around with the recipe." He smiled. "You might even call it magical mystery bread. All you need is love."

"Just don't sing." She blew across the top of her cup, sipped.

"How is it?" he asked.

"The coffee? Great. I feel better already."

He sidled up to her, took her by the elbow. "It's only the queen mother, you know. People say she's gracious when she wants to be."

"Now that you're a magician, maybe you can make this morning disappear."

"How about we disappear instead?"

"Where to?" she asked.

"Your choice." He opened the oven, tapped the bread with a fingernail, took it out and transferred it to the cooling rack on the table. "Or is that too much to deal with?"

"Kind of."

"Okay," he said, leaning back against the sink, "Cape Town is out of the question, since we can't travel there, although I'd love to see it. But we could go to Lourenco Marques or Mombasa."

"Too hot, too much sun. We'd fry."

"Inland then. Uganda, Rwanda."

"I was thinking more like Aspen in the summer," she said.

"Oh, I get it. Any place but here, right? Especially now."

She watched him watching her as she took another drink of coffee, neither of them saying anything until she asked if he thought she had time to dress before they ate.

He shrugged—"Don't see why you wouldn't"—picked up a towel and walked back toward the oven.

In the bedroom, she set her cup on top of the dresser and opened the curtains covering the window. At first, she'd noticed the bars all the time, her eyes lingering first on their weathered spirals before taking in the scene beyond. Now she saw them only if she focused directly on them.

She wished the air were cooler and less gritty as she gazed out at the fair-weather clouds floating over the valley. A column of red dust bowed in their direction behind a minibus that climbed along the market road past two young boys clad only in khaki shorts. She followed the path of the bus to the Y in the road, expecting it to steer along the curve to the right toward the market. Instead, it continued straight ahead, past the king's entertaining palace, a white stucco ranch-style house with a terracotta tile roof, and on until it topped the hill near the end of the eucalyptus grove that shaded the queen mother's compound.

They would soon be on that same road themselves. Last Wednesday Mr. Dube had dismissed students to their classrooms after opening assembly but had asked faculty to stay a moment longer. He announced that the queen mother had invited them to a reception at her Lobamba residence at eleven o'clock Saturday morning. Mr. Dube hoped everyone understood the honor the Indlovukati was bestowing on them and would have the good manners to attend. If there were questions, he would be in his office.

"What do you think?" she'd asked Brian as they walked away.

"About whether to go or not?"

"Yes."

"Like Mr. Dube said, if we don't, I think people'll be pretty insulted."

"Especially if we're among the missing."

"Yeah."

"That worries me."

Along with what to wear to the reception that wouldn't draw everyone's eye to her. She closed the curtain and tossed underwear onto the bed. She laid a navy-blue A-line skirt and lighter blue long-sleeved oxford cloth blouse beside them. Dressed, she sat on the bed and turned each shoe upside down to shake it out before slipping it on, advice she'd initially scoffed at until the morning a spider had spilled from a sneaker.

"Does this look okay?" she said, walking across the kitchen to the back door.

"Sure. Great. How can you go wrong with a dress?"

"It's a skirt and blouse."

"Same difference."

"I thought this blouse would be best because married women aren't supposed to have bare arms in public, remember? Is that what you're going to wear?"

"What's wrong with khakis and a polo shirt?"

"Mr. Dube'll have on a suit and tie."

"He always has a suit on."

"You could wear your sport coat."

"No, Meg."

"You wouldn't need a tie."

"It's not going to happen. Not on a Saturday morning in this kind of heat." He rested his hand on the soda bread he'd taken from the oven, a perfect round loaf with a crusty brown top. "Needs to cool a little more before we cut it."

"I can wait," she said, twisting to one side, the other, trying to catch a glimpse of herself behind, below her waist. "Do you think this skirt's too short?"

"Jesus, Meg."

"I don't want to embarrass anybody—myself included."

He slipped his arm around her. "You need to cut yourself a little slack. I don't think anybody will throw you out for something like sleeves or no sleeves. We're foreigners, for god's sake, and we're supposed to make mistakes. Besides, you'll be the most beautiful woman there no matter what you wear, so stop worrying about it."

She tried to pull out of his embrace.

He leaned in for a kiss.

She spun away, and they stood apart like wrestlers waiting for the other person to make the first move.

"Don't be mad at me," Meg said.

"I'm not."

"Yes, you are."

"No I'm not, goddamnit."

Plates clattered as he took them from the pantry and hacked a wedge of bread for each of them, which they took along with their coffee to the living room. They ate without talking, the voice on the radio weaving in and out of hearing.

"Fucking Nixon," he said through a last mouthful of bread. "Fucking Pentagon. They're all lying bastards. Turn that shit off before I really do get mad."

She shook her head, flipped the power switch to off, gathered the plates and took them to the kitchen to wash and put in the rack to dry. Sure, Nixon and the Pentagon and all the rest of it was maddening, but that wasn't what had set him off like some maniac. It was her skittishness at being touched, let alone hugged or kissed. And she couldn't even think about sex, but each time it came up, direct or implied, like now, and each time they didn't talk about it or think about it anymore than they had to, it got buried deeper, grew harder inside each of them. A boil, a cyst, a dark seething sealed off from each other and themselves, and she wondered what would happen if they continued like this, trying to say and do everything but the right thing, go through the right motions but not attend to what they needed to. Would that growth, that ugliness, atrophy over time and wither to some irritating lump that you finger but otherwise ignore until you take it with you to your grave?

But for now, in moments like these, they couldn't touch, let alone talk.

When she rejoined him at the living-room table, an exercise book lay open in front of him, his pen in the fold to mark his place.

"What're you doing?" she asked.

"Reading."

"I can see that. What are you reading?"

"Essays."

"Okay. Fine," she said, sitting, scooting a stack of math quizzes toward her. She still used a red pencil, which she held point down beside each answer before marking it. Check, check, check, X, check, check. 5/6, she wrote at the top. Good work.

Next sheet.

"Damnit, Meg."

X, check, check, X, check, X. 3/6. Rework the answers you missed and return this to me.

"Damnit what?" she said. X, X, check, X, check, X. 2/6. Please see me so we can talk.

"It's the assignment I told you about," he said, "what they would do if they found out they only had a month to live?"

She glanced up at him. "I do remember that one. How's it going?"

He held an exercise book out to her. "Here, if you're really interested."

"No, that's okay."

He closed the book, shrugged.

She sighed, put out at herself, at both of them, and laid her pencil diagonally across the quiz sheets she'd marked. "How about if you read it to me? I'd like that."

"I don't know. Maybe it'd be better if—"

She gave him what she imagined to be her best "don't start again" look.

"All right." He reopened the book, cleared his throat. "You're going to especially like the way this one starts: 'In this world, many things can happen. Some are good and some are bad. Today, I am going to talk about a bad thing that happened.'"

"I thought you got them to stop using that introduction."

"So did I." He glanced at her. "You sure you want to hear more?"

She nodded.

"Okay: 'This morning when I got up and left my hut to eat, I had a great dizziness in my head. It was like many gnats or bees flew in and were buzzing me. I told my mother and she sent me to the doctor. He looked in my eyes and ears and mouth and told me that he was too sad but I was going to die. I said, how can that be and he said he could not lie, even for me. I asked him when this thing must happen, and he said in exactly one month.'"

"Good detail," she said. "What happens next?"

"His words or mine?"

"His," she said.

"'I did not believe the doctor, so I went to find a sangoma. He can throw the bones and see what it is that is killing me. I walked that side and then came by the priest's house. He lives near the sangoma, so I went there and the priest said we must get on our knees. He prayed that I might be saved, and he said I must go now with his blessing. And then I came to the hut of the sangoma. He took me inside and brushed the ground with the tail of an ox and threw the bones and stones. He picked them up and threw them again. I was afraid. And then he spoke. He said I must have an evil enemy who wanted me to suffer and die. I said I had no enemies. He shook his head and said I must have done something very bad then. Something that offended the ancestors. And he sent me away and I found a *tjwala* pot that never grew empty. And there I stayed, far that side by the river, all the days of my life.'"

"Wow," she said. "Who wrote that?"

"Dumisa Masuku."

"You're kidding."

"I know. Most of the time he just stares out the window."

"Have they all been that good?"

"No, but they've been better than usual."

She reached up where Roger slept on the windowsill and stroked his tail until it twitched. "When you made the assignment, did you think what you would do in that situation?"

"A little maybe."

"And what did you decide?" she asked.

"I don't remember."

"Sure you do. Did it involve me?"

A light knock at the front door.

She shook her head.

"I told you. Magic." He leaned back in his chair to look out the door. "Ah, Percy. Come in, come in."

"Am I interrupting?"

"Not at all," Brian said. "We were just—"

"Working as always." Percy ducked his head as he entered, even though the doorway was more than high enough. "Weekends are for rest."

Meg went to the spare bedroom and brought out an extra chair. "Would you like coffee? Or tea?"

"Coffee will be fine, if it isn't a bother."

She cleared a space on the table for his cup and a slice of Brian's bread.

"Thank you so very much, Madam."

"Meg."

"Yes, um, Meg. And what, may I ask, am I, um, to have the pleasure of tasting?"

"Irish soda bread," Brian said.

"Ah. Is it made of potatoes, then?"

"No, but I can see why you might think that," Meg said before either she or Brian could smile.

Percy sipped his coffee, pecked at the bread. "Umm." He bit off a larger chunk, his Adam's apple bobbing up and down his neck as he swallowed.

"Glad you like it," Meg said. "Brian can give you the recipe, if you'd like."

"Perhaps another time," he said, a glint in his eye, as if in appreciation of the humor in her offer. As far as anyone knew, Percy never cooked. "But there is one thing, if you don't mind."

"What's that?" Meg asked.

He ran his finger around the rim of his coffee cup. "It is that just as I got to your door—and please do not think that I was, what is the word, eavesdropping?—I heard Madam, Meg, say something like 'what did you decide?' And I could not help but wonder what it is you might be deciding. I hope it is nothing serious like thinking you might wish to leave us. Because that would be too sad. The students, they would miss you terribly, I'm afraid. Not to mention others."

She glanced at Brian, Brian at her.

Percy blushed. "I'm sorry. I should not have—"

"No, no," Meg said. "It's not that. And don't worry, we're not planning to leave any time soon. What we were talking about is completely different, but it might be something interesting to you. Brian can explain while I bring more coffee."

By the time she returned, Percy was saying "I see" and tapping his fingertips together in front of his face. "Yes, it is interesting. Quite interesting indeed."

"And what would you do in the same situation?" Brian said.

Percy stopped tapping his fingers and folded them as if for prayer. "That was the very question from Mrs., um, Meg, was it not, that you left unanswered?"

"So you were eavesdropping," Brian said.

"Not on purpose. I do believe your door was open." He broke off a piece of bread, ate it. "But it is no matter because what you have asked, it is still interesting and I will answer in this way: one," raising a long, thin finger, "I would get what I believe you call a second opinion. Just as the Masuku lad did, although I would seek out a medical doctor rather than a sangoma. When that doctor also says 'yes, that is what will happen,' I would search for Mr. Bernard—Brian—and challenge him to a chess match."

"Which, I suppose, you'd expect me to let you win as usual?"

"That would be the courteous thing to do, would it not, if I am to die? And then." Percy raised his right hand like a conductor. "After reigning victorious, I would find a boy whose uncle can sell me a bank bag of *dagga*. And I would take my bank bag and go to a quiet place, perhaps to the mountain, and sit and smoke it and stay happy, until—" He looked steadily at each of them and settled back on Meg. "It is good for that, you know. It carries memories away. Without memories, there is no sadness."

He folded his hands on the table near his cup and bread plate, a faint smile on his lips, eyes half closed. Such a peaceable presence, she thought, like still waters or a clear blue sky. And yet there was the other Percy who had caught up with her last week as she was walking home after school and, in the same thoughtful, calm voice he would use if he were discussing the price of tomatoes at the market, asked if she would like for him to kill her assailant or find someone who would.

Percy's eyes popped back open when Roger jumped down from the windowsill. Brian cleared his throat. She stood to clear the table.

By 10:30, Sarah and Grace Mtetwa had joined them. Joseph had stayed home with Jabalile, and Simeon Maphalala had told Brian he wasn't going since Mr. Dube would be there to represent the school administration. Which was better anyway, Meg thought, since Grace would have left if he had shown up. Three of the other teachers had already made plans for the weekend and had said last Wednesday that they couldn't attend. So four in addition to the two of them. Mr. Dube had told them to gather at Meg and Brian's house and he would stop by to drive them to the reception a bit before eleven o'clock.

Meg brewed new coffee and a pot of tea which she served with thin slices of soda bread from a tray she carried person to person. The bread disappeared quickly, and Brian wrote the recipe for Sarah and Grace on pages he tore from the back of a ruined exercise book. The women looked on with a mixture of amusement and awe at a man who actually cooked and wrote recipes and washed dishes. They once told Meg that they'd even seen him sweeping the floor.

Percy, who had been alternately checking his watch and the market road, finally rested his coffee cup on the windowsill and said, "Here he is at last," with a theatrical wave of his hand. They all watched the gleaming dark-blue sedan glide along the dirt road beyond the ponds, a boxy dun-colored VW bus jittering three car-lengths behind it over washboard grooves cut by recent rains. At the intersection, both vehicles turned left and left again down the lane to the teachers' compound. Mr. Dube parked in front of Meg and Brian's house, the van pulling up beside him. Once the cloud of red dust had wafted past, Mr. Dube got out and leaned toward the passenger window of the van. A few moments later, he straightened and the van crept forward, the driver, a white man with red hair, wire-rimmed glasses and a dark short-sleeved shirt, ducking and straining across the empty seat beside him to peer at the house for several seconds before straightening, steering around the turning circle at the end of the lane and back to the main road.

"Who was that?" Grace said.

"No doubt someone lost and in need of directions," Percy said.

"Lost?" Mr. Dube stood just outside the open doorway, brushing dust from his brown wool suit. "I just spoke with the man. He was not lost at all."

"Well," Grace said, tapping her toe, "tell us then what he wanted."

Mr. Dube swept a hand over his face, as he did when nervous or trying to gain a moment to think, an annoying gesture that Meg thought left him looking more confused than in charge. "He had questions. He asked if this was teacher housing for Lobamba National Junior Secondary School. I told him it was. He next asked if Mr. and Mrs. Bernard lived here."

Meg stopped wiping crumbs from the table. Held insect still.

"I said they do indeed. He then asked if I knew them, and I said of course I did, I was their headmaster. So he said I must know then in which house they lived. This one, I said, and he wanted to know if they were at home, he needed to speak with them. I said I certainly hoped they were, since I was coming to collect them for an important meeting. The man nodded his head and said in that case he would go on along and come back another time." Mr. Dube paused, eyes narrowed, as if making sure he hadn't forgotten anything.

"He did not mention his name or where he's from?" Percy asked.

"Or why he wants to talk to our friends?" Sarah said.

Everyone turned to find Meg and just as quickly looked away.

"No, but he did say I must give this to Mr. and Mrs. Bernard." He plunged his hand into his coat pocket and brought out a small cream-colored business card.

Meg took it, scanned it, and handed it to Percy, in spite of protocol. "You can read it if you'd like. To all of us."

Percy stretched the card between his hands, as if trying to pull it apart.

Mr. Dube cleared his throat and nodded.

"Harry Philips, JD. In America this JD means he is a lawyer."

"Ah," Mr. Dube said, fingering his moustache. "He sounded like an American. You can tell, you know, the way they talk."

"Harry Philips, JD, Office of Public Prosecutions, Mbabane."

"Isn't that the office in charge of seeing after trials the government has some interest in?" Grace asked.

"Which is to say the king," Percy said.

"Of course," Grace said, with a curl of her mouth. "The king knows everything, is everything."

"Because he cares," Mr. Dube said, turning to Meg. "You and Mr. Bernard are guests in his country, and it is his duty to see that you… that you are… that everything is well with you. As well as it can be, that is. Even if that is not—" He raised his hands in a half-shrug, as if signaling that it was someone else's turn to speak, but Percy stood by the window, eyes closed, hand to his mouth, while Grace and Sarah stared intently at their feet.

Brian stepped forward. "Shouldn't we be getting ready to go to the kraal?"

Mr. Dube smiled, which seemed to relax everyone, and he went on to say yes, they should, but he wanted to mention first how they should behave in general to show respect for the queen mother, instructions given to everyone, although with his attention focused on Meg and Brian, his gaze finally moving from Meg's bare head down to her bare legs.

Mr. Dube didn't need to say anything more, and she asked Brian to clean up while she excused herself to go search through her dresser for the black shawl she'd knitted with Sarah's instruction. In the same drawer, she found two pairs of black tights she wore in winter for extra warmth, and she stepped into one, wiggling them into place around her waist.

The house was empty when she came out from the bedroom and saw Mr. Dube beside his car, Brian beside him, like an honor guard. She stepped outside, closed and locked the door, and walked toward the car, where Mr. Dube nodded and ushered her to her place in the middle of the front seat. Brian eased in beside her, and she turned to smile at Percy, Grace and Sarah in the back.

Stifling air, a thick mixture of sweat, dust and new leather, made each breath a conscious one, slow and shallow through the nose only. Trickles of sweat ran behind her ears, and Meg lifted the shawl off her head, letting it fall lightly across her shoulders. Everyone was silent, the less said and the less movement, the better.

Mr. Dube made one last survey of his passengers and slid in behind the steering wheel. "Mrs. Bernard is comfortable?"

"I am. This is such a nice car."

"Thank you." Mr. Dube stroked the faux walnut dashboard.

"It still smells new. My father always said there is no perfume more expensive than the smell of a new car."

Mr. Dube thought a moment, lips spreading in a smile. "He is a wise man." He turned the key in the ignition. The engine raced, settled into a low soft rumble.

"I see you even have air conditioning," Meg said.

"Indeed. It cost extra, but when the salesclerk turned it on for my wife to feel, well, I had no choice. Would you like to see how it feels, Mrs. Bernard?"

"That would be nice, but please don't do it just for me."

"No, no, by all means. I insist."

He raised a shiny lever and held his hand to a vent.

She lifted her face and turned it side to side in the cool blast. "I can see why your wife likes it."

"Perhaps it is too much?"

"Not at all," Percy said before Mr. Dube could make any adjustments.

"It couldn't be better," Grace said.

"A blessing," Sarah said.

Meg felt Mr. Dube's shoulders straighten, saw a smile crawl beneath his moustache as he put the car in gear and they inched forward, around the turning circle and up the lane, at the top of which he swung right then left after only a few yards and idled past the eucalyptus grove with its silver bark and emerald leaves to where the road curved into the confines of the queen mother's compound.

A semicircle of beehive huts bordered the back of the tin-roofed stucco house where the Indlovukati lived, and the kraal, a 15-foot-high circular enclosure of stacked spindly wooden poles, loomed beside it.

Two men in traditional warrior dress stood guard near the entrance to the house. They approached the car, each with a brown and white cowhide shield, a long blunt fighting stick attached to the back of it in one hand, a knobkerrie raised toward the car in the other.

Mr. Dube opened the window and the warrior nearest him leaned down, ebony face glinting in the dappled sunlight, reddened eyes studying Mr. Dube, Meg, Brian, and on across the back seat. The warrior said something and Mr. Dube's response included "Indlovukati," so Meg assumed he had asked the purpose of their visit. The warrior's gaze weighed each of them again before he straightened, stepped back and motioned them on with a sweep of his shield.

They parked in the shade beside a tunneled entrance to the house formed by the overlapping ends of a 10-foot-high reed fence that circled the compound. After they got out, Mr. Dube lined them up—himself, Meg, Brian, Percy, Sarah and Grace— adjusted the shawl over Meg's head and said, "All right, off we go then."

The bare ground around the Indlovukati's house still showed scratch marks from straw brooms that had swept away even the smallest twig and pebble. Steps led up to a long veranda, a Swazi flag tacked to the wall behind a single wicker chair and small sofa, a round end table between them. Shades covered the insides of the windows, and the door remained closed.

They all stood silently at the bottom of the stairs, heads bowed and hands folded in front of them until a willowy girl of 15 or 16 slid cat-like onto the veranda clad in a short red, black and yellow *emahiya* cloth under a brown checked calf-length *lihiya* that draped over her torso and left shoulder. A lourie feather crowned the back of her head and a multicolored bead necklace graced her throat.

The girl smiled and bowed, motioning for them to come up the steps. They climbed single-file and arranged themselves, at the girl's beckoning, in a row facing the chair and couch. Meg bent her legs back to the side on her right, hands folded in her lap to match how Sarah and Grace sat. The men squatted, their knees cocked straight up, arms hooped around their shins. The girl retreated next to the door, and everyone in the guest party followed Mr. Dube's lead by lowering their heads, eyes to the floor.

Two other women soon emerged from the house, older and larger and more conservatively dressed—*emahiya* cloth to their ankles, both shoulders covered, rolled leather bands on their heads supporting beehive hairstyles. The woman cradling a stenographer's pad, a ballpoint pen behind her ear, stood beside the chair, the other at the far end of the couch.

Again they waited, sweat trailing down Meg's temples as she watched Mr. Dube, to her right, eye the door from under his brow. On the other side of her, but out of sight unless she turned her head, Brian cleared his throat and someone sighed— most likely Grace, bored and wondering why she'd ever agreed to come—and she imagined Sarah and Percy, necks bent but otherwise as straight-up and silent as herons, hands waving now and again to shoo flies from their faces, and behind them all a wash of whirring grasshoppers, chirping birds, and motors whining up and down the market road.

Yet even here, amid such an exotic scene, it struck Meg how waiting was the same everywhere, whether in Swaziland, or Johannesburg or 10,000 miles away outside your boss's office in Chicago. Waiting was waiting, and the longer you did it, the more important and powerful the person you were there to see seemed to grow. At home, someone by now would have cracked a joke—the more disrespectful the better—and everyone would have sniggered and been done with it, tension relieved. But here, the silence and heat continued unbroken, until even Mr. Dube shifted and glanced back down the line, smiling for them to remain patient—head still lowered, of course.

Meg peeked up in spite of herself when the door creaked open and the Indlovukati shuffled out, a short block of a woman guided toward the chair by an aide in a lime-green nurse's uniform. Her swollen and cracked feet scuffed the cement floor as she made her way along, gasping, wheezing, lips twitching, nose running, but with black onyx eyes set deep in her lined face locking on each of her guests in turn.

Her bulk bowed the arms of the chair as she settled into it, sweat dampening the *emahiya* cloth and animal skins swathing her. The girl who had escorted them rhythmically waved an oxtail fly whisk around the Indlovukati, who motioned to the woman by the couch to bring the small silver box on her lap. She opened it and held it out to the Indlovukati, who took a pinch of snuff between her thumb and forefinger and sniffed it first into her right nostril, then her left. She sneezed, squeezed her nose shut with a bandana and greeted them in siSwati. The woman with the stenographer's pad, which was now opened, pen in hand, interpreted: "The queen mother says she is happy to see you." To which they answered, "*Yebo, Nkhosi*," yes, honored one. The queen mother then asked in her mumbling monotone about the health of their mothers and fathers, husbands or wives and children, aunts and uncles and cousins. She asked about the President of the United States and his family. She did not ask after the king of the Zulus. She paused and signaled for her snuff box and once again sniffed, sneezed and tended her nose before saying how she hoped the school year was going well and that their work was satisfactory and enjoyable. The woman with the stenographer's pad wrote furiously as the Indlovukati fell silent, eyes fixing on some point beyond the veranda, the kraal, fingers stroking and pursing her lips as she appeared to mull over what she wanted to say next and how to say it. She dropped her hand, swiped her mouth with her bandana and refocused on them as she asked if the children at school were behaving and were working hard and paying attention. They needed to, she said, so that they could get good marks and one day play important roles in the future of their country. She asked about good behavior, she said, because she knew that sometimes people did not act the way they should and did not do the things they should. They disobeyed their teachers and parents and the ancestors, which could lead to bad things happening. Sometimes they ran with bad people and did bad things. Sometimes they listened to bad people and thought bad thoughts. Sometimes they were just wicked, evil people and did what they did for no reason, but that was as rare as a white leopard.

By that point Meg had peeked enough to realize that the queen mother had focused on her and Brian only, and she said she hoped that the parents and grandparents of anyone who had been affected by the bad actions of a bad person could forgive her and the people of Swaziland, who walked in peace and wished harm to no one, especially special guests who had traveled a long distance across deep waters to help bring knowledge to her young people.

She drew back her head and cast a sweeping glance over the whole group and asked that they pass her greetings to their families and to accept her best wishes for their continued health and happiness.

The attendant with the stenographer's pad stepped to the Indlovukati's side and leaned down to whisper in her ear. A slight smile passed her lips and she thanked them for coming and told them to go well and to continue their important work, to which they said "Nkhosi" in unison.

The nurse and snuff woman helped the Indlovukati from her chair and steered her back into the house.

Once the entourage had cleared, the girl by the door escorted the guests down the steps to the tunneled passageway. Mr. Dube opened the car doors, and as they waited for the interior to cool, Sarah touched Meg's arm, drawing her aside, and asked in a soft voice if she was okay. Meg said yes, she'd be fine. Sarah nodded that she understood and said they could talk later if she wanted to.

10

Harry Philips parked in the welcome shade of a mahogany tree a hundred yards or so south of the school grounds, windows down to catch what little breeze there was. Behind him in the sideview mirror, a rutted dirt lane disappeared over a rise, heading vaguely in the direction of the Malkerns market. He'd never driven that route, preferring instead the paved highway in the interest of time, but sometime he would, just to see where he ended up. To the north, the same track joined the main road to Lobamba market a half-mile away, which gave him a perfect view of any vehicle coming or going in the immediate area.

He was waiting for Mr. Dube's—he was almost certain that was the headmaster's name—Chevy sedan to appear and drop off its riders at the teachers' compound. He had decided that, rather than driving back to Mbabane, he would wait until after the reception, appear at the Bernards' door and see if they would agree to meet with him after all. If they did, great, it saved him an extra trip. If they said get lost, no harm done.

He'd already run a basic background check on them by talking to the Swaziland Peace Corps director, who proved to be quite cooperative and supportive. He had even commented on how helpful it was to have an expat American involved in the logistics of the case, since it would be difficult for Peace Corps or American embassy officials to become involved. What he found out was that the volunteers' names were Brian and Meg Bernard, both American by birth, from the Chicago area, he 25, she 24. Teachers: she math and science, he English and history. Standard Peace Corps stint: two years with an option to renew, which might be attractive, depending on Brian's draft status. They were paid a minimal monthly living allowance by the US government, including airfare to the country at the start of service and home at the end. Each had a master's degree. Parents were living. She had one sister and one brother, both away at college. He had one older brother. No known "suspicious" memberships or associations in the US, other than involvement in student anti-war protests while they were in college, and no questionable activities or contacts since arriving in Swaziland. Employment evaluations superior across the board.

He had no idea what Gideon Dlamini would do with that information, except to make sure it was presented to the court in such a way that the Bernards were held up as excellent examples of the potential of the multiracial state, and Solomon Kunene, by contrast, would be shown to be a willing instrument in a nefarious scheme to undermine that ideal. The notion of which frankly tempted him to go away and hide until the whole damn mess had blown over, since the deeper he was sucked into it, the sleazier he felt.

Swiping his hand at the trickle of sweat inching down his jaw, he caught a glint from the eucalyptus grove at the royal kraal, Mr. Dube's sedan appearing in a burst of light that faded as the car crept around the curve in the direction of the school.

He imagined Dube living the way he drove—steady and smooth, slowing for every hole and bump, as though comfort and damage control were his primary concerns—and how trying that approach must have been as he weathered the exposure of his school and himself in the wake of the rape of one of his volunteer teachers, who was, Harry Philips imagined, young, white and idealistic, although he didn't know whether Mrs. Bernard—Meg—thought of herself in those terms.

He slid farther down the closer Dube's car came, until his vision was framed by the top of the steering wheel and the dashboard. The heads of two of Mr. Dube's passengers rotated in his direction when the car turned down the lane to the housing compound. He laughed, shot back up. So what if they saw him, even recognized him? What the hell difference did it make? It wasn't like he was there to arrest anybody or was playing private eye like Magongo. He just wanted to talk, give the Bernards what he hoped would be some useful information. Nothing more, nothing less, and certainly not something he should be secretive about or ashamed of.

Dube's car stopped midway through the turnaround at the end of the drive. People got out, stretching, straightening clothes, chatting a moment and drifting off toward their homes. Mr. Dube drove slowly up the lane, as if mindful about not raising too much dust.

Harry Philips waited a bit longer—time for people inside to have a bathroom break and change their clothes—before he drove to the compound and parked in front of the Bernards' house. No one came to the door or a window, not there or anywhere else for that matter, which seemed odd since everyone had gotten home only a few minutes earlier. He slipped from the van as quietly as he could, holding its door just shy of the pop that sounded like the hinge had broken when it swung too wide, and stepped across the cracked red earth to their front door.

He knocked, waited, knocked again.

A man with a dark-brown beard opened the door and stood before him barefoot in khaki shorts and an unbuttoned sport shirt, a woman with a cascade of blonde hair in the dim light behind him.

"Mr. and Mrs. Bernard?"

The woman tilted her head, brow furrowed.

"I'm Harry Philips. From the Ministry of Justice. I hope you have a few minutes for us to talk."

"Come in," the woman said, and they both backed away from the door.

"Thanks." Harry Philips stepped into the living room. "Sun's pretty fierce today."

"You can say that again." The man pulled his shirt closed and fastened the middle button in place. "I'm Brian. Brian Bernard. This is Meg."

Harry Philips shook both of their hands, said how glad he was to meet them.

Brian offered him a chair and disappeared again into the back of the house. Meg asked if he would like coffee or tea.

"No, I'm fine."

"Will you excuse me then while I make some for us?"

"Of course."

She raised a hand to finger-comb her hair behind her ear. Graceful, fetching, a hint of innocence that momentarily caught him off guard.

While she was gone, he browsed the collection of photos of the two of them, scenery, and what must have been some of their students, arranged on a corner shelf between knobby drinking gourds. A long blue and green sisal mat hung down the wall to the right, a medium-size bookcase next to it, overflowing with mostly paperbacks on African literature and history and other works on archeology, anthropology, knitting and crafts, guides on sketching and art, copies of *National Lampoon*, *Time*, *Newsweek* hanging limp over the rows of books. A black and chrome Grundig shortwave radio sat on the windowsill by the end of the table, and a series of pen-and-ink drawings, some with colored pencil shading, lined the wall from the front door to the center hallway.

"Didn't you stop by here earlier when we were about to leave?" Brian said, coming back into the room, shirt fully buttoned, sandals flapping.

"I did, but before we get into that, tell me who the artist is."

"She is," Brian said as Meg approached the table, tea tray in hand.

"Nice work. Beautiful line and composition," Harry Philips said. "I especially like the kitchen drawing. Is it the one in this house?"

"Yes," Meg said. "Are you an artist?"

"I'm afraid not, just an admirer." He pointed to a small cardboard bookshelf, which as he thought about it, seemed somewhat less permanent than he would have liked. "I see you have Kuper's book."

"Peace Corps gave it and almost all the others to us," Brian said.

Harry Philips tipped the Kuper book from its place on the shelf and thumbed through a few pages. "An amazing work when you think how much information she distilled into such a short book."

"Wasn't she the first white person to live at Lobamba while she did her research?" Meg said, both hands holding her cup in front of her, a mannerism he'd noticed many women tea drinkers adopted.

"That's right. Nineteen thirty-four, thirty-five, I don't remember for sure," Harry Philips said, slipping the book back into place. "Oh, and for the record, she wasn't just the first white person permitted to live here, she was the only one—until you two. Which I'd say makes you pretty special."

"Safe might be more like it," Brian said. "We're married Midwesterners, you know. Is there anything less terrifying than that?"

"Peace Corps staff spent a lot of time here talking to people," Harry Philips said, "listening to what they wanted, what they said they needed. So I think they put serious thought into where they assigned people, and they likely believed you had more to offer than just staying out of trouble. And from what I've heard, everything's been going fine—maybe until recent events anyway."

Meg frowned into her cup, as if she'd found a bug floating in it.

"So how do you know all this stuff, and why are you here?" Brian asked.

"Fair questions. I don't know if you saw the card I left with Mr. Dube, but I work with the Swaziland Ministry of Justice, in an office that follows judicial cases requiring scrutiny from the government. I'm an American by birth and education. I've lived and worked here for ten years." He paused to let some of what he'd said sink in and see if they had any questions. "As to why I'm here, my boss, the Minister of Justice, thought it might be a good idea if I came out to talk with you about the case."

"Does Peace Corps know?" Meg said.

"They cleared me to come, since, as they said, it's their policy not to get involved in the internal affairs of a host country, even if this involves foreign nationals. Besides, they don't feel they have the expertise to advise you, so here I am. I hope this is all okay with you."

They looked at each other, turned their gazes back to him.

"So where do you want to start?" Brian said. "We don't know anything about what's going on."

Harry Philips shifted sideways in his chair, crossed his legs and rested his right forearm on the tabletop, hoping to strike a more relaxed pose. "First, before I forget, I'm supposed to remind you that Peace Corps has someone available to help you in any way they can." Pause, no response. "And my job is to discuss and advise, nothing more." Another silent pause. "I want to assure you the ministry is moving as fast as it can on this case."

"Meaning?" Meg said.

"People are embarrassed, and they want to put this behind them as soon as possible. Which, I imagine we'd all like to see."

She squeezed Brian's hand, a tight smile on her lips.

"I think what she's wondering," Brian said, "is whether this case is receiving some kind of special—"

"We're paying close attention, if that's what you mean." Harry Philips spread his arms toward them. "You have to remember where this happened."

"And who it happened to?" Brian said.

"Of course. You're not exactly invisible out here. People see, they talk, they come to conclusions that may or may not be flattering to anybody. So, you know, lots of things play into how a case is developed."

"If this happened to one of my friends at school," Meg said in a barely audible voice, "would she get the same attention as me?"

"Maybe, maybe not. It would depend."

She took a deep breath and let it out in a slow, measured exhale.

"I'm only trying to be honest with you," Harry Philips said.

"Which makes me want to disappear."

"Hiding won't help." He closed his eyes and pinched the bridge of his nose, wishing he could learn to keep his mouth shut. "Look, I'm sorry. I know it's hard to talk about this, think about it. But when you say things like you want to disappear, it worries me what you might do, depending on how pissed off you are. Go back to the States before the trial? Refuse to testify? Decide you need to yell at somebody about how the government didn't do enough to protect you. How the Peace Corps didn't. As far as we know, you might do anything. But I want you to understand that the government is trying to keep this as quiet as possible. We have a good thing going with you guys volunteering here—all of you—and we don't want something to mess that up. Peace Corps feels the same way."

"That makes it sound like we have a choice," Brian said.

"Nobody can force you to go through with this. But without you, the trial probably gets canceled and Solomon Kunene walks away a free man."

"And it's our fault if that happens?" Meg asked.

"People might see it that way."

"Some choice," Brian said.

"Sorry. I imagine this is one of those times when you wish you'd never seen this place." Harry Philips stood and turned toward the window. "Am I safe in assuming we're ready to move forward—for now at least?"

Meg and Brian glanced at each other.

"Yeah, I guess," Brian responded.

"Good," Harry Philips said, stepping back to the table, Meg across from him wan and stiff-backed.

"I'll be so glad when this is over," she said, glancing away.

"So will I." Harry Philips reached toward their hands, still clasped on the table, drew back. "Believe me."

"Really?"

"Really. But remember, the trial is the worst part. Once the day arrives—and I wish I could say for sure when that'll be, although it won't be too long. Once we get going, everything'll be over before you know it."

Meg's face hardened, paled, as he thought how the girl at the market, the one taken by the crocodile, must have looked when she heard the initial lunge, claws scratching the dry earth and stone, a hiss maybe just before jaws locked around her leg and she was dragged into the water.

Meg shifted her gaze to him. "And you really believe that? Everything? Over? Presto-chango, just like that?"

"Sure. For all intents and purposes."

11

"You want some lunch?" Meg asked, turning away from the window where she had watched Harry Philips drive away, en route, she supposed, to Mbabane.

"Sure. What can I get you?" Brian said.

"No, let me. It'll be good to do something, you know, to actually do something."

"Fine."

She loaded a box of digestives, a jar of peanut butter with a knife plunged into it, and two glasses of water onto a tray, which she carried to the living-room table. They ate in silence, listening to the BBC drone on about the effect of America's war on the British economy.

After Brian cleared the table and washed up, he asked whether Meg minded if he went to the school library to work a while. He wouldn't be long. She was welcome to come with him, but she said no, he should go on, she had things she wanted to do at home, and he asked if she was sure, and she said she was, although as soon as the door shut behind him, she stood at the kitchen window, following his progress through the turnstile and up the short path to the school, wishing she were walking with him, only not to the school but somewhere beyond, out where she knew no one, and no one knew her.

But Harry Philips was right. Running away wouldn't accomplish anything and would likely end up making matters worse. So would brooding. She decided to write a letter home.

Dear Mother and Dad,

A man from the Ministry of Justice just left. Harry Philips. He's an American lawyer who has lived here about ten years.

151

He told us the trial is coming up soon, but he didn't know a definite date yet. That's going to be such a hard time.

Do you have to forgive to forget? I think I know the answer.

This morning several other teachers from our school and Mr. Dube and the two of us were invited to the queen mother's royal kraal for a reception. It turned out that the QM was mainly interested in seeing Brian and me to find out if we were okay—and (I think) to be sure we weren't going around badmouthing anybody, which we haven't been. She reminded us that Swazis are gentle and peaceful people who don't do the kinds of things the man who attacked me did, except, of course, he did and others do as well, way too often, and not just here. But she was trying to apologize and in the end did a sweet thing by leaning toward us—Brian and me in particular—and said to be sure to send you her greetings. Her way, I guess, of saying she was a parent, too, and understood what you were going through.

There is so much sadness and chaos in the world—I won't even get started on Kent State and the rest of it. I still have a lot to be thankful for.

I'm going to walk to the store to mail this and buy a loaf of bread.

All my love,

Meg

She followed the path beside the barbed-wire fence enclosing the school grounds to where it made a sharp right turn past the housing compound and angled down a gentle half-mile slope toward the main road. On the other side, a brick and stucco filling station hunkered against the ground, incognito but for red walls, a rust-streaked Caltex sign and a single gas pump. Inside, Mrs. Mabula collected mail, sold bread, milk, cigarettes, beer, soda, coffee, canned goods, and whatever she had cooked that morning, minced mutton curry with rice being the most common dish. When they had first come to the country, they had ordered carry-out curry from her, attracted by its delicious smell and eager to try local food, and later in the day had suffered the consequences. A month or two later, thinking the first incident was a fluke, they again took food home from the shop and again became ill. Since then, they had limited their purchases to bread, canned goods and an occasional quart of milk.

"*Sawubona, sisi,*" I see you, sister, Mrs. Mabula said from her usual station behind the counter, a short, thin woman with a hawkish face and fingers so crippled with arthritis they curled from her hands like catalpa pods.

"*Yebo, make. Unjani?*" Yes, mother. How are you?

"*Ngikhana. Wena ke?*" I am well. And you?

"*Ngikhana.*"

Each bowed slightly to the other to finalize greetings, and Meg handed her the aerogram and asked for two loaves of bread, a carton of milk, a can of coffee, and a Coke to drink before she started home.

Mrs. Mabula tallied the bill in the margin of a sheet of newspaper she used to wrap around the bread, which she packed with everything else into a brown paper bag. Meg paid her and carried the groceries and her drink to a small table near the front of the shop where she could look out. Several cars passed, one stopping for gas, and a bus pulled over across the highway to let someone off. Otherwise, the scene was empty but for the graceful swell of mountains behind the royal kraal and swaths of pasture and plowed fields leading up to them.

She took a deep breath, closed her eyes, and exhaled slowly.

A serenity about where she was and why washed over her, and she held it fast until she heard the scuffing of gravel outside. She glanced up to see an old woman coming around the corner of the building, a bundle of firewood on her head. The woman lowered the bundle, leaned it against the wall and came into the shop, where she greeted Mrs. Mabula and asked for a drink of water. Mrs. Mabula gave her one in a Styrofoam cup, and the old woman thanked her and turned to look out the window as she drank. When she noticed Meg, she asked Mrs. Mabula who that was, as far as Meg could make out, and Mrs. Mabula told her she was a teacher from Lobamba School. The old woman's face lowered and her voice quaked and she began to babble things Meg couldn't understand at all, louder and louder, flapping her hands and stomping her feet. "No-no-no!" she screamed in English as she staggered toward Meg and dropped to all fours in front of her. She wrapped her arms around Meg's calves and stabbed a bony chin into the tops of her knees as she weaved back and forth, sobbing and babbling.

Mrs. Mabula hobbled from behind the counter and clutched the old woman's waist to drag her away from Meg, but the woman tightened her grip and drove her chin even deeper into Meg's knee. Meg stood and tried to pull her leg free, but the old woman drove her back onto the chair. She sat with a jolt. She reached down to push the woman's arms down her legs, but she had uncanny strength for someone so scrawny. Meg drew herself up, one arm on the table, the other on the chair back. She twisted and wiggled, the old woman's arms slowly loosening from her calves, and with a limp-leg maneuver she remembered Brian describe once at a football game, she slipped her right foot free. She planted it and jerked her left leg so violently the woman gave up and lay panting and weeping on the floor.

Meg backed against the window so she wouldn't kick her. She'd never done anything like that in her life and certainly not to an old woman lying spent at her feet. The idea that she could even consider it shocked and frightened her, and she sank onto the chair on the far side of the table as Mr. Mabula helped the woman to her feet, gave her more water and walked her to the door. Meg watched as she rebalanced the bundle of kindling on her head and trudged off across the road.

"Who was that?" Meg asked.

Mrs. Mabula, who spoke only a little English, shook her head that she did not understand.

"Her name?" Meg said in her best siSwati.

Mrs. Mabula gimped back behind the counter, finger-dusting the chrome strip that rimmed it as she sat and whispered, "Blessed. Blessed Kunene, from that side at Zombodze."

Meg turned to find the woman, who though slow afoot, was now only a speck on the path that led to the school, and a half-mile beyond it, the market, where she must have been taking the wood.

"Why did she grab me like that? What did she want?"

Mrs. Mabula took a deep breath but turned away. "She said you cast a spell on her son and took him away. She said you must give him back."

Mrs. Mabula excused herself to do something in the little room behind the counter, and Meg sat a moment longer, trembling.

Her knees buckled as she opened the back door of their house and stumbled with the groceries to the kitchen table. She calmed herself and closed but didn't lock the door, since she doubted Brian had taken a key. She put the milk in the fridge and the bread in the pantry. She went to the living room and closed and latched the windows, drawing the curtains over them. She locked the front door and moved on to the bedroom, where she left the windows open but pulled the curtains across the bars. She closed the door, kicked off her shoes and lay down on her left side, knees raised toward her chest, arms wrapped as far around herself as she could manage.

"Meg?"

A shaft of light from the bedroom door spilled across her and the bed.

"What's going on?"

She clenched her jaw, pressed the side of her face into the pillow—and still, despite what she'd been warning herself against, she began to cry.

Brian sat on the edge of the bed until he fit snugly against her back.

"I just saw his mother," she said, her voice shuddering. "Kunene's."

"Oh my god."

"I went to the store to mail a letter to my folks and get some bread and milk, and I bought a Coke to drink before I came home. I was sitting at the table by the window—you know, the one in front?" And she told him the rest of the story in as much detail as she could remember. "It was awful, Brian." She draped an arm over her eyes. "She thought I'd cast a spell on her son, so it was all my fault. If I hadn't been here tempting him, nothing would have happened."

He turned to hug her, his face near the back of her neck.

She pulled away from him. "Please don't breathe on me."

"Jesus, Meg, I'm only trying to—"

"I know, but I need to be alone." She craned her neck to look at him. "I need to be away."

12

As soon as Magongo spotted Harry Philips approaching, he half-rose from his seat in Lena's to wave him over, one arm braced against the table as if to steady himself.

"Greetings, my friend. Sit, sit."

"You said you'd call me, Bertie."

"Yes. We must talk. You said you wanted underwear, I will give you underwear."

"Are you drunk?"

"You remember the day, do you not, when you sat here, perhaps in that very chair, and told me you wanted me to find out everything about this Kunene chap?"

"Of course I remember."

"Even his underwear you said."

"But I didn't mean that literally, for god's sake."

"Tomasto taught me to see what is necessary. Once he solved a case where a single speck of red powder led him to the thief. What a clever fucking fellow."

"You are drunk."

Magongo flopped back in his chair and sucked down the rest of his Castle. "Jockey. Boxers—plain, no pattern—drying on a rock by his mother's hut."

"How about something to eat?" Harry Philips said. "Maybe some nuts?"

"And…" Magongo wiggled his empty bottle.

Harry Philips signaled Noah and ordered two beers and a bowl each of peri-peri peanuts and cashews.

Magongo leaned in and said in a low voice, "You heard about the croc at the market?"

"I was there."

"You saw it happen?"

"No. I came just after."

Magongo held up a single finger. "So by the time you arrived everyone was talking about it, no?"

"Pretty much."

"All at once and each with a different story? And you listened and listened and by the end you were not certain what you heard. Is that not true?"

Noah brought their order, and they sipped beer and munched nuts, watching each other, until Harry Philips said, "So what's your point?"

"So it is with your Kunene chap. Much talk but little said." Magongo lit a cigarette, took a deep drag, and seemed to eye the drifts and eddies in the stream of smoke he exhaled. "When you listen, you hear he is one thing in Zombodze, another in Manzini, and another that side. You say you want to know everything about this man, but that is the problem. How can I know what I know?"

"So maybe I should leave and come back after you've figured it out."

"Oh no, that will not be necessary, my friend. I will start where I must, and we will see what we see." He flicked ashes off his cigarette. "I went first, as I said, to Zombodze, where I saw this Kunene's mother—and the boxers. Be calm. A joke, eh? Only a joke. We sat by her hut, and do you know what she told me? She told me I was not the first person to come asking questions. She said a tall white man with glasses and hair the color of the earth had been there before me. A man who spoke lie after lie about her son."

"All I said was he was in jail—and why—nothing else."

"No matter. She cannot believe any of it. This Kunene chap, he is her son, and she wept when she spoke of him. She told me he is the one who cares for her and gives her money when he works. He is the one who gives her food and sees that she rests, the one who puts new thatch on her roof."

"He's also a rapist."

Magongo's nostrils flared.

"I can't believe you didn't know that."

"Oh, no, my friend. Many people have told me. But never you."

"I wasn't at liberty to say anything."

"Because of the woman, who she is? American, white?"

"That's part of it."

"And the rest?"

Harry Philips shook his head.

"No matter." Magongo popped a palmful of cashews into his mouth, chewed, washed them down with a swig of beer. "It will not change that this Kunene's mother is a mother and thinks what she thinks, and that is that."

"Did she tell you she believes the American woman is some sort of evil enchantress who cast a spell on her son, or had someone else do it," Harry Philips said, "to draw him to Lobamba and her? Do you think that's what happened, Bertie?"

"I cannot say I believe such a thing. But I cannot say it must not be true if his mother says it is."

Harry Philips reached for a cashew, amazed that he was witnessing first-hand how myths came to have such power over people's minds. "Who else did you talk to?"

"Oh, there were many others. From his mother, I went to the *tjwala* pot and then to the place where he worked and then to Lobamba. I have been—how do you say?—here and there and there. All over."

"Good," Harry Philips said, and they both turned to glimpse the woman in the pillbox hat entering the pub. She strode straight to the bar and slid onto a stool. Noah picked up a glass and began making what must have been her usual. She smiled, toasted him, twisted this way and that on the stool, spoke to him again.

"She is looking for you but does not realize you are here," Magongo said. "I must go tell her."

"That isn't necessary."

"You are not interested?"

"We have business to attend to."

"Tomasto—"

"We know what he'd be thinking?"

Magongo laughed loudly enough that the woman glanced over her shoulder in their direction. He wiggled his fingers like a six-year-old.

"I don't have all night, Bertie."

He dropped his hand, worked a cigarette from his pack. "I am too worried, my friend. Even you Americans say all work and no play. How can it be you are happy, without—"

"Goddamnit, Bertie."

Magongo shook his head. "You are angry with me."

"Frustrated," Harry Philips said, glancing despite himself at a smooth swath of leg showing along the skirt's split.

"Then perhaps you can know what I mean when I say this Kunene, he makes me frustrated as well. He is like that lizard that changes colors wherever it goes."

"A chameleon?"

"Yes, a chameleon." Magongo raised his head and sucked on his cigarette, his words trailing out with the smoke that followed. "All those places I went and all those people I saw, they were like the ones at the market when you heard about the girl the croc took. One man in Zombodze—a man who said he knew your Kunene chap like a brother—told me he could be as sweet as honey one day and as nasty as a rat the next."

"Go on."

"This fellow said that he once asked Solomon Kunene for money to buy food for his children, and Kunene gave him all that he had. Another time, he did the same thing, and Kunene cursed at him, calling him a worthless scab, a lump of dirt. He even broke a branch from a tree and began switching the man with it."

Harry Philips tore a sheet of paper from the yellow pad and began taking notes.

"Another man worked with him at the Adolphus C. Mahamba Construction Company in Manzini. He was a big man, bigger than you, Brother Philips, with arms like posts. Together with this Kunene, they laid cinder blocks and bricks for new buildings—and, I suppose, repaired old ones, although I do not know that for a fact. This big man with the strong arms was a friend of our Kunene, just like the fellow at Zombodze. A good friend, who worked with him all day, all week, until, for some reason, Kunene was no longer there. One day, this big man said, he did not come to work, and the day after and the day after."

"Kunene you mean?"

"Yes, Kunene. Before that, he was never absent, even when he was sick. He worked and worked, and then he was gone, just like that."

"What happened to him?"

"No one can say. Not even his friend. There were—what is the word?—rumors all around: he fell and broke a leg, he hit another worker and was fired, he got into an argument with his boss and was fired, he quit to go work the mines in the Republic, he ran away with his girlfriend to Mozambique."

Harry Philips stopped writing and looked up. "He has a girlfriend?"

"They said so, but—"

"But what?"

"You know." Magongo shrugged, twirling the end of his cigarette to a point against the ashtray. "A girlfriend is a girlfriend."

"Jesus Christ, Bertie, you didn't even ask about her?"

"Why must I when they are all the same? They want to eat with you and drink with you and fuck with you—and perhaps even run away with you to Mozambique. But what happens when there is no more laughing and you must get up and return to work? Eh? What then? Here is what—first she will say you must get married and give her a home and all she can eat and perhaps children, perhaps not. But none of it will matter, for after some time she will grow tired of you and leave anyway. That, my friend, is why I did not ask."

"Maybe this girlfriend was different."

"Maybe. But think about our man. He is a laborer without a job. He has no father and no cattle and his mother sells firewood. He may be handsome enough a girl can want to have sex with him before she grows old. But other than that—" Magongo rubbed his stomach. "Perhaps some mutton curry?"

"I'm not hungry."

"Ah, but there are times when you are and do not realize it, and this frustration you speak of, it comes rushing back out worse than ever, just like that." When Harry Philips said nothing, Magongo shrugged and crushed out his cigarette. "Something else if not the curry?"

"Get whatever you want."

Once Noah had taken their order and turned to leave, Magongo leaned forward again, neck bowed, elbows against the table. "So this Kunene chap. I would be too happy if you could tell me what it is you wish me to say about him."

"Only what you know."

"But so far that has not pleased you."

"No, it hasn't."

"Perhaps it is because you are looking for more than I have to give."

"I don't think so," Harry Philips said, tapping the pen point on his notepaper. "There's something missing here that we haven't found. I mean, Kunene may be poor and down and out and all, and he may have spent too much time that night at the *tjwala* pot, but up until then, the guy had a clean record. He'd never been arrested. Did you know that? Not for drinking too much and smashing somebody in the mouth, nothing. And then he suddenly breaks into a woman's house and rapes her in her bed—a white woman, no less—with her husband asleep beside her? Don't you find that more than a little strange, Bertie? I sure as hell do. And I can guarantee you I'm not the only one who wants to find out why he did what he did."

The skin on Magongo's brow wrinkled, like a teacher about to explain something one more time to a slow student. "Men fuck, my friend."

"Yeah, they do. But they usually don't walk over a mountain to do it—especially in the middle of the night."

Magongo held up his hand. "Do not misunderstand me. What this man did, it is not right, and he will be punished for it. But this 'why' you and your friends speak of might be no more than he saw the woman on her bed and thought how nice she would feel and climbed through her window and took her, even though she did not ask for him and did not like it. So, yes, men fuck, and that may be as much an answer to your 'why' as you will find. Unless you also believe in curses and spells."

Noah brought plates, cutlery and napkins, set places for them and went back for the food. The bowls had hardly touched the table before Magongo heaped rice onto his plate and smothered it with curried meat sauce, the sight and smell of which made Harry Philips' stomach growl regardless of his earlier denial. He served himself while Magongo spread his elbows to either side of his plate and attacked his meal, using his knife to scoot a mound of curry and rice onto the back of his fork, which he ferried flawlessly to his mouth, over and over, washing down every third bite with a draught of beer. Finished, he laid his knife on the table and sat back, fork now raised like a pointer in his right hand as he recommenced his story of Solomon Kunene.

Before Kunene disappeared from his job, Magongo said, he had also gained a reputation as someone people would do well to keep an eye on. He apparently spent a good bit of his time talking to his fellow workers, two or three at once and always out of earshot, so no one knew for certain the nature of their discussions—drinking? football? women?—or that which worried the bosses most of all: poor wages and the only means workers had to improve them? Even before independence, the king had made his opposition to labor unions clear, since they could by force of numbers challenge his ability to rule with true authority. Consequently, he wanted no discussion of unions or attempts to organize them, under penalty of arrest and imprisonment. So it followed, Magongo thought, that, although the bosses couldn't prove that Kunene was feeding worker discontent, they didn't want to take a chance of incurring the king's wrath.

"And that, my friend, is, I believe, the real reason your Kunene came to be without work. It had nothing to do with any of that other business—arguments, fights, girlfriend—none of it." Magongo lit another cigarette and drained his beer.

Harry Philips held up two fingers. Noah nodded, opened fresh Castles, brought them to the table and cleared their dishes.

"Okay, Bertie, let's say you're onto something. What then? I mean, how does Kunene go from being fired as a would-be Wobbly to becoming a rapist? That's a hell of a gap. What happened?"

Magongo knocked a column of ashes from his cigarette, swirled beer in his bottle, and said that after he lost his job, Solomon Kunene began a loop around the country that took him first from Manzini to Bhunya, where he tried to hire on at the wood-pulp mill. They had no job for him, so he moved farther north to Ngwenya and the mine where his brother worked, loading hopper cars with iron ore on its way to Japanese foundries. But the current mine owners had begun cutting production a year or so earlier because of decreased demand and had no work to offer either. Kunene stayed on with his brother for a few weeks, picking up odd jobs here and there, but eventually moved north again to Pigg's Peak, where he had no hope of employment but knew some people.

"What people?" Harry Philips asked.

Magongo shrugged, glanced away.

"For god's sake, Bertie, are we going to have to play this game again?"

"You do not understand, my friend. It is not the same as the girlfriend. They told me in Ngwenya—even Kunene's own brother, he said that I should stay away from those people. They are not nice. He said they will beat you just like that—and maybe worse."

Harry Philips gouged a check mark on the margin of the sheet of yellow paper, laid his pen beside it. "So why would Kunene go see them?"

Magongo's face darkened, lines across his forehead and around his mouth deepening. "They told me in Ngwenya that these bad boys, they work for Piet Giesen. They said that your Kunene wanted to go there and work for him too."

"Run guns, you mean? Sell *dagga* and rot-gut whiskey?"

"And perhaps girls for sex," Magongo said.

"I imagine Giesen keeps that side of business for himself."

Magongo shook his head and clicked his tongue. "How does a man like that—?"

"Stay in business?"

"Yes."

"He knows a lot of people, a lot of people know him."

"But he has much hate."

"So I've heard," Harry Philips said, thinking of the file drawer at the ministry filled with folders labeled with Piet Giesen's name.

"They say he hates the king and all he stands for—people living together, whites and Africans, colored, everyone. They told me that for this Giesen chap, when he talks, it's fucking kaffirs this, fucking kaffirs that, no matter what. Fucking kaffirs are the reason for all that is wrong." He dug his finger into the crumpled cigarette pack and teased a last smoke from it. "Yet these fellows work for him."

"Money can make people do strange things," Harry Philips said. "Did Kunene finally get to see Giesen?"

Magongo held up the empty cigarette pack for Noah to see.

"All of this stuff, though, you don't know if any of it's a fact, do you?"

"I know what they told me."

"The men in Ngwenya, you mean? Kunene's brother."

"Yes, I trust them."

"How do you think that'll stand up in court?"

Magongo shrugged, blew smoke. "So many questions."

"I don't like to be made a fool of."

Magongo dipped his head and glanced to either side. "That is not my custom."

"May I ask what is?" Gideon Dlamini said, leather shoe soles swooshing the floor as he walked toward them in his Saturday dress-down dark trousers, gray sport coat and soft yellow polo shirt.

"Gideon," Harry Philips said, rising to shake hands. "What a pleasant surprise. I didn't realize you were a fan of Lena's."

"I am and am not, you might say, depending."

"Do you know Bertie Magongo?"

"No, I don't believe we have met," Dlamini said, stretching his arm toward Magongo. "A pleasure."

Magongo stood, straightening his tie, and held out both hands, left fingers to his right wrist. "Yes, of course. My friend has spoken of you often."

"And your reputation, as they say, also precedes you, Mr. Magongo."

"Have a seat, Gideon?" Harry Philips said.

"No, I am sorry to say I cannot. I am here for an appointment."

Dlamini glanced toward the bar, as did the other two. The woman smiled. A vague emptiness flashed through Harry Philips.

"Sure. Don't let us keep you."

"Well, on with your evening," Dlamini said, heels clicking. "I merely wanted to stop by and greet you. Delighted to make your acquaintance, Mr. Magongo."

"Likewise."

"I am certain, as they say, our paths will cross again soon. Perhaps then I will learn what it was that the two of you were discussing so earnestly."

"Chameleons." Magongo took a drag on his cigarette. "We were saying how difficult it is to see and catch one in the first place and then have to set the fucker free when you find out how useless it is."

"Ah. Well spoken."

Magongo smiled with the right half of his mouth, à la Tomasto, but said nothing.

"And on that note," Dlamini said, bowing and turning away.

They watched him saunter to the bar, climb onto a stool next to the woman and lean close to whisper something to her. She laughed and raised her shoulder as if to protect her ear, legs uncrossing.

"I don't know, Bertie. Sex is a strange goddamn thing, all right, the people it draws together, the trouble it can cause."

"Tomasto would agree, even as much as he loves his women: you must be careful who you fuck."

"Or get fucked by."

They sat in silence a long while. Magongo opened the new pack of cigarettes Noah had delivered, before Harry Philips said, "Well, all right, then, until next time," and pushed his chair back to leave.

"Just one other matter, my friend," Magongo said, fingers and thumb rubbing together in what seemed a universal gesture.

He worried all the way home that Dlamini had seen him pay Magongo. He also worried about how much he had given him — 200 rand — a lot of money for what amounted to no useful information. Which, in the end, he worried most about. Dlamini and his people wanted a connection between Kunene and something bigger they could hang on him so they could drag him before the public as an example of what happens if you dick around with the powers that be. But all Magongo had to report was that Kunene was fired for fomenting labor unrest and that trusted sources said he traveled to Piet Giesen country and hired on with him. Nothing but allegations. And the thought that he could become culpable in the creation of false accusations against Kunene made him bilious, even though the effort catered to his own suspicions that something more than "men fuck" drove Kunene to do what he did.

He pulled to a halt on the driveway beside his house, switched off the car engine. Elizabeth was nowhere to be seen in the deepening dusk, all signs of her weeding cleaned up and put away and only a single light on in the hallway. He unlocked the kitchen door and called her name. No answer. He listened for sounds of the shower in the bathroom. Nothing. He walked into the hall, the living room, the hall again. "Elizabeth?" He leaned into her room and saw with relief that the clothes he had given her were still there, washed and folded on the bed. Everything else seemed in order as well, so he began wondering if he should be worried about where she was and what she might be doing, although he didn't recall that keeping track of her every coming and going was part of the agreement for her to live there. But he did like her and cared about her and didn't want anything to happen to her. She was probably with friends and they had gone to a movie or to get something to eat or were walking up and down the street looking for boys, the way girls did everywhere.

He sighed and turned back to the kitchen, flipping on lights as he went, more aware than ever how empty the house seemed.

He wandered out to look at the flowerbeds and the lawn in general, pausing at the top of the slope beyond his garage to peer at the flow of lights across the valley below and up the hills to the west.

Before long he was slapping at mosquitoes on his arms and head, and he hurried inside to the living room where he tuned the radio. Saxes squealed, trumpets blared, drums thumped. He lowered the volume and opened the liquor cabinet for a glass and a fifth of Jameson that he tucked under his arm as he headed toward the overstuffed chair across the room. He shifted his book—a massive tome on the history of authoritarianism in sub-Saharan Africa—and set the glass and whiskey beside it. He should have picked it up—or a newspaper or a magazine—but he knew he had no intention of reading and let them lie. He poured a finger of Jameson, drank it down, poured another, as he sat back to listen to the soft wail of music drifting through the room.

He awoke sweaty and stiff-necked to a dark, quiet house. His glass was empty and the cap was on the Jameson bottle. He had a sour taste in his mouth and a dull headache. He closed his eyes and reconnected to the vision of the woman from the bar naked, but for her high heels and pillbox hat, in the living room of someone's home. She was leaning against an exposed brick wall, legs spread, back at a 45-degree angle, Gideon Dlamini behind her, naked also, pressing himself against her, hands sliding toward her hardening nipples, her abdomen, her thighs. He called for a basin of water and a sponge, which Bertie Magongo and Tomasto, a mustachioed man in a dark suit and black fedora, carried in from another room. Dlamini then turned to Harry Philips, who stepped forward, dipped the sponge in the basin, squeezed excess water from it, and washed where Dlamini demanded, theretherethere, music wailing from the radio, Magongo and Tomasto scat singing nearby, as Harry Philips stroked down and up in rhythm to the music, down and up, down and up, the woman's hips gyrating ever higher, until Elizabeth arched her back, twisting to look at him over her shoulder, eyes wide, mouth open, Carolyn's voice saying you bastard yes oh oh you bastard, before slumping to the floor, sponge clamped between her thighs.

He sat a moment, wiping his hand over his face, before he scooted forward in the chair and pushed himself up. He replaced the Jameson in the cabinet and carried his glass to the kitchen. Shoes under his arm, he padded stocking-footed to Elizabeth's room, where, ear to the door, he thought he could hear her breathing, but wasn't sure, and wrapped his free hand around the crystal knob. The door was locked. He backed away, nodding, smiling, and crept off to his own room.

13

"So this list," Joseph said, shifting the car into neutral a safe distance behind an overloaded bus waiting for its chance to turn onto the highway. "You say you do not need it?"

"No, not need-need," Meg said.

"The way some people need tobacco or alcohol?" Sarah adjusted her arm around Jabalile, who sat between them in the back seat. She'd brought up lists by asking if Meg had gotten everything on hers, or should they wait for her to recheck, a continuing joke between them.

"Exactly," Meg said. "I'm not addicted."

Sarah smiled. "But you still carry one."

"It's her security blanket," Brian asked.

"If I may ask," Joseph said, "did your mother make lists as well?"

"She's the queen of list makers."

"And now you make your own. What is the saying?"

"Like father like son," Brian said.

"Only with this it is like mother like daughter," Sarah said. "My mother never used lists. There was no need. We always ate the same thing—mealie-meal porridge with bread and whatever vegetable we could find in the garden. A chicken now and then. Sometimes a beast—a pig or goat—on feast days."

The bus belched a cloud of deep gray smoke, waddled over the lip of pavement at the edge of the parking lot and lumbered south. Once it was across the bridge and had started the long descent down Malegwane Hill, Joseph put the Cortina back in gear and pulled onto the highway.

"And your mother," Brian said to Joseph, "did she make lists?"

"Ha. Your wife's mother and mine could have been sisters. Mine had lists of her lists. She was a bookkeeper, you see, at a large dry cleaner's near Pietermaritzburg. She was quite a particular person."

"Yes, she was," Sarah said. "And still is. But nicely so."

"What about your father?" Meg asked. "What does he do?"

"Did, I am afraid. He died several years ago."

"I'm sorry," Brian said.

"Not to worry. He enjoyed his life and his work. He was a barber and was quite proud of his profession."

"Every day he went to the shop in a pressed shirt and tie and a long white coat," Sarah said. "One like doctors wear. It was his uniform. Everyone knew him by it. The coat had many pockets for combs, scissors, clippers and such. And the strangest thing to me was that even though he cut hair — African hair — all day, you never saw him with a single clipping on that coat."

"That was because of Clayton," Joseph said. "He was my father's assistant, who did nothing but clean up the shop and my father. As soon as my father finished with a new creation — that is what he called those who came to his shop, rather than customers — Clayton would go to work before my father started on another."

"It was comical to watch," Sarah said. "Clayton was a little man. Short. One and a half meters, perhaps. And thin. Joseph's father was quite tall. Taller than Joseph. He and Clayton made such a pair. Because he was so short, Clayton had a small wooden box that he stood on to dust off Joseph's father. Clayton would have him face away to begin with, and he would clean Joseph's father off with the softest brush you can imagine. Long bristles that would go this way and that without a care. He would attend to the collar and shoulders, then go down the back to the end of the white coat. From there, the backs of the trousers. Left side, right side, same treatment. The front was even more thorough because Clayton would unbutton the coat and brush down the shirt and tie, rebutton, and continue. Finally the shoes. After he finished Joseph's father, he swept the floor and put everything away for the next person."

The bus loomed ahead, brake lights bright against the steep downward grade. Joseph slowed, downshifting to slow the car.

"So with these creations," Meg said, "did your father try to keep up with what were popular hairstyles, or —?"

"Oh, no, he cut all hair the same, like mine." Joseph slid his hand over his short-cropped trim. "He did not like pomps or conks, that sort of thing. And he did not like putting chemicals on hair. Natural. That is what he liked, and he worked toward helping each person become more of who they already were, rather than making them into something different."

"Be true to yourself," Brian said.

"Yes."

"Did that mean be African?"

"Yes. Exactly," Joseph said.

"Sounds pretty subversive."

"It was. But he made his mark quietly. Otherwise he would not have stayed in business for long. Someone would have reported him to the authorities if he had been too — what should I say? — obvious. There are informers everywhere."

"Perhaps we should talk about other things," Sarah said.

"Why?" Joseph said. "We are with friends. Even white friends who are traveling in our auto and are about to have lunch with us. In the Republic we would be arrested."

A small yellow sign with black letters barely readable from where they were announced Mdzimba Mountain Lodge. Joseph steered in the direction the arrow pointed and followed a tarmac lane that rose slightly, before dipping down toward the Mbabane River, which they crossed on a one-lane wooden bridge. Then they began the serpentine climb up the mountainside. One last turn led to a level but narrow parking lot beside the lodge.

Meg liked the building — modest but pleasant, in keeping with much of the rest of the country, a timber and stone structure, topped with a green corrugated metal roof. A wide veranda crossed the front and continued along the far side, where in good weather they liked to eat and take in the view of Ezulwini Valley.

Coming here had grown into a ritual, a special occasion about once a month to pay Sarah and Joseph back for the rides here and there and to spend more time together.

Once out of the car, Jabalile took Meg's hand and they walked behind the others up the stone steps to the entrance. A young Swazi woman in a black cocktail dress and heels greeted them inside and escorted them through the main dining room, with maybe a half-dozen occupied tables, to a side exit onto the veranda. After everyone was seated, she handed each person a menu and told them that Thomas, their waiter, would be with them shortly.

Sarah craned around to have a better view of the valley. "I do not believe I will ever tire of seeing that."

"Me neither," Meg said, peering over the top of her menu at the scene that stretched uninterrupted for miles across treetops and verdant fields directly to the western border of mountains, where white wisps of cloud clung here and there, like memories of hair on an old man's head.

Thomas brought them each a glass of water and stood by to take their orders.

"A toasted ham, cheese, and tomato sandwich for her," Sarah said, nodding toward Jabalile, "and peri-peri prawns for me."

Thomas looked at Meg. "Oxtail stew and soda bread."

"Fish and chips, please," Brian said.

Joseph handed his menu to Thomas. "I would like the small filet. Medium, with béarnaise sauce."

"Anything to drink other than water?"

After they ordered drinks and Thomas had gone back inside, Brian said, "So you were talking earlier about informers being everywhere in the Republic. What happens to people who get turned in?"

"They might be fined," Joseph said. "Or arrested or lose their job or go to jail. Maybe worse, depending. And it can be for anything—what you might say or do, where you try to shop or live—if you are too ambitious."

"In what way?" Meg said.

"Do you remember the story about eyeglasses when we were at university?" Joseph asked Sarah, who put her arm around Jabalile and drew her closer.

"There was a man we both knew, Phineas Xhosa, the son of a chief who could afford to own the eyeglasses that he needed. His mistake was that he wore them to class the day after he got them. The professor—who was white, of course—came to Phineas' desk and asked him what he thought he was doing. Only whites could wear eyeglasses, not blacks, and then he struck him. Slapped his face so hard that his new eyeglasses flew off."

"That's awful," Brian said. "Maddening." He paused while Thomas served their drinks and told them their lunch would be out shortly. "But if it's any consolation, the same thing could happen in America. It's only four years ago that we finally got around to passing the Civil Rights Act. But even with it—"

"At least you have a law," Sarah said, slowly stirring her tea. "In the Republic we have apartheid, which is only getting worse. It has become a strange and crazy place. We know an English woman in Manzini—a teacher, like us—who is married—well, maybe not married—to a Zulu man. Our tribe. But she is white, and he is black, and they have a child who is, by apartheid policies, colored. She wants to go to her home in England to introduce her child to his English grandparents." Sarah sighed, tears in her eyes. "She wanted to drive with the child to Joburg to avoid the flight from here to there. When she got to the border at Ngwenya, the guards would not let her pass because whites and coloreds cannot travel together in the Republic. Her own child."

Thomas brought their food and everyone ate, but almost dutifully, it seemed to Meg. She sipped a spoonful of soup and dropped a bread crust into the broth to soak. "So how do things like that—like you're telling us—make you feel about going back home?"

"Not so good, I suppose," Sarah said. "It is better here. Not perfect, but better. More—what is the word?—tolerant."

"Do you think you'll ever go back?" Brian asked. "I mean to live there again?"

Joseph paused, a bite of filet halfway to his mouth, and lowered his knife and fork to his plate. "The time will come when we have no choice. When they are ready, Swazis will take our jobs, even if it is not to our liking. It is their country, and we will need to go back to ours."

"Surely you could find something else here, if you wanted to," Meg said.

"Yes, I believe we could, but would it be work we would be happy to do?" He raised meat to his mouth, chewed, swallowed. "Besides, going back might not be so bad. Things will change in the Republic. They cannot stay the way they are. It is only a matter of when the change will come—and perhaps how. So we will go back when we need to, and we will survive."

"What about you?" Sarah asked Meg. "What will you do?"

"We don't know yet. It all depends. On the trial. As it is, we pretty much have to stay to the end of our Peace Corps assignment. After that... There is the Vietnam War. Peace Corps volunteers are deferred from the draft while they're on the job, but once you resign..."

"It becomes a matter of life and death," Joseph said. "I remember reading that once a soldier enters combat in that war, his chances of dying—what is it you say?—skyrocket?"

"Yes," Meg said. "That's exactly right. So. Like I said..."

14

Gideon Dlamini's office door was open just wide enough that Harry Philips could see the prince standing at the window next to his desk, body and chin jutted forward, head posed to cast a sharp silhouette of his face against the bright sky. His left arm hung to his side, right elbow cocked to accommodate a Napoleonesque hand resting between the middle buttons of his suit vest. His mind seemed fixed on some distant horizon, perhaps lost in complex thought, or, more likely, what to do about the woman in the pillbox hat. Should he cast her off once he grew tired of her, or keep her on as the pleasant dalliance she must surely be, with the understanding that their relationship would never progress to anything more? Or ultimately, when he assumed the throne in place of his dead father, should he throw tradition to the wind and demote his current wife by bringing his new love into his household as his new chief wife and declaring her his Josephine, empress for life?

But whatever thoughts he might have had seemed to vanish when he turned his head and said, "Ah, Mr. Philips. Come in, come in. I have been expecting you."

Harry Philips pushed the door open and waited for it to close before stepping forward.

"Please." Dlamini gestured toward a chair opposite him. "Tea?"

"Sure."

The prince poured a cup and guided it to Harry Philips. "So this Magongo chap, he is a friend of yours?"

"Sort of."

"But close enough to have a discussion about lizards as I recall."

"Chameleons."

"Yes, of course. How difficult it is to identify one, and when you finally do, you wonder whether it was worth the effort. Rather an odd topic, I thought."

"Beer talk. You know how it is."

Dlamini stood and paced back toward the window. "But of course you and Mr. Magongo were not discussing chameleons at all, were you?"

Harry Philips shifted in his chair.

"He was reporting what he had learned about Solomon Kunene, was he not?" The prince faced the desk, feet spread, shoulders squared, hands clasped behind his back, a pose that drew a striking resemblance to his father in the photo portrait on the opposite wall. "Why did you feel it necessary to seek help outside the ministry?"

"Because you told me that you—and the king—wanted the job done as soon as possible."

"We have people here—"

"Sure, but you know as well as I do it can take a week at best to get a manpower requisition cleared."

"Even so, Mr. Philips, you no doubt recall our discussion concerning the need for discretion in this case. The utmost discretion."

"Of course I do."

"And that we were trusting you to conduct the investigation with that in mind."

"So if you're worried about Bertie, don't be. He is a little odd, I have to admit, but he's not stupid."

Dlamini's mouth curled into a half-smile as he strolled back to his chair and arranged himself in it.

"Or maybe you think I'm the stupid one," Harry Philips said, "and would love to get me out of the way. If that's the case, just tell me."

"No, no, Mr. Philips. You misunderstand me." Dlamini held his hands chin-high, fingers arched, tips tapping, as if carefully measuring his thoughts. "Rather than relieving you of your duties, I am far more interested in making certain of your continued commitment to the case developing around Mr. Kunene."

"Developing?"

"Yes. There is, for instance, that rather prolonged stopover he made in Pigg's Peak. Surely your friend mentioned it."

"He did."

"And what did he conclude was Mr. Kunene's business there?"

"I wouldn't say he concluded anything."

"Of course not, since he never went to Pigg's Peak, did he?"

"No."

"And he therefore has no evidence that Mr. Kunene did not in fact meet with Mr. Giesen, eh, when he would seem to have every reason to. He is out of work, out of money, out of friends, out of luck. So where does he go? To find the man everyone says is—what is the term?—made of money?"

"I'm not sure I like where this development, as you call it, is heading."

Dlamini rose, paced to his father's portrait, turned and paced toward the window. "As it stands, Mr. Kunene will be tried and sentenced to prison. That much is certain. But due to the circumstances—that no one actually saw him entering the house since Mr. Bernard was asleep—the case will come down to Mr. Kunene's word against Mrs. Bernard's. He will say they were lovers, she will say they were not. He will say she enticed him, she will say she did not. He will say she is lying, she will say she is not. And, in most cases, as we unfortunately know, the judge would believe his version of events over hers. But not this time. She is not just another woman. She is a white American, he is a black African. She has special friends, he does not. The case is closed. But," index finger raised, "he appeals for leniency. He tells the judge he has never been arrested and he has an

179

old mother who depends on him for survival. The judge grants his appeal and recommends much less than the recommended maximum sentence." Dlamini paused, brows raised. "Is that a satisfactory outcome, Mr. Philips, when another is within grasp that could increase his sentence significantly?"

"Involving Giesen?"

"Yes. I would even go so far as to suggest he ordered Mr. Kunene to carry out the attack on Mrs. Bernard."

"I don't know, Gideon. I mean, Kunene's in it for the money, but what about Giesen? Sure, he's a dirty player, we all know that, but he never does anything just for the hell of it. What's in this for him? What's his motive?"

Dlamini stepped to the desk, bracing his hands on its edge as he leaned forward. "He embarrasses the government, the monarchy, the people. He mocks everything we stand for. That seems motivation enough for me."

"We do have a constitution, you know. Maybe somebody should be watching the watchers here."

Dlamini's mouth tightened, his eyes narrowed. "You surprise me, Mr. Philips. In fact, you disappoint me with your attitude. As you recall, we agreed at the beginning that Solomon Kunene in all likelihood did not act alone in his assault on Mrs. Bernard."

"At that point I thought there really might have been something else, but—"

"Yes. Go on."

"I was thinking more in the lines of some existential crisis, something more personal. Definitely not this mega-political thing you're talking about."

"Mr. Giesen used Solomon Kunene to attack the monarchy, Mr. Philips." He had never seen the prince so stern and dour. "I will do whatever is necessary to protect the integrity of the king and his place in this society. Is that clear? Anything at all. For the good of our people."

"And you think Giesen's going to stay quiet during all this? He knows a lot of people, wields a lot of influence."

"Yes, he unfortunately does." Dlamini straightened. "But that will diminish considerably when he is no longer, as you say, in the picture."

"What are you going to do, have him killed?"

Dlamini laughed, slipped back into his chair. "No, as tempting as that may be. I was thinking more of sending him back to his Afrikaner friends in the Republic."

"Deport him? On what grounds?"

"Sedition, conspiracy, any number of things."

"Without a trial?"

"There would be no need for one in this instance. We would take care of everything right here," finger poking the desktop, "in the ministry."

Harry Philips raised his cup to his mouth. The tea was cold, but he drank the rest anyway in a single gulp. "What about Kunene? What happens to him?"

"We attach an additional charge to his case of carrying out acts injurious to state security. Depending on the judge, he would get another ten years, minimum."

"But that means news about the case would be everywhere— papers, radio, word of mouth."

"All in our favor," Dlamini said. "Who could possibly oppose us in ridding our society of such scourges?"

"I was thinking of the Bernards."

"It is kind of you to be concerned, Mr. Philips. But on occasion—and this appears to be one—people are called upon to make often unpleasant sacrifices for the sake of the greater good. Now, if there is nothing more..."

The door closed behind him with a crisp snap. A revolver loading. A vault sealing. The bastard. He would make Machiavelli proud. But as much as he hated to admit it, Dlamini's scheme to deal with Giesen was genius, even if it was a lie. And whatever happened to Kunene was okay, too. The Bernards, though, were another matter. They deserved better.

15

The storm had started with fluffy, innocent-looking clouds sailing over Mdzimba Mountain, as if to divert attention from what was coming. And they did. When Meg saw them, she'd smiled as she hand-wrung the last few items she'd washed, adding them to the pile on the table. When she'd finished, she rinsed the wash basin, stacked the laundry in it, and headed for the barbed-wire fence behind the house to hang the wet wash with the rest that was drying there. Other than underwear. That she draped over a makeshift clothesline in the spare bedroom.

"Oh my god," she said, halting in the doorway and staring out at the leaden sky that was lowering over the valley from behind the mountain. She could smell the coming rain and see dust and debris swirling in front of angry, sickly green clouds, a sign, her mother used to say, that they were really in for it.

She dropped the basin back onto the table and bolted through the doorway to the fence to retrieve laundry before it got shredded in the gathering wind. She removed shirts, pants, blouses, a dress from the barbs as carefully as she could, amazed, but grateful, to find that nothing was damaged beyond repair—nothing a stitch or two wouldn't fix.

As she scurried around the trash pit toward the house, she spotted Brian coming as fast as he could from the school, hair whipping over his head, T-shirt and jeans wind-plastered to his body. Puffs of dust raced ahead of him from each footstep, and scattered strands of coarse grass and weeds switched his legs as he hurried home.

He had reached the turnstile when the first drops fell. Large, cold splats that stung her bare arms. Meg ran inside and dumped an armful of clothes on the bathroom floor.

"You get the windows in the bedroom and the living room!" Brian yelled as he slammed the kitchen door. "I'll get these. Maybe leave cracks so we have some ventilation."

The storm engulfed them, rain hammering so hard on the asbestos roof she ducked her head and held her hands over her ears. Hail and rain scoured everything in its path, driven by wind that howled like some phantom beast. She backed away from the window, fearful it might shatter.

"Shit!" Brian shouted.

She found him on tiptoes at the kitchen sink, straining to look out.

"What's wrong?"

"Can't tell for sure, but—" He nodded toward a small semicircle of water edging under the door and kicked off his shoes, leaving his socks on and rolling his pant legs to mid-calf.

"What are you doing?"

"Gotta go see what's going on."

"You're nuts."

"Would you rather have a flood?" He opened the door and ducked his head out, glancing to the left and right.

Beyond him, debris that had been flushed out of the trash pit pushed past the doorway on a stream of runoff, banked by hail it had swept aside. The same scene repeated as far as she could see amid trees and grass roiling in the wind.

"Ah, there it is," he said, righting himself before stepping into the puddle of water outside the threshold.

She hurried for a chair, climbed on its seat, and bent as close to the window as she could. Brian stood almost directly below her, hands braced on his knees, backbone showing through his soaked shirt, water streaming from his hair. In front of him, a small but probably more than ankle-deep pond had formed from water that surged down the slope from the schoolyard and pooled against the base of their house, the ground just beyond the kitchen door rising enough to form a makeshift dam. The pool of water from under the door had widened now to cover a third of the floor and would only get worse unless Brian could somehow relieve the blockage. Maybe dig a spillway or something. But they didn't have a shovel, and even a big spoon wouldn't be sturdy enough to gouge clay and rocks. Her trowel. It was small, made for potting house plants, but might be better than nothing.

She ran to the spare bedroom and scooted a couple of boxes away from the bookshelf. There it was, shiny and blue-handled, together with a hammer, pliers, screwdrivers and a jar of screws and nails.

Climbing back up on the chair in the kitchen, she knocked on the window. Brian straightened and glanced toward the school. She knocked again. He turned to face her. She held up the trowel. He smiled and nodded. She opened the window enough to push it through.

"I thought it might help."

"Perfect. Thanks."

"Careful with the handle."

She winced as he hopped from one tender foot to the other over ground littered with pebbles and hail and who knew what else. Nothing sharp, she hoped.

He crouched beyond the doorway puddle and began stabbing the ground, both hands around the trowel to protect it. He piled clumps of clay, loose rocks and bits of cement left over from construction beside the channel he was digging down the slope to his right, deeper and deeper until the water began to drain away.

From inside as well, flowing slowly back out. She hopped off the chair and grabbed the broom and swept the water that remained toward the crack under the door.

She put the broom away and went to the spare bedroom for a towel. When she returned, Brian stood stripped and shivering just inside the door.

"You wouldn't believe how cold that rain is," he said, reaching for the towel.

As he dried himself, she hurried back to the spare bedroom for one of their extra blankets, which he immediately hugged around himself.

"So nice."

A flash and a crack of thunder, followed by lash after lash of rain and hail, drove them into the hallway, where they huddled like animals escaping to a cave.

"You're still cold." Meg wrapped her arms around him and squeezed.

"Feels good," he said, opening the blanket to include her.

She laid her face sideways on his chest and stroked his bare back. She'd forgotten how much she enjoyed touching him, smelling him, feeling his penis stir against her.

"I have an idea," he said, slipping his arm around her waist as he guided her toward their room, where he pulled the blankets loose from her side of the bed.

"I think we'd be more comfortable lying down."

She closed the curtains and began unbuttoning her blouse.

"You don't have to do that," he said.

"But I want to."

He lay down and drew the blanket back over him.

She finished undressing, and he lifted the blanket for her. She crawled in, her back to him. He draped an arm and a leg over her. She snuggled back against him. He held her hair away from her neck and kissed the back of it. Her ear. The side of her neck and across the top of her shoulder. She shuddered, wiggled even closer to him, felt his growing erection on her hip.

"Thank you for putting up with me," he said.

"I love you, Brian."

He reached over her, put his hand to her mouth, and turned her enough that he could kiss her lips. His other hand stroked her side, armpit to waist, up and back, more kisses on her cheek and ear, the crook of her neck. And ever so slowly, with gentle but gradually more vigorous attention to those places she'd loved for him to touch—her breasts, her hips, the backs of her knees, the soft insides of her thighs, and there, oh yes, there— he soon brought her past any remaining unease to an urgent, arching appreciation of what she'd/they'd been missing.

They lay afterward twined around each other, listening to what was now the patter of rain on the roof, until hunger drove them from the bedroom to the kitchen, where they made an early dinner of pasta and marinara sauce with dried mushrooms, stacked their dirty dishes in the sink and, with what wine was left in the bottle, went back to bed.

16

Thoughts of Carolyn—the way she looked, talked, walked, laughed—kept looping in his mind like a song lyric, especially a bad one—a jingle, Tex Ritter song, a hymn he heard as a kid, something along the lines of "ye who are weary, come home," the last word stretched over several wobbly notes. The first loop might bring a smile, but by the tenth he looked for anything to distract him, even if he liked the music, because he knew it would eventually plunge him into an ever more foul mood. His memories of Carolyn were initially enjoyable as well but always grew darker, descending into angry glares, angry voices and words he would rather forget.

He wandered into the living room, and there she was again, hanging above the mantel in the only piece of art she'd left behind. Why still mystified him. Did she do it deliberately so he'd have a reminder of her absence, like a finger jab to the chest, or was it more nuanced, trusting to his possession a work she knew he would never get rid of and would possibly one day return to her—in person? He'd always considered it one of her best works, a crayon sketch of a Swazi woman, sitting on a wooden chair and leaning forward, chin in hand. She was neither young nor old and was dressed in a bluish long-sleeved top and a cream-colored skirt that billowed over her lap and off the canvas. A close-fitting beige cap covered her hair and ears. Her eyes and mouth were closed, her face angled. He'd wondered from the beginning what Carolyn had seen in the woman—someone tired from a long day's work, someone unlucky at love, someone contemplating the world? Whatever the vision, the woman seemed bent but still strong and determined, and Carolyn's sympathy for her—or should it be empathy?—showed clearly. But that's the way she was, which made her all the more able to discover the emotional core of people. It was uncanny at times but was what breathed life into works like the portrait. Her life. Her breath.

He could take the picture down, store it away so he wouldn't see it all the time. Leaving it up made him as guilty of self-torture as those crazy monks who flagellated themselves. Purification by pain.

He spun away.

What he needed was to get out of the house to help ward off the stupor he felt coming on. If Elizabeth were home, he could maybe teach her to play hearts or some board game, but he'd given them all to the library, since he didn't have anyone to play them with. Besides, he was never comfortable with her for any length of time. They rarely carried on a conversation for more than a few minutes, and then with several long pauses. He'd love to be a fly buzzing her and her friends as they walked the streets and chattered, listening to what they said and how they said it, learning from their sociability.

He could do some yard work.

Go for a walk.

Go for a drive.

Maybe to Lobamba to see the Bernards, find out how they were doing. It'd been close to a month since he'd talked with them, so it really wasn't a bad idea. Maybe they could even go into Manzini for peri-peri prawns at the Portuguese restaurant. Or the Indian place, the name of which he couldn't remember, if they would rather, and order the spiciest samosas he'd ever eaten.

Or maybe not.

Maybe he'd drop by Lena's instead for a sandwich and a beer and see what was happening. He might even bump into Magongo, or maybe not, and reminded himself to take a book, just in case.

He opened the door to the soft squeal of African jazz coming from behind the bar. Long shafts of sunlight scored the floor in front of him and at the back of the pub, leaving the central area in a deep shadow enclosing two men at a table, a man and woman at another, a lone man on a stool at the bar, another far to the right haloed in a wreath of cigarette smoke. But no Bertie Magongo. He and his buddy Tomasto could be harvesting information on a new case or, more likely, he hadn't made it out and about yet after another long night at the office.

He laid his book on Magongo's table, out of habit as much as anything, since that was almost always where he sat, and went to the bar, where he exchanged the usual pleasantries with Noah and ordered a Castle, a ham and cheese sandwich, pickle and hot mustard on the side, and a bag of crisps. He carried the beer back to the table, setting it down across from Magongo's chair, took a sip, and opened his book so he would look busy, but didn't read.

He glanced up as Noah brought his order. After smoothing mustard over the top slice of bread, he cut the sandwich in half and opened the bag of crisps.

The salty tang of mustard and ham, the processed yellow cheese that was more a texture than a taste, the sour nip of the pickle and vinegar crisp melded with a wad of white bread into a magic, comforting familiarity of flavors and sensations that deepened even more the hunger which had already surprised him in its urgency.

By the time he'd finished eating, two more couples had come in and made their way through light shafts and shadows to the back of the pub, where they took seats on opposite sides of the room. He folded his napkin and set it and his plate to one side to make room again for his book, which, after ordering another Castle, he began reading in earnest.

Two chapters later, the light shafts had climbed halfway up the walls, with the sun rapidly setting behind the low hills west of the city.

Movement on the sidewalk caught his eye. The woman in the pillbox hat sauntered toward the entrance to Lena's, hesitating on the first step to turn to meet his gaze. He blushed but was almost certain—no, was certain—that he saw a brief smile cross her lips.

He concentrated again on his book, following the clack of her heels on the wooden floor as she walked to the bar. He peeked up and found her greeting Noah with a smile as she slid onto a stool and ordered a drink. She took a sip and said something to Noah which seemed to prompt the two of them to turn in unison to look in his direction. His face flushed again. She again said something to Noah, who nodded. She slipped off the stool, gathered her drink, and glided toward him.

He stood when she neared.

"Mr. Philips?"

"Harry Philips," he said, offering his hand.

They shook and he walked around to pull out the chair across from him. She sat, straightening her skirt.

"And you are?"

She said nothing.

"What is your name?"

"Constance. Constance Mhlongo."

"Nice to meet you."

"Thank you."

He lifted his beer. "Cheers, Constance."

She smiled and raised her drink until bottle and glass touched.

"And to what do I owe the pleasure of your company?" he asked. When she again didn't answer, he continued, "Why are you looking for me?"

"Bertie Magongo told me that I must come here. If I found you, I must give you something." She reached inside the front of her blouse, pulled out an envelope, and handed it to him.

The paper was still warm to the touch.

"How do you know Bertie?"

"He is a friend."

"Bertie's everybody's friend."

"He is." She paused for another sip from her drink, looking at the envelope.

He turned it over and caught a faint whiff of her perfume. He drew another breath, held it a moment before opening the letter and removing a single sheet from a yellow legal pad folded multiple times to fit into the envelope. He imagined Magongo hunched over his desk, pencil stub in hand, as he carved his message in heavy block letters mixed with hurried cursive script, dark smudges from a bad eraser here and there down the page.

To my good friend Brother Philips,

Tomasto says when you have a thing that is too important, you must always write it and make certain the person you write it for reads it. So if you are reading my letter, it is good so far.

I will be brief, for what I must say is too sad for many words. Yesterday I was at my place in Lena's Pub when a man in a suit, he came to me and handed me a letter. A fancy letter on fancy paper. It was from the Ministry of Home Affairs. It said that I must leave Swaziland. I am not welcome any longer because I have done things that the government thinks are dangerous and unfriendly. What those things are I do not know. I have done nothing. Tomasto he would say that it is because I worry them. But how? Is it because I know something that they do not? Or perhaps because I do not

193

know something they wish I did? If I did nothing and know nothing, why are they angry with me?

They say I have one week. If I am still in Swaziland after that they will arrest me and put me in jail. I still have my papers and will return that side to the Republic tomorrow. I am too frightened to remain here longer.

But not to worry, Brother Philips. I will be okay. I am only too sad that I must not say goodbye to my friend.

Stay well,

Bertie Magongo

PS: My friend, she is lovely yes?

"The sonsabitches." He dropped the letter in front of him. "Did he tell you what this is about?"

She shook her head no.

"They're kicking him out of the country. He's going back to the Republic."

"This cannot be so."

"According to the letter it is. And you know who's behind it?" He should shut up, but he couldn't help himself. "Your buddy, that's who. The prince."

Her eyes narrowed. "No, that one is not my friend."

"You could have fooled me."

"You are angry."

"Yes, but not at you."

And he didn't quite understand why he was so upset with Dlamini, either—it was exactly what he said he was going to do with Magongo. Which meant Piet Giesen was next. And what about the Bernards? No, they'd probably be okay, or as okay as they could be until this mess was over with and they weren't as useful anymore. Besides, Dlamini would have to be outright stupid to do anything to them, and he was anything but stupid.

Better to let things for them come to a more natural conclusion and avoid ruffling international feathers.

He handed Constance his handkerchief as she swiped a finger over the tears on her cheeks.

"Thank you. He is a good man, you know. Bertie Magongo. A very good man."

"To Bertie." He raised his bottle and she her glass and they drank to their friend. "He says in his letter that I—and I should now say we—shouldn't worry. He says he'll be okay."

"Yes. He will be. He is more than good, that one, he is clever." A flicker of a smile played across her lips again. "And he has many friends and family that side. A brother and a sister near Ladysmith. Others too."

He wondered just how friendly she was with Magongo. They were apparently close enough that he shared personal information with her but not close enough that he'd told her ahead of time he was being deported. Yet even at that, Magongo still trusted her to deliver his message. Meaning she'd just seen him? Had she come directly from his house? If so, what were they doing there?

"Are you hungry?" he asked, not knowing why.

She seemed not to understand or was taken aback by the question.

"Would you like something to eat?"

She glanced at his empty plate, back at him, and smiled.

What he would rather have asked was whether she would like to go home with him, but he didn't, of course, and after Noah took her order and returned with her baked chicken and vegetables, he inquired about her family, as was the custom. How everyone was, where they were, what they were doing. And in the course of their discussion, he learned that ties between Magongo and her family went back years. They were both from the same area of Natal in the Republic. Not long after her parents came to Swaziland, Magongo followed, only her family eventually became naturalized citizens but Magongo did not, which in the end was what made his deportation feasible and much less awkward. No charges, no trial, no jail time.

Constance was born in Swaziland and said Magongo was a young man by then, making him a good 15 to 20 years older than her, and remained an on-and-off presence in her life from as long ago as she could remember. Like an older cousin, from what Harry Philips gathered, which relieved his mind as to their relationship.

He wondered what Carolyn would see if she were there. The rakish tilt of the pillbox hat, of course. But what about the spacing of her eyes, the prominence of her cheekbones, the way she sat straight but relaxed and used her fingers to pull chicken flesh from the bone, grasped loosely in her hand, as if afraid it might burn her?

How would she draw or paint Constance beyond what anyone could see? For that matter, how would Carolyn paint him, what he was thinking? How would she paint jealousy, which surely she would sense? Or anger? Or despair?

He hadn't noticed until now that the sun had set and shadows had consumed the room, except where a couple of weak bulbs near the ceiling and behind the bar cast faint light. Constance's face was more profile than detail, and he could barely pick out the other customers.

Excusing himself, he made his way to the restroom and stopped at the bar as he returned to the table to ask Noah for a candle. He leaned slightly to his left and brought out a votive candle in a clear glass bowl-shaped holder. He pulled the wick free from the wax and lit it.

"Now you may see better," he said, nodding toward the table.

"That'll be nice for me, but I don't know what she'll think."

"Oh she will not be troubled. She has stayed with you this long, no?"

The flame flickered, held.

"So do you know her? Constance?"

"Yes, a little."

"How often does she come in here?"

Noah took a glass from the sink beside him and began drying it. "Once, maybe twice, a week." He held the glass in front of his face, as if focusing Harry Philips through it. "She is usually alone." He set the glass at the end of a row of others like it on the counter behind him. "Sometimes she is with a girlfriend but not often. And never with a man. There are plenty of them here to talk to and to buy her drinks, if she wants."

"I can imagine," Harry Philips said. "Do you have any idea what she does, how she makes a living?"

"Oh, she is quite the modern woman, that one." He picked up another glass. "She said she works as a clerk," which he pronounced clark, "in an office in Mbabane. A government office, I believe, but I am not certain."

"It doesn't matter. I was just curious." Harry Philips picked up the candle holder and cradled it in the palm of his left hand, as if he were about to transport something far more delicate than it was. "But I'd best get back over there while I still have somebody to talk to. And, by the way, bring us another round of drinks when you have a chance."

Constance smiled at his approach and raised her hand in a half-wave, but whether for him or Noah, he didn't know, since he couldn't tell for sure where she was looking.

"Thank you," she said as he placed the candle between them, his fingers inadvertently brushing her forearm. "Sorry."

She gazed at the place he had touched.

"It really was an accident."

"Not to worry," she said, looking up at him. "Bertie says you are a good man. He says you treat him well and are kind." She reached her hand toward him. "He says he is honored to call you his friend and that I should shake your hand goodbye for him."

Her fingers were soft and warm, sandwiched between his palms, as was the custom. He bowed slightly to her and she to him, and they continued the shake far longer than any European or American would normally find tolerable. When he at length started to pull his hand away, she tightened her grip. Holding hands with her was pleasant enough, even if it was a bit like they were eighth graders who had finally worked up the courage to touch each other. Maybe that had been her intention all along—to be touched again by him and him by her—and she'd fabricated the story about Bertie so that could happen. Or maybe Bertie had been preaching Tomasto's dictum that if you find someone attractive, don't hesitate to pursue the opportunity as far as possible.

My god, how long had it been now, two, three months since he and the divorced solicitor from the ministry had had their one-night fling after a party? Mary, wasn't it? Mary Wilkinson, and she'd wanted him to call her Muffin during and after, which he couldn't bring himself to do. And that had been the pattern since Carolyn left—the few flirtations that had ended in sex—attraction, pursuit (usually on their part), giving in with enough to drink, and always parting the next day. But what about here, now, when she raised her head with that look in her eye that said she was ready for more than holding hands? Could this be different? Not just for one night. If things worked out, maybe this could be good for as long as they wanted. Maybe not forever, but for a long time, a long, long time.

They could leave now and drive to his house, where he would show her around and they would eventually end up in his bedroom. They would hug and kiss—pecks at first, nibbles that would begin to linger—lips, tongues, hands in long strokes up and down bodies. She would lift the hat from her head and stow it on the dresser, fluffing her hair where it had sat. He would kiss her again as he lifted the hem of her blouse and drew it over her head. He would reach around her waist to unbutton and unzip her skirt that would slide over her hips to the floor. She would step free of it and undo one of his shirt buttons, two, on down to his belt. She would untuck the shirt from his trousers while he unbuttoned the cuffs. Shirt and undershirt would drop behind him. She would unbuckle his belt, loosen the clasp, draw the zipper down, his trousers finally draping around his ankles. He would kick his shoes off, pull his legs free, and draw her toward him, burying his face in the crook of her neck. In a long, graceful movement she would sit on the bed, pulling him beside her, and in a flurry of hands, bra, panties, and boxers would disappear and they would lie bare skin to bare skin, and he would relish the taste of her, her hardening nipples. She would lie back and reach down to stroke his penis and they would wait no longer.

They would nuzzle afterward, kissing gently, stroking each other over and over, their touch saying all that was needed. And soon, aroused again, they would rejoin, more slowly, more deliberately, mouths and tongues, hands everywhere, on and on until spent.

In the morning she would still be there, she would not have slipped off before he woke, and so it would begin.

What a fool. But wasn't her hand in his telling him she was as fervent for him as he was for her, or had he misunderstood everything and she was trying to tell him something else? Something bordering more on *what the hell have I started here, how do I get out of this?* And now, as he watched her across the table, he noticed a subtle change in her face. Less a look of lust than a ghostly question mark running across it, as if she were trying to reconcile what she saw with what she might have felt moments before. Here he was, a no longer young white man (maybe even old enough to be her father), who wore glasses, had unkempt wiry red hair, and was taller and more lanky than most and walked with a slight stoop. What was there to like in that? What was there to induce her to surrender caution and take to his bed? Not much that he could see, nor, it seemed, could she either as her grip on him loosened and she drew her hand back into her lap.

"Thank you for the food and drinks," she said in a quiet voice. "You have been too kind—just as Bertie said."

"Not at all. I've enjoyed your company. Oh, and please remember to return my handshake to Bertie and wish him well, if you see him again." He stood. "And now I should be going. May I give you a ride somewhere? Home, or…"

She smiled and shook her head. "No. I must walk. I am going just there."

"All right then."

He signaled Noah to bring the tab.

17

The first time Sarah had seen Meg with a needle and thread, she asked if Meg would teach her how to sew. Meg had said she would be glad to if Sarah would teach her to knit. They'd begun with simple things—an apron, a scarf—and gradually moved on to more advanced tasks—a pull-over blouse, a sweater vest. Now it was a dress and hat for Jabalile.

Meg held up the last pattern piece Sarah had cut. "You're going to make a little girl very happy."

"I hope so," Sarah said.

"Have you thought about what you want to work on next?"

"No, not really."

"How about something for you—a skirt or trousers or—I know—a pair of shorts for summer?"

"Oh, no. Joseph would not like that."

"Why?"

"He thinks shorts are for inside only so that other men may not see a wife's legs."

"What about women who aren't married? Is it okay for them to wear shorts? Like Grace, for instance?"

"Grace is Grace," Sarah said. "She will do what she wants, that one. Perhaps it is why she is not married."

"Because she doesn't think she needs a man to decide for her how she should live her life?"

Sarah glanced away.

"I'm sorry. I'm just trying to understand. You wear skirts and people can see your legs."

"But not so much." Sarah tugged at a hemline which was already below her knee.

"Not like Grace, you mean? Or me? Does Joseph think our skirts are too short?"

"He has not said so. But you are different. Grace is different."

"So the same rules don't apply to us?"

"They are not rules," Sarah said. "They are the customs of our people. Americans must have their own."

"Sure we do, except we have so many cultures there's not a single custom about clothes. Where I lived, it was my father who usually said something like 'Hold on now, young lady, you're not going anywhere looking like that.' Which meant your skirt was too short or your neckline too low."

Sarah smiled. "So far apart, here and your home, but not so far perhaps? A husband here, a father there. Each must do what he must do."

"But it doesn't have to be that way. Things can change."

"Why should they?" Sarah said, rearranging pattern pieces on the table.

"So you could make up your own mind about what you say and do and whether you wear shorts."

"Joseph is a good man, a kind man. He is a good father. I am not bothered that he does not want me to wear shorts or to be like Grace." Sarah again shuffled the pattern pieces. "This freedom, it is a strange idea, yes? You say I am not free because I pay attention to what Joseph thinks. But what about you? Perhaps you would like to go to your home to be with your family, but Mr. Bernard—"

"Brian."

"You know if he returns, he might have to fight and be killed or injured in a war he does not care for. So because of him you do not go. What has happened to your freedom now? You might ask where freedom is for anyone, if we truly care for and listen to the wishes of others?"

"We call that situation being stuck between a rock and a hard place."

"Not at all comfortable," Sarah said.

"Painful, in fact." Meg reached for pieces of pattern. "What do you say I help you baste these and they'll be ready to sew?"

18

Harry Philips watched Dlamini's Mercedes loom larger and larger in his rearview mirror as he backed out of his parking space and wondered whether he should keep going until he smashed into the car, claiming later, with false contrition, that his foot had slipped off the brake pedal. As juvenile as the thought was, it nevertheless gave him a rush and made him smile. He doubted there was anything the prince prized more highly than his car, unless maybe his suits or his women.

Turning the wheel at the last moment, he stopped, shifted into first gear, and idled out of the parking lot, heading, as he often did, in the direction of Lena's. But maybe that wasn't such a good idea. Constance Mhlongo might be there and decide to come over to say hello. And what then? He wasn't sure he would have the will—nor the desire, for that matter—to resist her a second time. And what would that make him if he tried something and she really wasn't interested? A chill crawled across the top of his shoulders at the thought, and he changed course to drive instead to the bottle store to stock up on whiskey. Better to drink alone at home.

Which he wouldn't have any choice about now that Elizabeth was gone. He'd come home from work three days ago to find a note from her on the kitchen counter, saying her mother had sent word that she wanted Elizabeth to come back home as soon as she could and thanking him for his kindness. Her suitcase and book bag were gone from her room. The bed was made, the floor swept, Carolyn's clothes he had given her for gardening washed and folded in a stack on the bed. He missed her immediately. He couldn't say it was due to the lack of her company, since she had never really been good company in the normal sense of the word. But it might have been more her presence that he missed, just knowing she was there, even if in her room with the door closed.

She'd left with no warning and no explanation other than her note. But why would her mother suddenly say she had to come home? Had her father demanded it? Had he or her mother or her brother or sister gotten sick? Had her mother realized how much she needed Elizabeth's help after all? Had Elizabeth said something about him or the way he treated her that had prompted her mother's request? Was it something he'd said or done or not said or done? Hell, he wouldn't be surprised if Dlamini had had a hand in it. He had gotten rid of Magongo and would eventually do the same with Piet Giesen. So why not send Elizabeth packing, too? He wouldn't put it past the man, particularly after his meeting with him late that afternoon.

The prince had called and asked him to drop by before leaving for the day, there was something they needed to discuss. As always, they started with tea and the usual litany of inquiries about his family, but Dlamini soon got to the point:

"Your friend—"

"Which one?"

"Mr. Magongo, he is well?"

"You'd have a better idea than I do."

Dlamini's hands lay flat on the desktop to either side of the blotter that held his cup and saucer. "He was a talkative man."

"So you got rid of him to keep him quiet."

Dlamini straightened, a slight smile on his lips. "We prefer to express it in other terms, but, yes, that is the essence. Although you said it, and I did not."

"Why are you so afraid of him?"

"He knows too much."

"Or maybe not enough?" Harry Philips said, remembering what Magongo had written in his note.

"Yes. That as well."

He took a sip of tepid tea, catching the look on Dlamini's face. "So you got rid of him to keep him from saying that, no, he didn't see Kunene hanging around with Giesen in Pigg's Peak, which wouldn't be lying, since, as you found out, he never went there. But somebody could get the wrong idea and think he was saying Kunene wasn't ever there in the first place. And if that story got around, you could have a lot harder time convincing anybody about Kunene, right?"

"Precisely," Dlamini said.

"But Giesen's still here. How does he fit in?"

"Rather than send him away immediately, we have decided to call him as a witness at the trial to testify that Mr. Kunene did in fact work for him, and that he personally ordered Mr. Kunene to go to Lobamba and attack Mrs. Bernard as a way to discredit the nation and the king."

"And then what, after you've gotten what you need from him?"

Dlamini's eyes narrowed with near reptilian malevolence. "As part of our arrangement, he will be allowed to leave the country after his testimony, without charges and with whatever of his personal business he desires. Oh, and he will also be under instructions never to cross back into our country, upon threat of arrest and imprisonment, or even death."

"Clever. Self-deportation. So much cleaner that way. No disputing the facts, no contradictions, no bodies to get rid of." He smiled and shook his head. "I have to hand it to you, Gideon. You've really outdone yourself with this one."

Dlamini straightened his cup so its handle was parallel to the edge of the desk. "As sometimes happens, Mr. Philips, I am not entirely certain how to interpret what you have said — in this case, whether or not you intended your remarks as a compliment."

"Oh, it was a compliment all right. But I still have one question: do the ethics of this scheme trouble you?"

"No, and there is no need for you to be concerned, either," Dlamini said.

"But what happened to the common good you're always talking about? The people? The constitution, the rule of law?"

Dlamini pushed himself back from the desk and rose slowly from his chair. "As you know, the king is the law. And now, Mr. Philips, I suggest that you might want to go somewhere and— how do you say?—cool off."

He was amazed the man hadn't fired him on the spot. If he'd been Dlamini, he would have, no question. But Dlamini seemed determined to keep him around. Maybe so he could monitor him, neutralize him if necessary? Except that didn't make sense. There wasn't anyone he could think of to talk to about what was going on. Members of parliament wouldn't pay attention to him. They were almost to a person royalists, and all of them were aware that the king viewed their institution as a purely symbolic check on his authority. He had agreed to a parliament during independence negotiations, with the proviso that he would maintain the power to dissolve it at any time, for any reason. And talking to the press was equally out of the question. Editors, reporters and managers at the newspaper and radio station all understood that they held their jobs at the pleasure of the king. The small opposition that was allowed to exist was in effect muted by their low numbers and intimidation from the king's cronies. Nor would anyone in the American diplomatic corps pursue action that they would consider interference in the internal affairs of a foreign nation, unless the matter was in their immediate interest, which Giesen's situation wasn't. And were he to try to take the issue outside the country, no one would blink an eye at something so trivial in a world where rape, murder, and torture were commonplace. Even if he were to find a friendly ear, how could he prove what he was saying?

In the end, it would come down to his word against Dlamini's, and there was little doubt how that would turn out.

But maybe the real reason Dlamini still tolerated him had to do with his usefulness in placating the Bernards, if they somehow learned about the ministry's plot and objected to it because they felt guilty at being unwitting partners in something so sordid, let alone how hurt and angry they might feel over the way it trivialized the real crime. And Dlamini would understand that if they balked and refused to play their parts, all would be lost, and he couldn't afford that much damage to his reputation.

Such had life become in the house of Dlamini.

19

Meg stood inside her kitchen doorway watching Brian and a group of Form III boys tour the barbed-wire fence marking the boundary of the field beside the school that everyone now called the football pitch, after Mr. Dube dubbed it that.

The space was Brian's pride and joy. His brainchild, his determined creation—along with most of the school's athletic program. He'd first convinced Mr. Dube not long after they arrived that no education was complete without attention to physical as well as mental exercise. Students learned better if they moved more, and they also benefited from working together as members of a team. Mr. Dube asked Brian to draw up a proposal, which he did, including a financial plan that would seek support from Barclays Bank and the US embassy. Both gave generously and even sent representatives to the ribbon-cutting ceremony that was reported both by the *Times of Swaziland* and Radio Swaziland. Everyone talked about partnership and progress and the bright future that was at hand.

And today, this very Friday, was the day a year and a half later when, beginning at one o'clock that afternoon, all the planning and hard work was to culminate in the first-ever Lobamba National Junior Secondary School Invitational Athletics Competition. Three other schools had been asked to participate, and before opening assembly that morning, Meg had watched Mr. Dube scurry about like a nervous wedding parent, directing students who had arrived early to set up every folding table the school owned in the entryway and teachers' lounge and to cover them just so with real tablecloths. He sent five Form II girls to his office, under the supervision of Glory Khoza, to assemble trays of fruits and vegetables, crackers and cheese, and assortments of biscuits, which he said would, at the appropriate time, go there and there and there and should be draped with dishtowels to keep flies off. He instructed the same students to be sure, once the trays had been laid out, to arrange pitchers of water and glasses between them and to place on a table by itself a single chocolate cake Meg imagined would be gone in a matter of minutes. He told the best art students to make a sign that said

WELCOME ONE AND ALL!
WE ARE TOO HAPPY YOU ARE VISITING LNJSS THIS JOYFUL DAY!
MAY THE BEST TEAM ACHIEVE VICTORY!

and to decorate it with bright-colored flower borders and tape it to the entryway wall.

He put still other students to work sweeping and tidying classrooms, the veranda, the toilet blocks. Later, after the last trays had been laid out by students he'd pulled from class and all seemed in order, Mr. Dube called students and staff to the veranda where he announced that all was ready for the grand event and that school was dismissed and everyone could leave for lunch, except for Glory, who was to stay and watch over the food. They were to reassemble for the competition at half past twelve. Many left for the market. A few wandered toward Mrs. Mabula's shop. Anyone who had brought food sought out the deep shade of the eucalyptus grove near the queen mother's kraal. Teachers went back to their homes, Meg included.

Form III math had been her last class before the early dismissal. She had been five minutes late to it after staying behind to clean up a shattered test tube at the end of the science lab. She thought she heard laughter as she hurried toward the room, an undulating wave of sound, like a weak radio station going in and out of hearing, until she entered the room. Silence. Full and complete. She always expected them to settle down when she came in, but this seemed different. They were too quiet, embarrassed maybe for doing something they knew they shouldn't have been? If so, what was it?

She leveled her gaze at Dumisa Zwane, who seemed the most likely ringleader of anything questionable. Everyone on the faculty thought of him as a troublemaker, some of them going so far as to call him a dunderhead, a deadbeat, a spoiled brat. Grace Mtetwa claimed he was allowed to remain in school only because he was the son of a chief close to the royal family and would otherwise have been on his hands and knees cleaning toilets at the Royal Spa and Casino.

She could ask him directly what had been going on but had no evidence anything was and realized that, rather than escalate the situation, she should wait and talk to him away from his friends, if at all.

She laid her teaching material on her desk, took out an outline she'd made for that day's lesson and carried on as usual.

After class, she noticed a piece of paper beside Dumisa's desk. It had been folded over and over into a small square—obviously a note, which she unfolded but couldn't read since it was written in siZulu by several different people. The only words she could make out were Madam Thishela Bernard. She refolded the note and slid it into her pocket.

"A penny for your thoughts."

Meg started.

"I did not mean to frighten you," Sarah said, hand to her mouth.

"It's okay. I just didn't hear you coming."

"I practice creeping at home so I do not waken Jabalile."

"Where is she, by the way?"

"Nandi Mbisi in Form II has agreed to watch after her during the competition—perhaps even bring her to see a bit of it."

"Come in. Do we have time for tea before we have to go back?"

They retreated into the shade of the kitchen. Meg filled the kettle and set it on the propane burner.

Sarah backed up to lean against the wooden table in front of the pantry. "I worry that I did not say it correctly."

"What?"

"A penny for your thoughts."

"You said it perfectly."

Sarah clicked her tongue. "English is too difficult."

"And siZulu and siSwati aren't?"

"Not so much."

"I wish," Meg said, shaking her head. She assembled the tea service and carried it to the living room, where they each sat at the table.

"Well?" Sarah said.

"Well what?"

"I asked a penny for your thoughts when I came to you."

"I doubt that you really want to know them."

"But I do. I can see that you are not happy, even while you try not to show it."

Roger climbed onto Sarah's lap, and she stroked his back.

"Is that okay?" Meg asked. "The cat?"

"Of course it is. I can even say that I like it. He just stays there and makes that wonderful sound and wants nothing more."

Meg sipped her tea, sighed and said, "Well, you're right, as usual. I'm not happy."

Sarah rocked forward. "Why, if I may ask?"

"Dumisa Zwane."

Sarah's hand stilled on Roger's back. "What mischief did he brew this time?"

As Meg related the story of the laughter and chatter, the strange silence and, of course, the note, Sarah listened intently.

"What did it say?" she asked when Meg finished.

"I'm not sure. I could only tell that it had something to do with me. Maybe you can help."

Sarah took the note from Meg and sucked in her cheek as she read. "This Dumisa and his friends, they are old enough— Dumisa is seventeen, I believe. They should not be playing such games."

"Maybe not," Meg said. "But I'd like to know what the note says."

"It is mainly questions."

"Go on."

Sarah lifted Roger to the floor and scooted forward in her chair to lay the note between them. "It appears that different people wrote it."

"I thought so, too."

"This one asks if what people say happened to you is true. And this one says if it is true, how could it have happened the way they have heard. Another says you must have invited the man to sleep with you." Sarah turned from the note. "I can say no more."

"I want to hear the rest," Meg said as calmly as she could.

"One more." Sarah's voice dropped. "It asks where was your husband? What kind of man must he be?"

Meg sat silent, blinking back tears, finally fingering them from her cheeks. "If this is what people really are saying—and maybe even worse—they think I'm a slut, a loose woman, and Brian a spineless excuse for a man."

"You are nothing of the sort," Sarah said with her sternest teacher face.

"You and I may know that, but what does the truth mean against what people are thinking and saying?"

"Probably nothing," Sarah said, eyes welling.

"Do you remember that girl at the market?" Meg asked. "The one the croc took?"

"Yes. That was too sad, the poor child."

"Can you imagine what that must have been like for her? I saw a film once of a crocodile coming out of the water to grab an animal on the bank of a lake—a young antelope or piglet or maybe even a zebra colt that had come to drink. And the photographer got this camera angle so you were looking directly into the face of the croc—horrifying beady eyes and teeth sticking out of its closed mouth, and it was moving so fast I couldn't believe it, planting its feet and launching itself like it was on springs or something. I'd never seen anything like it. The animal being attacked seemed frozen in place, even as it was about to be killed. I wonder if it was the same for the girl, if she just stood there."

Meg hesitated. When Sarah said nothing, she went on. "It's weird, but I think I know why someone in that kind of situation doesn't move. They can't. There's no place to run, no place to hide."

Sarah ran a finger under the front edge of her *kitenge* cloth head wrap. "When a woman from my people is attacked in the way you were, she goes to her grandmother, her mother, her aunties, her sisters. You must be too sad that yours are so far away and out of reach."

"That would be wonderful—for me at least—but it can't happen for lots of reasons," Meg said, "which makes it all the more important that I have you."

Sarah smiled and reached toward her. They clasped hands. "There is also Mr., um, Brian and Joseph and Grace and many others."

"I know. I appreciate them all." She squeezed Sarah's hands a final time before she slid her chair back and stood. "I suppose we need to get back."

Sarah glanced at her watch. "Yes but let me tidy up before we go."

"You already have, you know. By being here. Thanks. That's all. Just thanks."

20

A white business envelope lay unopened on the oak sideboard in the entry hall of his house. The address was written in Carolyn's hurried yet graceful hand, a recognition that filled him with dread.

Not a peep for all that time, and now who knew what to expect?

Maybe she was writing to tell him she was pregnant, except she'd always been perfectly clear about not wanting kids. But maybe she'd had a change of heart. Maybe the bozo she was sleeping with had talked her into it. The more he thought about it, though, the more he realized it would be more like her, knowing all along the effect the symbolism would have on him, to have planned to mail the letter so it would arrive just shy of the day she'd walked out the door ten months ago to load her luggage into the car that was taking her to the airport. He'd offered to give her a ride, but she'd said no, she would rather go alone, hoping to escape, he assumed, any last-minute melodrama. It had seemed odd at the time that she would leave on a Wednesday, although, in truth, there were only three weekly departures of Swazi Air from Matsapha to Johannesburg. Once she'd decided what she was going to do, she would want to take the earliest possible flight, even if he didn't like it, so she wouldn't have to stay around any longer than necessary and risk having to rehash everything again.

He liked to think—rather, to believe—that he'd gradually grown more used to her being gone and that, if a time like this ever came, he wouldn't stand as he was now, nearly paralyzed by fear of what, besides a perverse birth announcement, the letter might contain. It was a business envelope, after all, and not an aerogram, which would have been faster and cheaper. But you couldn't send enclosures in aerograms. He picked up the envelope, hefted it in his palm to gauge its weight, and decided it was too light to be anything other than a letter. Or, he supposed, a one-page document of some kind, except he couldn't think of anything so short that would have much legal or financial importance. So what probably happened was that she didn't have an aerogram handy and didn't feel like going to the post office to buy one. And she had block-lettered AIR MAIL in the bottom right corner, hadn't she? Whatever that meant.

Turning, he made his way to his desk with measured steps, still palming the letter, which he held like a tray waist-high in front of him. He slid the envelope onto the blotter and, before sitting, retrieved a glass and bottle of Jameson from the liquor cabinet.

He poured a finger of whiskey, gulped it down, poured another.

Maybe she wanted a divorce. He could understand why, given the time that had passed, the 10,000 miles that now lay between them, the silence that had consumed them both.

Or maybe something had happened to her father.

His letter opener, a recognition of his service as a student representative on one college committee or another — academic affairs? — lay in a shallow drawer next to the typewriter. Its wooden handle had lost what luster it may have had and dark, oxidized splotches had appeared along the blade where the brass veneer had long ago peeled. He lifted the opener and ran his thumb along the cutting edge, wondering why he'd kept such a piece of junk for so many years. Misplaced loyalty, he supposed.

Or maybe she'd run out of money, thus prompting her to ask him to tide her over. He liked the idea of her needing him, even if only for money. It would at least be a connection, no matter how fraught, which was far better than what he'd had up until now.

He put the opener beside the letter and took another drink of whiskey.

What a spineless creature he'd become.

He picked up the opener and, after steadying his hand, slid it into the gap left at the top of the flap when it was sealed. First the tip, followed by the blade slitting the envelope open.

"What the—"

He dropped the opener, reached inside the envelope to pull out what?—a letter? a note? a document? No, not a document, seeing as how whatever it was had been composed on a sheet of typing paper, which he let fall, still folded, beside his glass.

A deep breath, another sip.

Dear Harry,

Not Dear Sir, at least, or To Whom It May Concern, or Dear Mr. Philips. But why only Dear and not My Dearest?

This is more than a little awkward. I don't quite know what to say or where to start. Kind of like being on a first date or something.

First date? What was she saying—or trying to say? The page—and there was only one, he'd been right about that—trembled in his hand.

You know, because you feel like you don't want to make a fool of yourself and every word seems important and is being scrutinized by the person across the table. Like you're doing now, right, reading and rereading everything and picking it apart, looking at every possible interpretation? I can see you in your leather chair or at your desk. But probably the desk. That's where you like to be with your handy glass of

Jameson when you're doing something stressful, and this must be after such a long time.

Despite himself, he turned to glance over his shoulder, as if to be sure she wasn't there watching him.

So maybe I should start by asking how you are. I'm fine. Still painting. Painting up a storm, in fact, and I like almost everything I've done. I've even sold a few works but not for enough to pay the rent. For that, I need to get hooked up with a reputable gallery, which will take a while yet, and since I don't want to be the starving artist, I went to work as a waitress in a decent restaurant near me. I've been doing okay with tips and all,

And what exactly does "and all" mean?

although again it's not enough to quite make ends meet. I finally decided the best way to do that was to get a roommate, and I did.

At least it wasn't the other way around and she was living with somebody else. Why that would matter, he couldn't say, but it felt like it would. The same sort of difference as who was on top during sex. That person had the most control over what happened and how. He smiled to himself. A nice image. Her on top, head thrown back, breasts swaying as she moved. On him, not some roommate who was called that in name only. As in, I'd like to introduce you to my roommate, when everybody already knew roommate shroommate.

Her name is Clarissa Scott. She's a waitress, too, at the same restaurant, but she only works part-time since she's also going to school. Which doesn't leave her with much extra money, so what rent she can pay isn't all that much. But it's enough. We both get by now. Between work and school and rehearsals on top of everything else—she's a theater major— we don't see each other a lot. But it's still nice to know somebody else is around. I didn't realize how much I would miss that. And what about you?

He took another drink, the rim of the glass resting against his chin, as he let the whiskey and her words sink in. Did he miss having someone else around? Was that what she was asking?

How are you doing in that regard? I think a lot about where we are now and what it means. Do you?

He smiled, set the glass down, and gazed over the top of the letter at a sheaf of paper near the back of his desk, something he probably should have read days ago but was either at Lena's or in the gazebo, doing just that—thinking about her, them, and what it all means. Although he would never admit as much.

Well that's enough for now.

For now? Meaning she must have had another letter in mind. Otherwise, why would she have raised the possibility?

I imagine you're thinking it's more than enough. I never have known when to leave well enough alone. And that said, let me just add one more thing: I seriously believe there were a lot of things unsaid before I left—and I'm sure there've been more since then. That was a big part of the motivation behind my sending this to you. So, if you have the time and inclination to write back, please do.

Carolyn

Just her name and nothing else? He brought the letter closer to his face and scoured the area above her name for any evidence that she might have written something there and erased it. Love, for instance?

.

21

The night had been fitful at best. Getting up as quietly as she could, she rounded the foot of the bed to pull the curtain back from the window and watch the sun rise over Mdzimba Mountain. Brian turned to his side but didn't wake. Roger sauntered in from the hallway, jumped onto the bed and curled up in the place where she had been. She shook her head. For anyone else on any other day, the scene would have been perfect. Cat, lover, clear sky, decent temperature. But today wasn't just any other day.

They were to be at the courthouse in Mbabane by ten o'clock to rehearse what they could expect to happen during the trial, which was scheduled to begin at eleven and be over, according to Harry Philips, in a couple of hours, if not sooner. Mr. Dube had asked Joseph to take them to the capital, they could leave after first period, but they shouldn't worry, their classes would be covered for the rest of the day. He said he'd thought of driving them but decided he shouldn't leave the school for that long. Just in case. He never finished the sentence, although it was clear that he would be more comfortable staying where he was.

She closed the bedroom door on her way to the bathroom, leaving enough of a crack for Roger. She didn't flush the toilet and slipped into the kitchen, where she ran a slow stream of water for tea and turned the BBC on to a barely audible newscast covering the war Nixon said he would end but recently had expanded into Cambodia; the war that set a new record death toll each week; the war that brought on ever more shrill and violent protests, with flag and draft card burning on one side and shouts of "America right or wrong, love it or leave it" on the other.

She switched the radio off.

Maybe Mateus Da Silva was right. He owned Casa Grande, the Portuguese restaurant in Manzini Harry Philips was driving to when he stopped by to check on them and tell them the trial now had a definite date. They'd had a drink to celebrate, and he asked if they wanted to join him for dinner. They said sure, it would be nice to get out of the house, if it wasn't too much bother, and he said if it were, he wouldn't have asked.

The restaurant was set back slightly from Ngwane Street, a single-story building with green and red stripes on either side of the sign above the door announcing Casa Grande. The dim interior was more spacious than she'd expected from the outside, an open floor dotted with tables and chairs framed by curtained booths lining three walls of the room.

A stout man with dark, slicked-back hair approached them, menus under his arm, the tips of his drooping moustache swaying like antennae as he navigated his way between tables. Meg leaned back as he scurried closer, but two steps away he veered off and came to a stop, hand extended, in front of Harry Philips.

"*Meu amigo americano.* How good it is to see you again."

Harry Philips smiled. "I'd like you to meet my friends, Meg and Brian Bernard. They live at Lobamba."

"Ah, yes, the teachers. Americanos."

"Mateus Da Silva," Harry Philips said, "owner of this fine establishment."

Da Silva shook their hands, saying pleased, pleased and giving each a quick nod of his head. "And one of you is a teacher of science. Is that not correct?"

"That would be me," Meg said.

"Ah."

"You expected it to be Brian? That happens all the time."

"No, no, it is only... Later we talk. But now I must be off. After I see you to your table."

Harry Philips asked if a booth was available, and Da Silva led them to one directly across the room. He gave each of them a menu, bowed as he stepped back, and said, "Yes, then, later."

The seats were comfortable enough and the choice of food broad enough. When the waiter came, Harry Philips ordered, with their approval, a bottle of wine and small plates of stuffed mushrooms and potato-chorizo bites as appetizers.

Once the wine was poured, Harry Philips held up his glass. "Cheers."

"Cheers."

They each had a sip and Meg said, "Did anybody else think he was a little strange?"

"Mateus?" Harry Philips asked, swirling his wine.

"Yeah. Is he always that aggressive?"

"No, not always, but he can seem a little odd at times."

As if to emphasize the point, Da Silva reappeared, scooted in next to Harry Philips and hunched forward, moustache drooping nearly to the tabletop and asked, eyes locked on Meg, what did she teach? Before she could answer, he went on, so as a science teacher, had she taught about the trip to the moon? Yes. Did she tell the truth about it, that it was all a lie, designed to make America look strong? Or did she say like the others that men truly had walked on the moon? Sweat popped out on his brow as his agitation grew, even though nearly a year had passed since the moon mission. How could such a thing be possible in the first place? he wanted to know. Flying into space? Walking on the moon? What nonsense. What an insult. It was like poking your finger in the eye of God, was it not? Think of his anger. What form his vengeance might take.

Da Silva seemed to see her as a false prophet who would deserve any punishment she received, including Kunene and anything that might yet happen—a notion she found so unbearable she set her teacup on the table harder than necessary—lifted it, set it back down, harder still.

But she could do that all day and never wake him. For that she would have to go and sit on the bed and say his name as she touched or lightly shook his shoulder and watch him rouse, eyes blinking open, casting around to make sure where he was before finally licking his lips and saying good morning in a croaky voice—his attempt at civility. If she stayed long enough, stroking his shoulder and back, he would eventually sit up and put his feet on the floor and try to shake the fuzziness from his head. He'd never been a morning person, saying little after getting up, but this morning in particular she needed him beside her, silent or not.

As if he had somehow been alerted, his eyes popped open as she neared the bed. Taking her in with a look that asked if she was okay and, deciding she wasn't, he flipped the sheet away, scooted over to make room for her and patted his pillow.

"We can't chance going back to sleep," she said.

"We won't."

"Not that I could even if I wanted to," she said.

"It's going to be an awful day for sure, but you'll get through it. We'll get through it."

"I hope you're right."

"I am." He paused. "Otherwise…"

"Otherwise what?" she asked.

"Nothing."

"Really?"

"Really."

At 9:20, the time they and Joseph had agreed on, he steered his Cortina to a stop in front of their house. Early enough for an unhurried trip to Mbabane, unless something were to happen en route, as it had with the police van. It was a calculated risk to be sure but was one they were willing to take since the last thing they wanted was to have time to kill as they waited to go into the courthouse.

Joseph got out of the car, dressed as usual in a tie and white shirt, sleeves cuffed to mid-forearm, a pair of gray pleated trousers, and black laced shoes. And, as usual, he freed a cigarette from the pack in his trouser pocket, smoothed it, and lit it, even though he likely wouldn't have time to finish it.

"We need to go," she said, without turning from the window.

As they made their way to the car, Joseph took three quick drags on his cigarette, dropped it and ground it under his shoe before opening the back door for Meg.

She scooted across the seat and motioned for Brian to join her.

"This looks pretty weird, don't you think?" he said. "Like we have a chauffeur or something."

"I don't care. Not today."

Joseph slid behind the wheel and, addressing their reflections in the rearview mirror, asked, "Are you ready?" before setting off on the same route past the same river and trees and rocks they had seen countless times. But today hardly anything seemed recognizable, let alone herself in it.

"We're here," Brian said.

She raised her head and peered out the window. Had it not been for the High Court, Kingdom of Swaziland sign beside double white doors at the center of a long veranda, she might have mistaken the building for a dormitory or even a hotel. She didn't know what she'd expected. Something more stately, maybe? More dignified? Something to signal that matters of concern and generally higher purpose went on inside?

"What time is it?" she asked.

Brian glanced at his watch. "A little before ten."

"He said he'd meet us, right?"

"Yeah."

"So where is he?"

"I don't know. Inside maybe?"

"I don't see his bus anywhere."

"He might've walked over," Brian said. "It's not that far."

She turned her head to blink back tears.

"Let me go see if I can find him," Brian said.

She smiled as much as she could. "Thank you."

After Brian left, she caught Joseph again looking at her in the rearview mirror. It was hard to know what he was thinking.

She touched him lightly on the shoulder. "I hope you don't think we're too silly. Or that I am anyway."

"Not at all, not at all. The truth is that I admire you for what you are doing. It takes courage, and not everyone has so much."

She drew her hand away and glanced down. "Thank you, but I don't feel very courageous. What you said means a lot."

"Ah." He ducked, as if to get a better view, or to avoid further conversation, and nodded in the direction of the courthouse. "There, someone is coming. Is he the fellow you are wanting?"

"Yes, that's him."

Harry Philips led the three of them down a building-length corridor lined with closed doors and hardly any adornment other than an occasional chair and, midway along, a large photograph of the king in a gray three-piece pinstripe suit and a muted blue tie, a Swaziland flag pinned to his lapel.

They stopped by the next-to-last door. A small brass plate identified the location as Courtroom A. Harry Philips turned the handle and pushed the door open a crack, then wider, and stepped inside, motioning for the rest of them to follow.

She was pleased to see that even though the room seemed small, it didn't feel cramped or claustrophobic. The back half had bench and chair seating for maybe 30 people, she guessed. It was divided from the front half by a spindled railing with a swinging gate in the middle to allow people to pass through.

Two solid but plain tables, each outfitted with a pair of chairs, stood on either side of the opening. A heavy dark wood bench stretched across the front of the room, a Swaziland flag to either side and between them a looming photograph of the king dressed in red-and-white *emahiya* cloth, a bead necklace, and a single red lourie feather in his hair.

Harry Philips ushered them toward the bench. "This, of course, is where the judge will sit in the middle, just like in the movies. The clerk will be over here and a messenger or two there. The translator and court reporter will be at those two tables in front of the bench." He pointed to the right. "And over there—the cubicle with the door on front—is the witness box. Behind us"—he turned to face the rear of the room—"the defendant will sit at the table to my left and the prosecution to the right."

"So everybody's in here at the same time?" Meg said. "And they see and hear everything?"

"That's the way it works here," Harry Philips said, holding his hand to his cheek. "So let's see, what else?"

"Where will we be?" Meg asked.

"There, just behind the prosecutor's table in the front row. That way you won't have so far to go when you're called to testify. And, Joseph, you can sit anywhere you like, since the trial is open to the public, although I don't expect many people to be here."

"Ah, yes. Thank you. But for now I must find a cup of tea and a newspaper, if you do not mind."

Meaning, she assumed, that he had no intention of coming back, which was okay with her except it meant she would be the one to have to tell Sarah what had happened, and she wasn't sure she'd be ready for that right away.

"Good timing," Harry Philips said after Joseph left. "I was going to ask him to step outside anyway so I could talk to you in private."

He gathered enough chairs for them to sit at the prosecutor's table, positioning himself across from them. "I wanted to go over a couple of things before the trial gets underway. First, the charges that'll be brought against Kunene. There's breaking and entering. That can bring him five years in prison and nine lashes. Next is sexual assault. Around ten years. Third—this one's a little trickier." Harry Philips uncrossed his legs and bent forward. "What's going on is this: there are people in the Ministry of Justice who refuse to believe Solomon Kunene did what he did for no apparent reason. That it was just out of the blue. They were sure there was a deeper motive involved and tried to find out what it was. So they've tacked on a charge of conspiracy against the Kingdom of Swaziland."

"That's heavy," Brian said.

"It is."

"How will it affect us?" Meg asked.

"I don't think it will at all," Harry Philips said. "I just wanted to let you know it'll come up."

"So what is this deeper motive?" Meg said.

"Conspiracy to undermine the authority of the Kingdom of Swaziland. The story they plan to present is that Kunene got laid off from his bricklaying job a couple of years ago and started wandering around, looking for work. He ended up in Pigg's Peak where he got involved with some unsavory characters."

"Like who?" Brian said.

"The ringleader is a guy named Piet Giesen, an Afrikaner apartheid supporter who immigrated from South Africa maybe twenty years ago. He hates the idea of multiracialism and will do anything to make the king look bad. Ministry people claim Kunene fell in with Giesen and ended up working for him."

"Is that true?" Brian asked.

"They say so."

Meg stiffened against the back of her chair.

"Later this year," Harry Philips said, "Swaziland is planning to host an international conference around the theme of multiracialism and cultural diversity in southern Africa, with Swaziland as the central focus. What the ministry's saying is that Giesen and his crew came up with a plan to disrupt the conference in a way that would embarrass the king, make him look foolish and even cause people to ask if he is as strong as everyone's always thought. Which is where the ministry says Kunene and you come into play. Giesen pays Kunene, a black African man, to go to Lobamba and assault you, Meg, a white American woman who is a highly visible presence at a school founded by the king to educate black African kids at the same level as any white kid in the country. So an attack on you at Lobamba not only damages the reputation of the school but the king too."

"So the idea is that Kunene's basically a hired gun?" Brian said.

"I'm afraid it's more complicated than that. According to the ministry, when Kunene agrees to go to Lobamba, he becomes a co-conspirator. And if he's found guilty of that along with everything else, the king looks even stronger and wiser for exposing the kinds of riffraff who'll stoop to god only knows what to oppose him." He took off his glasses and massaged the bridge of his nose. "Sorry to be so long-winded, but I wanted you to know what to expect. Oh, and one last thing: Kunene likely will act in his own defense, for several reasons. But the thing you need to remember is that he therefore has the right to cross-examine you." He leaned in and rested his hand on her arm. "But when you're on the stand, keep your cool when you're testifying. You're there to answer questions. Nothing more. Try not to think or feel anything other than what's required at that moment, and you'll be fine. It'll be over before you know it."

He lifted his hand. She moved her arm away.

Following her testimony, a guard had escorted her to a drab cubbyhole down the hall from the courtroom where she now waited until the end of the trial. The space reminded her of the room at the police station where she'd written her original statement—the wooden table, two chairs, a bare lightbulb hanging above her. The same sense of isolation and dread as she shooed away bits of memory of her time in the courtroom that swarmed like yellowjackets in her mind. She remembered, for instance, someone—the bailiff?—calling the court to order. She remembered standing when the judge entered the room. He was sixtyish, a short gray-haired white man, who appeared sober and serious, qualities she supposed you would want in a judge. He spoke with a clear British accent as he asked the accused to rise and hear the charges against him. Breaking and entering, with intent to commit a crime, in this case rape, and with further intent, by way of conspiracy, to undermine the integrity and authority of the Kingdom of Swaziland. How did he plead? She remembered looking at Solomon Kunene. He wore a dark-blue jumpsuit, his arms and legs shackled, two guards standing at attention next to him. She remembered him looking in her direction and her meeting his gaze without glancing away, holding it until he, in fact, turned his head back toward the judge and said, through his translator, "Not guilty." Because he was drunk, he claimed, and possessed of a spirit that came to him and told him she, that woman there, wanted him to come and sleep with her, and if the judge had seen her, what she was wearing, he wouldn't have been able to stop himself either. She remembered the judge telling Kunene to be silent, he would have his opportunity to speak later, and if he didn't remain silent, he would be held in contempt and removed from the courtroom. She remembered trying to control her breathing and not flush when she heard her name called and was directed to the witness box. After her oath, the prosecutor asked her to please give the court her account of what occurred on the night of the incident. She remembered how surprised she was to hear the strength in her voice. And how surprised she'd been that there were no questions from the judge and no cross-examination from Kunene. She didn't remember for sure whether she'd been asked if she wanted to leave or had been told she should or had simply been dismissed and led out through the side door near the guards. She remembered trying to catch Brian's eye and being stunned by the size of the gallery. Where had they all come from? Why? She didn't remember recognizing a single face.

And now that she thought about it, she wondered why she'd been dismissed in the first place. Was the judge being compassionate because things might be said that could upset her? Or things he didn't want her to hear? The move had seemed strange at the time and still did.

The door swung open.

"It's over," Brian said.

"So what happened after I left?" she asked, breaking a long silence as they walked toward the exit.

Brian ducked his head, glancing to either side, and led her by the elbow a few paces back in the direction from which they'd come. When a group of people on their way out neared them, Meg twisted away enough that she wouldn't see their faces, nor they hers, although she could feel them looking at her.

Once they'd passed, Brian braced his arms against the wall on either side of her, as if to make sure she stayed where she was.

"Tell me everything," she said.

He glanced up and down the hall. "Aren't there chairs around here?"

"I saw a bench over there," she said, pointing to her right.

They found it and sat.

"Okay," she said. "No more stalling."

"As soon as you were out of the room, I was called to testify. I told them everything I could from when you called my name. Like with you, nobody said anything afterward. Sergeant Gama came next and described what he saw and did. Then the doctor from the stationhouse gave the results of the tests he ran and whether he found evidence that a rape had occurred. Finally, the judge called Kunene to the stand. Do you want the long or the short version of that?"

"All of it."

"Okay," he said closing his eyes, as if to reset the scene in his mind. "First, Kunene claimed everything was consensual. He said he'd met you—I don't know when, exactly, maybe a week before, maybe more—somewhere in Mbabane. And you talked for a while, he said, and you took a liking to each other—my words, not his—which he seemed to assume meant you wanted to sleep with him. You want me to stop?"

"No."

"So as a way to support his mutual consent bullshit, he said he got drunk on *tjwala* to try to forget about you but couldn't and got to the point he didn't know what he was doing and started up Mdzimba Mountain. On the way, he was possessed by a spirit you'd sent to tell him how much you wanted and needed him to come to you. And he did, of course, because you can't ignore what a spirit tells you to do, etc., etc. Oh, and his mother's old. Can't forget that. She depends on him." He sat up straight. "And that was pretty much it. That was his whole defense."

Meg sighed and shook her head. "And the judge, how did he react?"

"I think he would have laughed if it wouldn't have looked bad. Instead, he said he should give Kunene life in prison for such an absurd story, because none of it made sense, except maybe the drunk part. Even then, how could you perform sexually if you were so drunk you didn't know what you were doing? And he wasn't going to comment on the nonsense about spirit-possession. Kunene whined about his mother again, and the judge told him to shut up or he'd be charged with contempt."

"That seems kind of—"

"What?"

"Well, harsh, don't you think? I mean, it *is* his mother."

"I doubt if you'd have felt that way if you'd been there. Kunene was crying crocodile tears at best over the fate of his poor mother. The judge was pissed at him but not as pissed as he got when the prosecution presented the conspiracy charge. He kept asking what grounds the government had for bringing the charge in the first place. He wanted to know where proof of guilt was. If they quoted a person as saying this or that, was their statement taken at a deposition, or was it hearsay? And why didn't they have witnesses? Where were their facts and how could they verify them? He said what they were presenting seemed completely circumstantial—at best incompetent and at worst libelous. At that point, he pounded his gavel and dismissed the charge outright."

"But only that one, right?"

"Just conspiracy. He was convicted on the rape charge."

"Did the judge sentence him?"

"Yeah but—" Brian's head dropped. "He only gave him two years."

She slumped against the wall behind her.

"I hated having to be the one to tell you."

"And that's seriously it? For what he did? Didn't Harry Philips say he was supposed to get nine or ten?" She glanced down the hall. "Where is he anyway? I thought he'd be here by now."

Brian stood, stepped to the window, peered out a moment, turned back. "The judge said he had to take into consideration that this was a first-time offense. And there was also the mother thing you were talking about. He said she's old and needs her son around and any longer than two years might be too long."

"But that means in two years he's going to be free."

He sat again, took her hands in his.

"To do anything he wants. And besides that," she said, looking at Brian with tears in her eyes.

"I know. Believe me, I do. I've been thinking about it since I heard the sentence, and no matter how you look at it, we're screwed—or I am anyway—unless we go to Canada or I go to jail."

As they neared the car, Joseph got out and said, "So sorry. I meant to, you know," gesturing toward the courthouse, "but—"

Brian held up his hand. "No apologies. Are we ready to go?"

Once underway, Joseph . asked Brian to tell him what happened.

All she heard was the drone of Brian's voice coming from the front seat but not what he said, which was fine with her.

At the end of Brian's account, Joseph double-clicked his tongue and said, "Such a pity," but nothing more.

What else could he say when she thought about it? A pity or I'm sorry was generally all she would hear for the foreseeable future, even from her parents and friends like Sarah. Words fail when someone announces the death of a loved one or, like her, reports being a victim of a terrible crime. And that's what it was, a terrible crime, without the resolution it demanded and now would never come.

22

He tossed back a shot of whiskey, chased it with a swallow of Castle lager and waited for the warm glow to wash through him. But there weren't enough shots and beers to drown the fact that he'd stood up the Bernards. That instead of seeking them out after the trial, he'd left, like the coward he was, via a side door, no less, so he wouldn't have to see the look on Meg's face after she heard about Kunene's sentence. By the time guilt turned him back and he barged through the front door, the car they were in was pulling away from the curb. He saw her in the back seat, although he wasn't sure she'd noticed him. If she had, she showed no sign of it.

As he was about to order another shot, Gideon Dlamini paused inside the door of Lena's, smiling and nodding as if to congratulate himself on how right he'd been as to where he would find Harry Philips.

"May I?" he asked.

"Why not?" Harry Philips gestured toward the chair across from him and raised his arm to catch Noah's attention. "What's your pleasure?"

Dlamini glanced at the shot glass and bottle. "That should do."

Harry Philips held up two fingers. Noah nodded.

"So are you celebrating or grieving?" Dlamini said.

"You mean you haven't heard?"

"No, I have not. Otherwise, why would I feel the need to ask?"

Noah set their drinks on the table and left. "Kunene got off with a two-year sentence."

"How can that be?" Dlamini said after a sip of whiskey. "Are you certain you did not mishear and the sentence was for twenty years? Accents can be difficult."

"Oh, I heard loud and clear—two years."

"But that is a meaningless, useless sentence. Surely it can please no one. Who was the judge?"

"Kemperman."

"Ah," as if the mere mention of the name explained everything. "He should not have been appointed, Mr. Philips. He is too temperamental. You saw him. Did Mr. Kemperman seem upset during the trial?"

"I'd say so, yeah. He was definitely pissed."

"Why?"

"The conspiracy charge. The way it was presented."

Dlamini stiffened, his hand clutching the shot glass.

"He didn't buy any of it. He said the whole thing was without warrant, a waste of time and unsupported by evidence, so he dropped the charge. I think in the end that affected the sentence he handed down."

Dlamini, a cornered lion-who-would-be-king, showed a rare flash of fear in his eye as he raised his shot glass and finished the rest of his whiskey. "Sorry to rush, but I must be off."

"I have an appointment myself, so I was planning not to come back to the office today. With your permission, of course."

"No, by all means. I understand fully." The prince rose and, after a cursory royal bow, left.

Harry Philips took a deep breath and signaled Noah to bring the tab.

The cerulean sky, skiffs of cloud skimming it, the fierce button of sun, the trees and grass and craggy slopes that all looked the same as he nosed his bus down once again into Ezulwini Valley. He took another deep breath, recalling the wonder of the rock paintings at Sheba's Breast, the rush of Montenga Falls, the gentle grandeur of the mountains, the thrill of simply being there, everything new and exciting, discovery after discovery.

But now he had the disquieting suspicion that something had changed. Not Swaziland itself. The country remained as haunting as ever. Nor his sense of it—the awe he experienced whenever he surrendered himself to it. Rather, who he was now, at this time, in this place had changed, a shift as subtle as seasons in his old life, like the first rustle of leaves scattering on a cool October breeze.

"I'm sorry," he said as soon as the door opened.

The Bernards stood side by side, faces drawn, Brian gazing straight forward, Meg's head turned slightly toward her husband, red-rimmed eyes peering not at but past him— *American Gothic*, sans overalls and pitchfork and 40 more years.

Shifting a bag from his right hand to his left, Harry Philips asked, "Okay if I come in, or would it better if—?"

They stepped back in unison, like a gate swinging open.

The bag thumped on the table.

"I wanted to stop by to see how you're doing and to apologize for not catching up with you sooner, but by the time I got away, you were already gone. I'm glad you're home. That must mean you have the rest of the day off."

"Mr. Dube told us we shouldn't come back," Brian said.

"Until tomorrow," Meg said.

"That's probably for the best." Harry Philips reached into the bag and drew out a bottle of Jameson. "Can I buy you a drink?"

Meg and Brian looked at each other.

"Why not?" Brian said for them. "Let me grab some glasses."

He brought back coffee cups. "Everything else we have is too tall. I thought these would be better."

Harry Philips poured each of them a dram and raised his cup. "To survival."

"Survival," Brian said. "But kind of an odd toast, considering."

"More ironic than odd," Meg said a second later in a quiet voice.

"Bad choice. Sorry," Harry Philips said, sitting back and pivoting his cup.

"Anybody hungry?" Meg asked.

Brian shook his head.

Harry Philips said no, he was fine and asked after a brief pause how they were doing, how they were feeling.

"Shitty," Brian said.

"Insulted," Meg said. "Used."

Harry Philips nodded.

"Two years sure as hell isn't nine," Brian said.

"I was as shocked as you were."

"What went wrong?" Meg asked. "Was it something I did? Something I said? Didn't the judge believe me?"

"It had nothing to do with you. It was the prosecution—my people. They got greedy and instead of going with a sure sentence tried to tack on the conspiracy nonsense. The judge saw the move for what it was and got mad."

"But aren't judges supposed to be above that?" Brian said.

"Sure. Except they're also human and hate like hell to have somebody try to make a fool of them. So he basically blew his judicial cork and as punishment for his tormentors gave the lightest sentence possible. Which he, as judge, has every right to do—judicially speaking. The trouble is that everybody but Kunene ended up losing in one way or another—with you two getting the worst of it."

"But even if that is what was going on," Meg said, "two years still stinks. It's ridiculous."

"Yes, it is," Harry Philips said.

"Is there anything we can do about it?" Meg asked.

A question he wished hadn't been asked but knew would be. He straightened, drank the rest of the Jameson in his cup. "The short answer is not much. The trial is technically over and done with. Kunene's been convicted and sentenced. There wasn't a mistrial. You can argue the results but not the fact. There is an appeals process, but it usually has to do with asking the Supreme Court to lower a sentence or dismiss charges altogether. I don't think that's where you would like to go."

"That's it then?" Meg said. "It is what it is, so get used to it, even if it means..."

Harry Philips poured another round of drinks. "There are a couple of things outside the regular channels. One would be to petition the Minister of Justice, my boss, to reconsider the sentence. But he was the one who came up with the conspiracy business in the beginning, and he's not likely to swallow his pride after the drubbing he took. The only other thing I can think of would be to appeal directly to the king. Nothing gets done without his approval, and he can change anything he doesn't like."

"So the idea is for me, the aggrieved white woman, to go on bended knee and beg for special treatment?" Meg said.

"Like it or not, he is your—our—last best hope. My guess is he'd be happy to do whatever he can to keep you happy and here."

"Because we help create such a lovely picture?" Meg said. "All contented and harmonious? But what if it isn't? What if it's just smoke and mirrors? Who wants to be part of something like that?"

Harry Philips studied the two of them as he finished his drink and stood. "I need to run. Keep the whiskey." He turned at the door. "But you might want to think hard about doing nothing. The alternative doesn't look so great, if I understand it correctly."

23

Sarah appeared at the kitchen door, tea tray in hand, minutes after school was dismissed for the day.

Meg stood on tiptoe to peer over her.

"If you are looking for Jabalile, she is there with her father," Sarah said, nodding toward her house. "It is better without her so we can talk. But only if that is what you want. Or we may sit and sip. But first, this." She put the tray on the kitchen table and raised her arms toward Meg.

"You must have talked to Joseph," Meg said, leaning into the hug.

"He told me that you were upset," her voice soft yet reassuring. "So I came quickly to find you."

"Thank you."

Sarah picked up the tray. "Shall we go now?"

Sarah had just finished serving tea when Brian emerged from the bedroom, greeted her and turned to Meg to say he was going to the library, since she now had Sarah with her, he would see her later.

"He did not look so happy," Sarah said after the door closed. "But I am sorry, I do not mean to pry."

"We had a disagreement."

"Ah." Sarah blew on her tea and sipped.

"Aren't you going to ask what it was about?"

"That would be rude," Sarah said, taking a shortbread from the plate between them. "However, if I did not ask and you told me, it would be different."

Meg thought how best to describe her combined sense of stress and strength when Brian had stood behind her as soon as Harry Philips left and she said no before he could start, she wasn't going to do it. But shouldn't they at least think about it? The answer was still no. She'd stood her ground until the bedroom door slammed shut.

"Our disagreement was about the trial."

"Joseph said you were not pleased with how it ended. He said that you thought the sentence was too little."

"Everybody did. Except the judge. And Kunene, I suppose."

Sarah sucked in the walls of her cheeks, let them go, slowly, in out, in out, like fish gills. "And what did others think would be the outcome?"

"Nine years, if not more."

"But at least he will go to prison. Some have not even that much satisfaction."

"I know. I'm not asking for special treatment. I hate the whole idea of that."

"So what is it that you do want?" Sarah asked.

"I want to feel like somebody there cared—really cared— about the fact that I was raped. And the only way I can even come close to knowing that is by the sentence. Two years seems like a slap on the wrist to me, instead of punishment to fit the crime. I'll have to live with what happened to me forever. And he—he's going to be free in two years. This is a small country. Can you imagine what it would be like to go to the market and see him, or have him come to find me?"

"Which would not happen if you were not here."

"But even that's complicated."

"Yes," Sarah said. "The war."

Meg explained how Harry Philips had come to Lobamba right after the trial to talk about the sentence and what they could try to do about it, none of which he thought would work. Except maybe for talking to the king. Harry Philips believed he had a keen enough interest in the success of their school and the Peace Corps being in the country that he might be open to their appeal and grant it, seeing as how he controlled everything that went on.

"Will you go then to speak with the king?"

"Brian thinks we should."

"But you do not?"

"I do not."

"I have heard," Sarah said, "that he is quite—that he is easy to approach. If he truly is, perhaps it might not be so terrible to go to him."

"That isn't the problem. What is—" Meg stood, walked to the window to peer out, returned to her chair. "Remember earlier when I said I wasn't looking for special treatment? Well, I meant it. I'm not. I won't. Do you understand the position that would put us in, how it would look?"

Sarah tilted her head, eyebrows pinched. "If that is your only hope—Brian's only hope—why not risk going? No one would blink any eye. It is a common way, you know, to get done what you wish. Going to someone with the power to make change."

"It would have been better if real justice had been served in the first place."

Sarah's gaze rested on the tabletop.

"So the way it looks now," Meg said, swiping a hand over a space in front of her, as if preparing to draw a diagram, "Peace Corps service is for two years. We've just started our second year. Kunene's sentence is for two years, and we still have eight months before the end of school when we could extend our service. But that would be for another two years, meaning Kunene could be released while we still have eight months to go before we could leave. That's just not workable."

"I understand," Sarah said in a quiet voice. "A simple question, if you do not mind: have you given thought to perhaps asking Peace Corps for a one-year contract?"

"To be honest, neither of us has thought about that. I don't even know if it's possible."

"Might it not be something to try?"

"I suppose," Meg said. "Except in the end, wouldn't that only be prolonging the inevitable? I mean, we'll leave sometime anyway, won't we? Will have to. What difference will a year make in terms of that?"

"But perhaps by then a miracle will have happened and the war will have ended and the draft will be no more."

"Maybe but not likely."

Meg walked Sarah to the kitchen door and watched as she made her way to her house and rounded the corner toward her own kitchen door.

Back at the table, she smoothed an aerogram against the Formica top, three strokes of her hand, bottom to top. A useless habit, really, since the sheets came from a folder ready to use, not a wrinkle or crease on them.

Dear Mother and Dad,

The trial is finally over. It was this morning and took less than two hours. I suppose it would have seemed fairly boring if we hadn't been part of it. Nothing like in movies or TV shows. No melodrama. My story, his story — and that was about it. With one exception — the sentence the man received. Harry Philips thought he would get nine years at least. He got two. That just doesn't seem right to me. Not for what he did. I didn't want him to be locked up forever, but I did expect something that might make other people like him think twice. The biggest problem for us is that the sentence basically forces us to not extend our time here, which we'd been thinking of doing. What that means for Brian — for all of us — is pretty serious, unless the war suddenly ends and the draft disappears.

Mr. Dube gave us the rest of the day off, so after school was over, Brian went to work in the school library. It was good for him to do that, but he didn't leave me alone. Sarah came over as soon as she got home and stayed a long time. Of course, we spent most of her visit talking about the trial. She's a good listener, and she helps me keep things in perspective.

I know it doesn't do any good to tell you not to worry, but by the time you get this letter, we'll have been back to work and trying to focus on other things. We made it this far and will come out okay.

I trust everything at home is all right. Life as usual. I'll assume so unless I hear otherwise.

Love,
Meg

24

Dlamini was in place, as usual, behind his desk, with Harry Philips across from him, again as usual. What wasn't usual was that Dlamini hadn't offered tea and remained seated, rather than promenading to and fro, his attention seemingly riveted to the view from his west office window. Was the pose only that—a pose—or did it signal something deeper?

Dlamini swiveled his chair to face his guest. "Remind me, Mr. Philips, how long have you been in our country?"

"Just over ten years."

"Has your life here been satisfactory?"

"Sure. I guess so. Why do you ask?"

"Ten years is a long time to be away from your home."

"I've been back a couple of times."

"But never with the intention of staying, I take it."

"Not yet."

"But it must be even more difficult now," Dlamini said, "with your wife gone."

"She had things to do. Her father is ill."

"I see." Dlamini arranged a stack of papers that didn't need arranging. "Do you ever feel the need to return to America to be with her?"

"No. I think there's still a chance she might come back here."

A look of consternation swept the prince's face, so Harry Philips asked if Dlamini had expected him to say something else, like he was planning to return to the US to save the prince the complications of firing him.

Dlamini pressed his forefingers to his lips a moment before saying he was disappointed that Harry Philips didn't know him better than that. The truth was, the prince continued, that, quite to the contrary, the ministry still greatly appreciated the wise counsel he provided for king and country and had no desire whatsoever for him to depart, regardless of the reason. Words scripted and delivered, it seemed, without an ounce of sincerity. He might as well have been reciting the grocery list his wife had handed him on his way out the door.

"As a matter of fact, Mr. Philips, I believe we have a proposal for you to consider that might help you regain confidence in our continued commitment to you and your work." Dlamini leaned back. "What I want to discuss with you came to my attention only recently, perhaps since we last talked. When I heard the idea, I thought immediately of you."

He supposed he should have been intrigued, or flattered, although he wasn't, necessarily. A general wariness of Dlamini's schemes, or more a general weariness?

"As you may know, talks will soon begin in Gaborone between Swaziland, Lesotho, and Botswana concerning the recent revision of the South African Customs Union agreement."

"Yeah, I heard something about that."

"The general feeling—at least among our three countries—is that the Republic has maintained far too much control over the pact and receives more than its fair share of financial benefit from the arrangement. The idea is for us to come together to determine what, if anything, can be done to change the situation as it now stands. The talks will not be easy." Dlamini lowered his head and voice. "And that is, I hope, where you come into the plan."

"Oh?" Harry Philips said in the flattest tone he could muster.

"I would like for you to join the negotiating team as a representative from the Ministry of Justice. There will be others from the Ministries of Trade, Foreign Affairs, Labor, and so on."

"When you were thinking about me as a possibility, I hope you realized I know next to nothing about trade policies, or labor and commerce. Foreign affairs, maybe a little, but still."

"You can learn, can you not? And you have good ideas and a strong ability to argue a case. I think you would make a fine addition."

"And I also know how to talk with Europeans, right, even if they're South African? And neocolonials from everywhere else?"

"That would clearly be useful as well."

"How long do you think the talks will last?" Harry Philips said.

"The complete process might take some time, I have been told, but the initial meetings should not last more than a week or two, perhaps a month, if problems arise. And there is always the possibility that you will need to go and come back and go again, until matters are resolved. More than anything else, in the end we want a strong settlement." Dlamini paused and straightened. "I trust that you will consider the offer seriously."

"Absolutely. But tell me, what'll happen if I say no?"

Dlamini gazed at him, fingers drumming the desk. Harry Philips met his eyes until Dlamini stood as if at attention and said, "That, of course, is up to you, but we must know your decision as soon as possible."

The prince walked him to the door. "Please keep in mind, you were—"

"I know—the first person you thought of."

He paced the floor of his office, shaking his head. Clear was clear: he either accepted the assignment—or what? Or else, he supposed. That threat alone was bad enough, but perhaps worse was the notion that Dlamini might be using the proposition to sidetrack him, get him out of the way for so long that if and when he did come back, his position might have disappeared or been filled by someone else. Either way he seemed to be on borrowed time, and it was likely up to him to figure out how to survive the remainder of his tenure there with even a trace of dignity.

Although he had a couple of small jobs to finish up, he took the rest of the day off, giving him time to stop by the post office—a habit that had become a near obsession.

He unlocked the mailbox door and pulled out two bills, a newsprint grocery ad, a notice for the new production of *Romeo and Juliet* at the Theatre Club, and a list of upcoming holidays for government employees. But no letter. He'd almost resigned himself to never hearing from her, although he wasn't yet willing to surrender all hope.

Clouds shielded the sun, making Lena's seem darker and more shrunken than ever. There was a small crowd as usual, although it was difficult to see faces. Even if he could, he doubted he would have known many of their names. There was Noah, of course, in place behind the bar, Constance Mhlongo perched across from him at the end of the bar, hat tipped to the side of her head. She caught sight of Harry Philips and gave a long look before moving toward him across the shadowy floor.

He stood to greet her and, after clasping his hand, she settled into the chair opposite him. He signaled Noah to bring them each a drink, and she leaned in his direction, saying she hadn't seen him in a while. Did that mean she'd missed him specifically or had simply noticed his absence from Lena's social fabric? He told her he was sorry, he'd been busy, which seemed to satisfy her for the moment. He asked if she wanted anything to eat as Noah approached with their drinks. Peri-peri cashews or prawns or whatever? She said the prawns would be good, with some bread to go with them.

"You seem worried," he said after Noah had taken their order.

She glanced away and sipped her drink. "I have spoken to Bertie Magongo. He said I must find you and give you the message he sends."

During the pause that followed, he wondered if Magongo—through Tomasto, of course—had coached her on how to deliver the message. How to draw it out just so to create as much dramatic effect as possible, cheap though the tactic was. Another time, he might have been less tolerant, if that was the right word, more impatient with this sort of antic. But for now, he was enjoying her performance and realized how much he would eventually come to miss her and Lena's, even Dlamini—all of it.

"But before I say more, I must ask how is it with you, you are well?"

"You can tell him that I have no more scars than when he left."

She twisted her lips and scratched her head lightly, with a single finger.

"Just tell him those words. He'll understand it means I'm okay."

She nodded. Noah delivered the prawns and bread, and they both ate, she with the mannered peeling off of enough shell for a single bite, inching her way along until she reached the tail, which she dropped into the bowl Noah had brought for their debris, before taking another prawn and beginning again. He, on the other hand, ripped the meat of the prawn out of its shell and stuffed it whole into his mouth. Each of them following with bread dipped in the serving-bowl broth.

After two more prawns, finger-sucking, wiping and a swig of Castle, Harry Philips said, "So what is Bertie's message?"

"He sends you his greetings and a handshake." She rose and leaned, arm outstretched, toward Harry Philips.

He likewise stood. They clasped hands, hers as warm and soft as before, and sat back down.

"He also said he wants you to know he wishes for you to stay well."

"And that's it?"

"Yes."

"You're sure there's nothing else?"

She glanced down and, after a moment, back up. "Perhaps I can say one thing more."

He inclined his ear toward her.

"He said he is frightened, Bertie Magongo."

"What of? What's scaring him?"

"Oh," she said, "it is not for him that he is frightened—it is for you."

"Me?"

"He said so."

"Where would he get an idea like that?"

He tried not to smile at the image of Bertie Magongo hunched over a beer, talking in a low, conspiratorial voice to some shadowed figure across from him. The conversation would go roughly along the lines of how the Swaziland government had come up with a cock-and-bull story about him to shut him up and get him out of the country. With a healthy measure of Tomasto mixed in, that story would grow into a larger government scheme to purge from the country anyone who had not been born in Swaziland or become legally naturalized. From there, Bertie could convince himself that Harry Philips would eventually be included. It was a plan that to some parties, such as Dlamini and his father, might seem a logical, and maybe even desirable, extension of independence.

Unfortunately, that hypothesis didn't hold up, considering the king's public statements in support of a multicultural, multiracial state. Also, ushering every foreigner out of the country was impractical at best and could be disastrous. The government would likely collapse, along with the infrastructure most people had come to depend on.

So he wasn't convinced anything dire was going to happen soon, if ever, although Magongo's fear on the heels of his discussion with Dlamini did give him pause.

"Thank you," he said to Constance. "Please send Bertie my greetings and best wishes. Tell him also that I understand and appreciate his concern."

She finished her drink and scooted her chair back.

"You're welcome to stay."

"No, I may not." She glanced at her watch. "There is a place I must go."

He stood to see her off.

25

There were still times she couldn't sleep for fear that Solomon Kunene would appear in a dream. His image, partially remembered, partially conjured, had taken residence in her mind and she now seemed unable to keep it from materializing whenever her attention wandered too far. Was this how you begin down the road to madness?

She got up and stood, arms wrapped as tightly about herself as she could manage, and moved to the predawn gloom of her kitchen. But the promise of brighter skies ahead grew from behind the silhouette of Mdzimba Mountain and she decided to dress and go outside, maybe even take her teaching materials and head to school early. The change of scene might help break her mood, especially to be alone in the teachers' lounge before the bustle and babble of the day.

By the time she got there, though, she was already too late for complete isolation. Students had come even earlier and now lounged in the shade of the veranda, under scattered trees, in classrooms, reading, chatting, writing on chalkboards. Although nowhere to be seen, Mr. Maphalala must have been there to unlock the school and perhaps still was, having stolen away to the library or Mr. Dube's outer office. Unless invited by Mr. Dube, no one entered the inner office.

She greeted the few students who either wished her a good morning or waved before she stepped into the entryway en route to the teachers' lounge. Luckily, no one followed her with a question or story or a need to be with her. And, as she'd hoped, the lounge was empty. She dropped her book bag on the chair next to the one she intended to sit on, with a clear view of Mdzimba Mountain, remnants of morning shadow dissolving into the valley below. For the first time in recent memory, a measure of peacefulness settled over her, and she savored the moment with each breath.

Her serenity was short-lived as she heard the clack-clack of heels echo around the entryway. Grace Mtetwa stopped when she saw Meg. She turned to peer behind her, as if checking to make sure she had come to the right place.

"Good morning," she said. "I did not expect to find you here. Not so early, at any rate."

"I was enjoying the peace and quiet."

"I am sorry to—"

"No, no, please join me."

Grace arranged her book bag and purse on the table and sat two chairs away from Meg, also with a view across the valley. "Would you care for tea? I am brewing a cup for myself."

"Thank you. That would be wonderful. But no sugar or milk, please."

"Yes, I remember your strange American ways."

"Some Americans think tea with milk and sugar is strange, too. Not to mention the plates of pastries and tiny crustless sandwiches."

Grace laughed. "When you describe it that way, it does sound fussy."

"I suppose it's the ritual."

"Yes." Grace set a cup and shortbread biscuit on a saucer in front of each of them. "Food draws people together, no matter how much or how little there is."

"We call that breaking bread."

Grace thought a moment, moving her hands as if snapping a twig. "Yes. Exactly. I like that. The sound of it. The meaning. I must tell others." Her smile dimmed. "I learn so much from you. I am only sorry that—"

"What?"

"Someone said that you must return to America."

"Yes, that would be—that's true. We will."

"Well, I for one—" She broke off at the sound of more footsteps approaching.

"Go on," Meg said.

"Perhaps later."

"Please tell me."

She sighed and said quickly, quietly, "I will miss you."

"Thank you," Meg said, laying her hand on Grace's forearm just as Sarah reached the doorway and stopped, eyes lowering, as if embarrassed by what she'd seen.

Meg withdrew her hand and sat up straight. "Good morning."

"Sorry, but there are things I must attend to before school begins, and here there is no Jabalile."

"Don't be silly. We were just talking." Meg lifted her book bag from the chair next to her and patted the seat.

Sarah slid into place and began leafing through a notebook. "I must give an exam today and have not written it yet."

"What does it cover?" Grace said.

"Verbs. Irregular ones."

"Oh, my." Grace shook her head. "Good luck."

"Thank you."

"To your students and you."

Sarah chuckled, any discomfort she'd felt seeming to have disappeared.

Without asking, Grace rose and busied herself preparing another cup of tea, this time with powdered milk and sugar, as well as a biscuit, which she placed in front of Sarah. "You'll need this."

Meg covered the top of her cup with her hand when Grace, brow raised, glanced in her direction. A casual silence followed, three friends in a room together before the start of a busy day, and she realized how much she treasured such moments, how she wanted so much to enter a new dimension occupied by the people and things she loved and cared for, and everything

else would disappear as she went about the task of writing—
rewriting?—her own history.

Glory soon called them to assembly and they gathered their
things to stand outside, backs against the wall, students in the
schoolyard just beyond the roofline of the veranda, arrayed in
ranks according to what form they were in, running left to right,
most junior to most senior.

"Good morning," Mr. Dube said. "Welcome to another day."

"Good morning, Mr. Dube."

Percy Mavuso stepped forward to lead the national anthem.
As everyone sang, Meg studied the upturned faces, the close-
cropped hair, male and female alike, girls in white blouses,
navy-blue skirts and white knee-high socks, boys in white shirts
that were for now still crisp, clean tan khakis, behind them the
trees and hills and sky rising with their voices. She continued
studying them as Mr. Maphalala began his daily message, this
one about how to achieve success through diligence, hard work,
and no funny business, her spell ending when assembly was
dismissed and Brian stopped by on his way to class.

"Are you okay?"

"Better. How about you?"

"I could have overslept, you know."

"You haven't since we've been here, so why would you
today?"

"There's always a first time."

She paused. "Yeah, I suppose that's true."

26

His pulse quickened as he downshifted the VW to slow for the final curve before Sibebe Rock burst into sight, gray and shimmering, like a breaching three-billion-year-old humpback whale.

At the parking area, he got out and, bracing himself against the side of the car, leaned as far back as he could to peer along the 1100 feet of solid granite past a row of erosion-etched teeth halfway up, to find the boulder and tree on the summit that he had rested under so many times, the Mbuluzi River valley spreading into the distance below. The view always struck him dumb in its majesty, much the way Ezulwini Valley did—the permanence, the splendor, the timelessness which had nothing to do with who laid claim to it, as it seemed Dlamini did by virtue of birthright and royal status.

But even as king, who in the eyes of most Swazis embodied the country, he couldn't own it, any more than his father did now. People had been present there for 25,000 years, if not longer—hunter-gatherers who roamed the land and eventually settled in fertile valleys where they took up raising livestock and tilling the soil. Around 1600, a band of Bantu people from the north and east entered the area, and it wasn't until the mid-nineteenth century that a group called Swazis grew strong enough to subdue and incorporate smaller clans under their rule. And wasn't that the point? "I came, I saw, I conquered." Everyone, including the Swazis, came from somewhere else, saw something they liked or wanted, took it and made it theirs—until someone stronger, richer, more powerful came along and the cycle repeated, as happened with the Boers and British.

Swaziland wasn't anyone's, even the king's, although he did have a unique relationship with the nation and its collective memory. Harry Philips certainly felt little of that connection, and he doubted that the Bernards did either. Or other expats, black, white, Asian. But did that mean they shouldn't be there, doing what they were doing, which, regardless of what he said, seemed to be at the core of Dlamini's thinking.

His mood had soured earlier in the day when he'd read the note he'd gotten from Carolyn that, out of fear, he hadn't read right away. It was newsy—job, roommate, painting—and polite, which seemed to be the best way for him to categorize it. But it said nothing about the unfinished business she'd mentioned in her last letter and to which he'd invited her to tell him more about. But zilch, *nada*. What should he make of that? Was she still mulling over the unsaid things she'd brought up, or had she decided to drop the subject altogether? As well as him? Was she telling him thanks, but no thanks, she wasn't interested in talking after all and maybe eventually reconciling?

Fuck it, fuck her.

And fuck Dlamini, although when Harry Philips stopped by Dlamini's office on his way to his own later that morning and said he wanted the prince to know that he respectfully declined the offer to serve on the treaty negotiation team, Dlamini said ah. Ah. Thanks for telling him so soon. The ministry would move ahead with an alternative arrangement.

Did that mean there would be an alternative for him as well? He had a fairly good idea what that might be. With so much free time, he could finally write the book he had in mind that would describe his first-person experiences with the Swazi legal system. Not something for scholars, like Hilda Kuper, but more for a general reader. Or he could do some serious gardening, putter around the house on small projects he'd put off for ages, become more social.

Or he could make a clean break from Swaziland. Having a law degree allowed him a fair amount of flexibility in the job market. Where to go, though, was a mystery, although it could be almost anywhere now other than the States, since he apparently had no real hope for being with her again.

There were a few other places where he'd rather not go and probably some that didn't especially want him either. The Republic, for instance, wouldn't give him the time of day after he'd spent so many years fraternizing with blacks. Mozambique was mired in a civil war that had no end in sight. Zambia would be great, except for the constant border skirmishes between African Nationalists in Zambia and ruling White Supremacists in Rhodesia that were bound to evolve into something more widespread and deadly. Malawi, called the warm heart of Africa, was beautiful although poor. He would nevertheless consider going there, if an opportunity came up—except for Hastings Banda, who, after independence, was elected president and immediately declared himself head of the only recognized political party in the country, which signaled to Harry Philips a political direction he wasn't willing to live with.

He could look farther north, but he wondered whether Tanzania would be as welcoming of another white man as somewhere else. Kenya, on the other hand, would be fine but not Uganda, where there was also widespread unrest. And he knew too little about West Africa to have even a faint clue about what might be a good place to look into. Everywhere north of the Congo to the North African Mediterranean states was either too dangerous or of little interest to him, save maybe Ethiopia. To his mind, his choice pretty much came down to Botswana. He knew the country and liked it, and he and Carolyn—there she was again—had enjoyed a wonderful vacation in the Okavango Delta, including the best photo safari they'd been on. Gaborone was large and busy enough he should be able to find a decent job. Maybe most intriguing was that diamonds were rumored to have been discovered west of the capital. No confirmation yet, but the DeBeers Company was in on the exploration, and they rarely got involved if possibilities didn't exist, which could mean a financial bonanza for the country and a myriad of legal issues to solve. For all those reasons, he found the prospect of going to Botswana reassuring, liberating. Now what he needed to do was act on it.

If he didn't leave and for some reason Dlamini kept him on at the ministry, it would be in a role he imagined would settle into a mind- and soul-numbing routine that would cause him to welcome even the most tedious and irritating interruption, whether in the form of a meeting or someone coming into his office with an inane question or complaint. His life would consist of a get up, go to work, go home rhythm so enervating he would need to remind himself each morning what the day and date were, until he finally glimpsed the fundamental truth of Sisyphus: that life is largely futile and any victory over its pointlessness is survival and that alone. Get up, go to work, go home, repeat until the boulder is no longer needed to flatten you.

27

It must have been the scent of the chocolate chip cookies Meg had just taken from the oven that drew Percy to their kitchen door. He bowed and apologized for the intrusion, all the while glancing over her shoulder at the baking sheet on the table.

"Would you like to come in?" she said.

"If it is not a bother."

"Brian's in the living room if you want to join him. I'll be there in a bit."

She loaded a plate with cookies, took an extra cup from the shelf and joined them.

"Help yourselves," she said and went to retrieve an extra chair, which she sat in at the end of the table.

She took a cookie and without thinking steeped it in her tea and bit off the softened section.

"It's an American custom," she said as Percy watched her. "Cookie dunking, but we usually do it with coffee or milk instead of tea."

"But it is not only American," Percy said, "people everywhere do the same and have for ages. Romans soaked their unleavened bread—their *bis coctum*, their biscuits—in wine. Sailors in the British navy used beer for their hardtack. Australians do it. The Dutch do it. South Africans do it. We do it. I believe you could even say that biscuit dunking is as much a part of our lives as tea itself."

"That's too bad. I was hoping to leave you something to remember us by."

"Oh, not to worry. There are many other things."

"I'm not even going to ask what those are," Brian said.

They were quiet until Percy slid his cup toward the center of the table and said, "I, um, I do not wish to be impolite or to make you feel uncomfortable after such a delicious treat, but there is something I would like to ask you."

"What's on your mind?" Meg said.

He straightened, looked directly at her. "Are you sorry that you came here?"

"Sorry in what way?"

"You left America," Percy said. "The Republic I can understand. Many of us have fled from there. Or Rhodesia, Mozambique. But America?"

"It's not the paradise you must think it is," Brian said. "We have a lot of problems. For one thing, we assassinate anybody we don't like."

"We're fighting a war half the country doesn't support," Meg said.

"We have race riots and the Ku Klux Klan," Brian said. "We still lynch people."

Percy squinted one eye, as though weighing what to say next. "So you left and came here because it would be better?"

"But we weren't running away from things, if that's how it looks," Meg said. "We thought long and hard about what to do."

"Peace Corps seemed like a good fit when we looked into it," Brian said. "Go someplace for a set length of time and do something you could feel reasonably good about and have an adventure at the same time."

"I've heard some people say Peace Corps is just a lark," Meg said, "a chance for twenty-something mostly white middle-class Americans to go, do their thing and try not to make too big a mess. And if along the way they unintentionally become cultural ambassadors garnering goodwill for America and Americans, so much the better. Cynics are more likely to think they're cultural imperialists or secular missionaries out to save the world. But Brian and I have never seen it that way."

"Volunteers are young, yes," Percy said. "Eager and energetic, yes. Idealistic, perhaps. But agents of anything sinister, no — at least to my experience. You have chosen to be here and not there, and I wonder what you will think about your experience when you look back on it through the years."

"So do you have any idea what Percy meant when he talked about looking back on our time here?" Meg asked as they cleaned up in the kitchen.

"He said he was wondering, right? Percy's always doing that. He always sees a bigger picture than most of us."

Meg inspected a cup she had dried before setting it back on the shelf. "I do believe we came here for decent reasons, don't you, even if extending your draft deferment was one of the big ones?"

"I don't have any doubt, especially about that."

"Some of the others seem a little naïve now," she said, "since I feel like I have a better idea of where I am and what I'm doing."

Brian emptied water from the dishpan and flipped it over to drip dry in the sink.

"I love this country," she said, "warts and all, okay? And I love the people in it. And our friends. And our students."

"And me?"

"Of course you."

She gazed out the window at the fence, the fields, hills beyond, wondering why, if she did love all the things she said, she was not a more loving person. The answer seemed all too obvious — in order to be that person she would first need to be a forgiving person. And she was clearly not that yet.

28

Constance Mhlongo came toward him, smiling, head tilted, drink glass cradled in the palm of her hand. As Harry Philips stood to greet her, she turned her cheek toward him. He hesitated, wondering what was going on, but she held her position until he kissed her, lingering a moment to savor the clean herbal scent of her skin, and offered her a seat.

She set her nearly empty glass on the table as she arranged herself on the chair. He held up two fingers. Noah nodded.

"There is news from Bertie," she said with special accent on the T. "He is going to America."

"What?"

She smiled and nodded. "He told me just today and said that I must come to find you so you can be happy with him."

"I am, or think I am, except 'surprised' might be a better word."

Noah set their drinks before them and backed away.

"He said an old friend, someone he had not seen since long ago, wrote to another friend, a man who lives near Bertie, and said if he saw Bertie to say to him that he should come to America. The old friend has a job for him, and he can live with the old friend until he gets a home of his own." She paused and took a sip of her drink, as though trying herself to believe what she had just said. "The old friend also told Bertie that he thought about inviting their other friend to come as well, but he remembered that man is married with children and has a good job. The old friend did not believe the other friend would have any reason to come to America. But Bertie, he hoped Bertie would have a reason to. Bertie told his old friend that he would say yes, he can come, but he had some things he had to take care of first." She rummaged through her bag and withdrew an envelope which she held out to Harry Philips. It was wrinkled and marked with a jagged brown stain from god knows what. His name was carved on the front in Bertie's heavy hand, with two underlines. "This came in his post to me. He said I must give it to you."

He opened the envelope.

Dear Brother Philips,

I am too happy! The lovely one, she has told you my surprise? I am going to America, my friend! Perhaps when you go back there, sometime we can meet as we always have and drink Castle together. Do they drink Castle in America? No matter. There will be something in a place like America. Because there is so much something everywhere in that place. And now I can go there, me, Bertie Magongo. My old friend from school went to university in the Republic and later to America to study more. He is a bright one, that man. Soon he decided to stay that side because his work was good and he was getting rich. America. I do not know why he remembers me after so long, but he does and has asked me to come to be with him in such a fine place. I can be pleased if you are happy, too, Brother Philips. Tomasto is. He says it is fucking fine there. Fine food, fine times, fine women, and everybody is rich. I know you are rich, Brother Philips. You buy drink and food and pay me to harvest information. Is it possible that you can also pay for me to go to America? To meet my old friend in Miami? What is this Miami like? No matter. I think I will be happy there. But I have been away from Swaziland and have no work. But now I have a chance to go that side to Miami for work and money and a rich life. Can you be able to help me? I must find the fare for the airplane or ship. And money I may need for travel papers. Also enough to have with me that I may not be turned away for having nothing. But do not worry, my friend. Your money will be safe with me and you may have it again as soon as I can pay you. May I please learn of your answer soon. The lovely one may say how to reach me.

Your humble and thankful friend,
Bertie M.

PS: Tomasto asks that I thank you for him as well.

As he raised his head, he could see that Constance had been watching him — maybe to report back to Bertie? "Did he tell you about the letter, what it said?"

"No."

"He wants me to pay for his trip."

She smiled, as though not in the least surprised and was wondering why he seemed to be.

"A fair amount of money." He tipped up his Castle and swallowed.

She glanced down. "He is your friend."

He was looking at a couple of thousand dollars, maybe twenty-five hundred. It could be even more with passport and visa fees, a medical exam, vaccinations and such so he could pass through immigration. It wasn't the money that bothered him. He doubted he would even miss it in the long run. But Miami, for god's sake? What was this friend doing to get rich there, as Magongo said? It wasn't even clear who this friend was. A school buddy, but what did that mean? What kind of buddy? Why, after all this time, did he suddenly remember Bertie and invite him with such open arms? To do what? Miami was Miami, after all. His friend could be involved in anything, perhaps owning an import business selling African goods or a restaurant that specialized in African-Indian food, and he needed Magongo to help him manage things. He could just as easily traffic in drugs and people, run a brothel or a chain of sex shops or an illegal gambling operation. The possibilities were endless in Miami. As was the potential for Magongo to end up in prison or be, again, deported.

The pulp fiction cesspool the Tomasto Tomassino/Bertie Magongo mind dwelt in came washing over him, and he fought being sucked ever deeper into it.

But what if the story wasn't a fabrication and Magongo really was going to America—even to Miami—what then?

He smiled at the irony of Magongo leaving and him staying— at least in Africa—as he refolded the note along its original creases and slipped it back into the envelope. Carefully, as if saving it for his Magongo archive.

"I'll need Bertie's address so I can write to him and also a phone number where I can call him if we need to talk."

Constance rifled through her bag to find a scrap of paper and pen. When she'd finished writing, she slid the information toward him.

"Thank you."

"What did you think would happen?" Sarah asked.

"I don't know, but I didn't expect all of this," Meg said.

"People want to celebrate."

"Because we're finally leaving?"

"You know very well that is not what I mean. Everyone is fond of you and Brian. They want to show you how much they will miss you."

Their going away function, as Mr. Dube called it in his best bureaucratese, had been in the works for some time now — more than a week that Meg knew of and maybe longer — even though the celebration/function/party/event wasn't scheduled until closer to the end of the school term two months away. But to Mr. Dube's mind, it was always better to err on the side of caution, so he had as usual put Glory Khoza in charge of fleshing out and executing the details of his plan.

"You must also remember," Sarah said, "that the students will be going home for a summer holiday. So that makes it an even happier occasion for them."

Meg tried to picture herself at her parents' home, drinking coffee at the kitchen table, eating dinner, sipping wine in the family room, people talking or not talking as the mood struck. An image that blurred out of focus as soon as she remembered she was here and not there, with Brian and Sarah and others who also cared about her.

"Are you well?" Sarah said.

"I'm fine. I was just, you know, thinking."

Sarah laid her hand on Meg's forearm. "It will be a lovely affair. You must relax and allow yourself to enjoy it."

"I don't know how you put up with me."

"It is not so difficult. In fact, I rather like it." She straightened in her chair, glanced down at Jabalile who was playing on the floor with a small ball of yarn Sarah had given her. She rolled the yarn toward the window where Roger perched on the sill. He raised his ears as it neared, tail twitching, before he pounced with a cat grunt, swatted the ball into the corner and chased after it, Jabalile squealing with laughter as he reared up, ball between his front paws, as if to toss it back to her.

"I have been wondering," Sarah said, looking again at Meg, "what will become of Mr. Roger?"

"I asked Glory if she wanted him back, but she said they had no more room for animals. Then I thought of giving him to a student but decided I would probably get the same reaction as Glory's. And I suppose there's always the Humane Society, or whatever it's called here."

"The Welfare Society, I believe," Sarah said. "But you know they are not always so kind to the animals sent to them. Or so I have heard."

"I didn't know that." She sighed. "It would be so hard just to leave him."

"Of course it would be, and I have been thinking it might be nice for her"—again glancing at Jabalile—"to have a companion until…"

"You have another child?"

"Yes."

"But what would happen with him then?"

"Oh, I am sure that would not be a problem," Sarah said, smiling. "He is small, you know."

"And he doesn't eat a lot."

"We would feed him just enough. It would not be good for him to become fat. But if he grew hungry, he could catch a mouse or a bird or a locust."

It was nice to think of Roger living next door with a family that appreciated him, and she could easily imagine him on the windowsill in Sarah's living room, watching for anything that moved, tail twitching in excitement, settling again as the moment passed.

But what if one day he pounced from the open window? He was after all a house cat, not accustomed to the dangers of the outside world. Anything could happen to him, none of which she could allow herself to think about, although she realized she would no longer have control over what he did or did not do.

"I think that's a great idea," she said. "But first let me check with Brian. I don't imagine he'll have any problem with it. One less thing for him to deal with, if you know what I mean."

A quick look at Meg and a nod. "Oh, yes, I know, I know."

As the end of the school term drew closer, day passed into day, week into week, like a valley breeze, felt but otherwise unnoticed. A routine of personal and school prep each morning, teaching, eating, working in the evenings, sleeping as best she could brought on, through daily repetition, a certain welcome relief she gave herself over to as often as possible. Brian had never been one to float through anything, let alone surrender himself to it. She had noticed, though, that he seemed to attach less urgency to tasks at hand, perhaps realizing he would never accomplish all that he wanted to and understanding that was okay, someone else could finish up.

She couldn't remember when for sure, but one Saturday afternoon during that final stretch of time, Harry Philips reappeared at their door with a new bottle of whiskey he said he'd brought to toast their departure, since he didn't know if he would see them otherwise before they left. They sat at the living-room table and hoisted their drinks to safe travels, good health, and new adventures. Speaking of which, what did they have planned—straight home or stopping to play on the way?

Brian told him they intended not to rush back. Maybe drop by Nairobi, then see the pyramids, Greece, Rome, that sort of touristy thing. They'd saved some money, and Peace Corps was paying them a readjustment allowance and their airfare home, so they should be okay money-wise. What about him?

Harry Philips sat back, saying he supposed he did have some news. As of the end of December, he would be leaving Swaziland and taking a new job in Gaborone. Meg asked what brought that on? Restlessness, he said, the ten-year itch, he didn't know. She wanted to know why he wasn't going back to the States instead of Botswana. He took a sip of whiskey and said that the last word from Carolyn had made it sound like he was free to do pretty much whatever he wanted to, so... Brian asked how soon he was leaving, and he said he started his new job at the end of March, which left him plenty of time to find a place to live in Gaborone, ship his furniture and put the house he had now on the rental market—maybe even sell it. You know, things like that. He might sneak in a little travel himself—say to Madagascar or the Seychelles, both of which had always intrigued him. But he wasn't going to go anywhere until after the Incwala Ceremony. Meg asked why. He said he guessed it was because he'd seen the parts of the ceremony other times and found the rituals that renew the relationship between the king and the nation fascinating. And he frankly didn't know if he'd ever get to see it again. Was there anything special planned here to celebrate the end of the year and the fact that the two of them were wrapping things up?

A lot of the normal stuff, Brian said, the kids throwing their usual going home party, singing and dancing and such, eating. Only this time Meg said the two of them got brought into the picture. Honors, goodbyes, and who knows what else. Too much, she thought. Brian said he didn't know, it seemed kind of sweet to him. Brian asked Harry Philips whether he had any interest in coming by to see what was going on, and Meg said she was sure he had better things to do, but Harry Philips said it sounded like a blast. Let him know when, and he'd come if he could and if they were sure it would be all right with the headmaster for him to show up.

Mr. Dube had no objections, of course, and the day of the ceremonies arrived despite her misgivings about being the center of attention. Sarah stopped by to walk with her to school, but rather than getting there in time to drop by the teachers' lounge for tea and talk, they went straight to assembly.

They lined up as usual—teachers and staff along the wall in the shade of the veranda, students in the schoolyard. Percy Mavuso led the national anthem as he had every day they'd been there. Mr. Maphalala told the students in his typical fashion that they still needed to apply themselves regardless of the special significance of the day.

But it wasn't until Mr. Dube's announcement that immediately after second period everyone should reassemble in the classroom on the far end of the building for closing ceremonies and all eyes seemed to drift toward her and Brian that she was seized with a pang so sharp she crossed her arms and squeezed herself to ease it, wondering, if only for a moment, whether they—she—had been wrong by insisting that they leave.

After assembly, Sarah took Meg's elbow and guided her toward the room where the ceremony would be held. Over her shoulder, she saw Mr. Maphalala with Brian in tow headed in the opposite direction toward the library.

"What's going on?" she asked.

"The students have a surprise for you."

Sisi, Domezile and Prudence from Form III met them inside. The girls ducked their heads to hide their smiles.

"Come, please, Madam," Prudence said, holding out her hand.

Meg glanced at Sarah.

"They want you to go with them. There," pointing toward a makeshift screen.

"Why?"

"You will see. Go. I will follow."

But there wasn't room for everyone in the space behind the screen, so Sarah stood within view just outside the entrance as the girls huddled, heads down, whispering so softly Meg couldn't make out what they were saying.

Domezile and Prudence soon stepped back, leaving Sisi alone. They waved her forward, and she shuffled a half-step closer to Meg.

"Excuse me, Madam. But I have been chosen to ask you to — how do you say? — undress? No clothes."

"What?"

Sisi looked again at Domezile and Prudence, but neither even lifted her head.

Sarah came toward and leaned close to say, "All but your underclothes."

"Not before I know what's going on. You can't just take a person someplace and tell them to undress. Especially —"

"I understand, but it is important for you to obey their instructions. They have worked hard to please you."

Undressing anywhere, even in the privacy of her own bedroom, was unnerving now and the thought of doing so in public... But the hint of warning in Sarah's voice made her stop before responding. Not to cooperate would be considered the height of rudeness, like refusing food or drink when offered. Or a gift of any kind for that matter. And aside from the strange request, everything else seemed benign enough.

She turned her back to Sarah and the girls and began to unbutton her blouse.

"Come now, come away," Sarah said to the girls.

Meg folded the blouse and laid it on a nearby bench. And her skirt and slip. She wondered about her shoes and socks but decided to leave them on.

"Okay," she called out, unsure how to stand or what to do with her hands.

The girls, Sarah behind them, stopped in the entryway and stared, soon dropping their gaze.

"Now what?" she said. "You can't just leave me like this."

The girls turned to Sarah who nodded.

"They have decided to make you a Swazi—an honorary one, but even then—by dressing you as one," she said. "Except we must first—" She stepped forward, pointing at but not touching Meg. "Those. The straps. It would be better if..."

Meg again turned her back to Sarah and the girls. She unhooked her bra, holding it to herself with one hand as she freed the opposite arm, switched and freed her other arm before rehooking it. The straps dangled awkwardly to her sides but were soon covered by the orange-and-black *emahiya* cloth Prudence wrapped around her torso and knotted over her right shoulder. Domezile fitted another, dark-brown cloth around her waist under the top. Sisi tied a Swazi flag beaded necklace around her throat. She flinched at every touch, hoping that her random movements—a turn, a flex, an adjustment—would divert the girls' attention enough they wouldn't be offended.

Finished, they all stepped back to inspect her.

"Now turn so we can see from behind," Sarah said.

She heard whispers.

"Your shoes," Sarah said, "and stockings. Please remove them."

"But—"

"It will be okay. You will walk only on pavement, not the ground. Afterward, you may wear them again. They believe, and I agree, that this will make you look more—how should I say?"

"Authentic?" Meg said.

"Yes. That is the word. More authentic, like a true Swazi."

But how could clothes alone do that? she wondered, her bare feet adjusting to the cool cement floor. She could see dress as a way to identify a profession—police officer, clerical worker, farmer—or position—chief, warrior, king, queen mother, princess. But authenticity? Didn't that have more to do with what you believed and valued, how you acted, how you approached life and the world around you?

What she was most keenly aware of, standing there in her new clothes, was how inauthentic she felt.

But Sarah and the girls were smiling and nodding their approval, so she smiled back and said, "Thank you. This is so nice of you. I feel honored." Thinking as she spoke how she hoped she could live up to their expectations.

Sarah motioned to Meg. "Come. We must go back now so final preparations may be made. We will wait in the lounge."

They met Brian, barefoot as well, coming from the opposite direction with Mr. Maphalala. He was dressed similarly in a beaded necklace, an *emahiya* top, darker skirt under it with an animal-skin loincloth tied over the top. He held a new olive-wood knobkerrie, like ones she'd seen for sale at the market, in his right hand. She wished she could ask him what he was thinking.

Mr. Maphalala veered off toward the office, while Sarah went ahead of them into the lounge. As they entered, everyone turned to stare, eyes roaming up and down their bodies.

"My," Grace said, "the students did a lovely job. You both look so... so..."

"Authentic?" Meg asked, smiling at Sarah and sitting.

Percy cocked his head one way, the other. "In a way, perhaps, but I might say more interesting than authentic?"

"What do you mean?" Joseph asked.

"You know," head cocked again, "interesting."

"Well, it's not something we would have done ourselves," Meg said. "Sarah told me it's because the students wanted to do something special for us, and that's really nice. We do feel honored."

"Definitely," Brian said.

"But it *is* embarrassing," Meg said. "I wish it wasn't only us."

"There is no reason to feel that way," Grace said. "You are American. No one else here is. In fact, many of us are traditional—how should I say—rivals of the Swazis and could never be honored as one of them. You, on the other hand..."

"Are harmless?" Brian said.

Grace smiled and looked down, as did everyone but Percy, who said, "I do not think anyone believes that, but America does not have the same history, the same relationship, with Swazis as the Zulus, for example, or the Xhosa or other groups in the area. Less is known about Americans, so you have had less opportunity for people to misunderstand you. Hence, you have been chosen and we have not, just as she said."

"Grace," Grace said, "not she."

Percy bowed toward her. "Grace it is then."

"Time to go," Glory said from the doorway. "Closing will begin soon."

The ceremony was held in the same room where she'd been dressed. They filed through the doorway, and Mr. Maphalala directed them to a row of chairs under garlands of colored chalk flowers, vines, gourds, mealies, finger bananas, mangoes, a crocodile, bundles of reeds surrounding signs in empty spaces to either side announcing HOME GO!! HOME GO!!

Students filled benches in the middle of the room, eyes bright, hands covering their mouths as they whispered to each other, some smiling but not laughing at Brian and her. Harry Philips sat alone at the back of the student section, hands clasped around a crossed knee, camera dangling from his neck.

Once faculty had taken their seats and adjusted themselves, Mr. Dube rose at the front of the room to address the assembly, a single row of people behind him, none of whom she recognized.

He first welcomed everyone to the gathering. Not only was it the end of the final term of the school year (cheers)—he wished all students a pleasant time away and the greatest success on their exam results; it was his desire that every deserving student be rewarded for their seriousness and hard work—but it was also a time he wanted to thank Mr. and Mrs. Bernard, who would soon be returning to their home in America (applause and groans). In addition, he wanted to thank representatives of the king, the queen mother, the local headman, the Ministry of Education and the Ministry of Justice for joining them on this special day.

While Mr. Dube took a moment to explain events to follow, her attention focused on the photograph on the opposite wall of the king resplendent in his traditional dress, the red lourie feather nestled at the back of his head. She'd once heard—or maybe read somewhere—that if you take away a person's personhood, all you have left is a body, an object you can imagine to be whatever you want, to dress however you want, to use however you want. As she looked around at the king, herself, Brian, Mr. Dube, the faculty, the students, even Harry Philips, it dawned on her how like dolls they were—everyone everywhere being controlled by everyone else. Dressed, as it were, played with, being made a Swazi for a day. Or would it last longer than that? What would happen tonight when she took the clothes off? What would happen if Sarah were to put them on? Would she want to? Could she, even if she did? Or was the line between Swazis and Zulus so deep it truly couldn't be crossed? Did something like that exist between her and Sarah that neither of them had ever acknowledged? Was it deeper now that she was an honorary Swazi and Sarah was not?

"Earth to Meg," Brian said, taking her by the arm to help her stand as Percy directed the national anthem.

Mr. Dube followed Mr. Maphalala's invocation by recounting how excited he had been to learn that two American Peace Corps volunteers had been assigned to his school. How anxious he then became as he thought about having them—he knew little about Americans: were they like the British? would they fit in at Lobamba? would they be good teachers?—so many questions. He told of his relief when Mr. and Mrs. Bernard arrived and he could immediately sense their enthusiasm and their seriousness about teaching. He said how pleasant it had been to work with them the past two years and how he truly wished they had decided to stay longer but understood why they did not. From the corner of her eye, she caught Brian glancing at her but didn't face him. Mr. Dube continued by saying how much he and everyone at the school appreciated their efforts and contributions to the future of Swaziland by helping educate its children. *Hambani kahle.* Go well. (Cheers and applause.)

Mr. Dube turned to those seated behind him and asked if anyone wanted to add to what he'd said. They smiled and shook their heads. He looked at Brian and Meg and asked if they had comments they would like to make, which meant of course that one or both of them should say something.

She was relieved when Brian stood. He turned and bowed in acknowledgment to the row of dignitaries, to Mr. Dube, teachers, students, Harry Philips. He thanked everyone for being there to help celebrate a wonderful day. He was sure he spoke for Mrs. Bernard as well in saying how honored they felt, how genuinely touched though humbled they were by the attention shown them, since in the end it was the students, Mr. Dube and their fellow teachers who should be honored and recognized most. He applauded them. Students, he said, were the main reason they'd come to Swaziland in the first place, and they were the ones who helped make their time in the country so meaningful to them. They and the kind, generous, accepting people they'd met. The friends they'd made. They'd had the experience of a lifetime—a quick glance at Meg, who studied her bare feet—and had learned far more than they could possibly have taught in return. Swaziland and its people would remain in their hearts forever. Thankyou thankyou thankyou, he said, hand to his chest and bowing again to all points in the room.

Cheers and applause.

Brian sat and Mr. Dube stood to announce that tea and treats would be available after the ceremony in the teachers' lounge.

In closing, Percy led them in a song sung in siSwati that wished a traveler a safe and peaceful, though fruitful, journey, which he later told them he thought was especially appropriate for the occasion.

Harry Philips stood back while she and Brian personally thanked everyone for coming. When they reached the group of faculty members still there, Harry Philips said he would like to take a picture of all of them together, Mr. Dube included, if no one minded. Hearing no objections, he arranged them in a single row, Meg and Brian in the middle, Mr. Dube next to Brian, Sarah next to Meg, and so on down the line. Sarah took Meg's hand in hers, giving a light squeeze of recognition, and continued holding it as friends there of any age did, men included, until Harry Philips finished and asked Meg and Brian to go outside with him. There he took even more pictures of them with one after another group of students, with Glory Khoza, and finally one of them alone in front of the school veranda, awash in the high African sun.

He told them he was sorry to rush off but before he did, he wanted to say goodbye and wish them well. He knew that, even at home, there were going to be some rough times ahead—not just about what happened here but, well, the war and all that. He would be thinking of them. He hoped he would get to see them again before they left, but that might not work out. Anyway, no matter what, he would make sure they got copies of the pictures he'd just taken. He shook each of their hands and said how nice it would be if they kept in touch, even though he understood all too well how often even the best intentions got waylaid. And the longer you didn't follow through with those intentions, the easier it was to ignore them. He would do his best to hold up his end of things. They said they would, too, and Meg watched as Harry Philips passed out of sight around the corner of the building, without looking back. Until that moment, she hadn't quite realized the full extent of what was happening. She glanced into the vestibule but decided with Brian's agreement not to join the others.

A week or so later Glory, who still worked Tuesdays and Thursdays even though school was not in session, hand-delivered to their house a manila envelope that had arrived in that day's post. It was from Harry Philips, but Meg decided to wait to look at it until Glory had left, which Meg thought would never happen. She chattered on and on, seemingly about anything that came to mind, all the while smiling, pacing around the room, hands fluttering to smooth her hair or her skirt or to straighten a stack of books to be packed. Meg finally stood and walked her toward the kitchen door, stopped and, hand to Glory's shoulder, said goodbye.

Slicing open the manila envelope, she dumped out another, smaller one with a note clipped to it:

As promised. Enjoy. HP.

She spread the photos in no particular order in front of her and scanned them, maybe 15 in all, before starting over again from the top to take a longer look.

What struck her most was the two of them at the center of each, so blanched compared to everyone else. But rather than fading into the background, they seemed to stand out even more, a sea of joyful beings swirling around them, nearly all of whom she recognized and nearly all of whom she could call by name. She spread her hands across the pictures, as if to gather the life present there, but instead felt only the glossy finish of the paper.

Was that the moment the hole opened, and in 20 or 30 or 50 years she would no longer remember names or recognize faces, her recollections dissolving into time as surely as the photos back into light itself, except for the one image not on the table but in her mind she knew would remain there always, rough and vivid as a scar?

ROUNDFIRE
BOOKS

FICTION

Historical fiction that lives

Put simply, we publish great stories. Whether it's literary or
popular, a gentle tale or a pulsating thriller, the connecting theme
in all Roundfire fiction titles is that once you pick them up you
won't want to put them down.
If you have enjoyed this book, why not tell other readers by
posting a review on your preferred book site.

Recent bestsellers from Roundfire are:

The Bookseller's Sonnets
Andi Rosenthal

The Bookseller's Sonnets intertwines three love stories with a tale of religious identity and mystery spanning five hundred years and three countries.

Paperback: 978-1-84694-342-3 ebook: 978-184694-626-4

Birds of the Nile
An Egyptian Adventure
N.E. David

Ex-diplomat Michael Blake wanted a quiet birding trip up the Nile – he wasn't expecting a revolution.

Paperback: 978-1-78279-158-4 ebook: 978-1-78279-157-7

Blood Profit$
The Lithium Conspiracy
J. Victor Tomaszek, James N. Patrick, Sr.

The blood of the many for the profits of the few... *Blood Profit$* will take you into the cigar-smoke-filled room where American policy and laws are really made.

Paperback: 978-1-78279-483-7 ebook: 978-1-78279-277-2

The Burden
A Family Saga
N.E. David

Frank will do anything to keep his mother and father apart. But he's carrying baggage – and it might just weigh him down ...

Paperback: 978-1-78279-936-8 ebook: 978-1-78279-937-5

The Cause

Roderick Vincent

The second American Revolution will be a fire lit from an internal spark.

Paperback: 978-1-78279-763-0 ebook: 978-1-78279-762-3

Don't Drink and Fly

The Story of Bernice O'Hanlon: Part One

Cathie Devitt

Bernice is a witch living in Glasgow. She loses her way in her life and wanders off the beaten track looking for the garden of enlightenment.

Paperback: 978-1-78279-016-7 ebook: 978-1-78279-015-0

Gag

Melissa Unger

One rainy afternoon in a Brooklyn diner, Peter Howland punctures an egg with his fork. Repulsed, Peter pushes the plate away and never eats again.

Paperback: 978-1-78279-564-3 ebook: 978-1-78279-563-6

The Master Yeshua

The Undiscovered Gospel of Joseph

Joyce Luck

Jesus is not who you think he is. The year is 75 CE. Joseph ben Jude is frail and ailing, but he has a prophecy to fulfil …

Paperback: 978-1-78279-974-0 ebook: 978-1-78279-975-7

On the Far Side, There's a Boy
Paula Coston
Martine Haslett, a thirty-something 1980s woman, plays hard
on the fringes of the London drag club scene until one night
which prompts her to sign up to a charity. She writes to a
young Sri Lankan boy, with consequences far and long.
Paperback: 978-1-78279-574-2 ebook: 978-1-78279-573-5

Tuareg
Alberto Vazquez-Figueroa
With over 5 million copies sold worldwide, *Tuareg* is a classic
adventure story from best-selling author Alberto Vazquez-
Figueroa, about honour, revenge and a clash of cultures.
Paperback: 978-1-84694-192-4

Readers of ebooks can buy or view any of these bestsellers by
clicking on the live link in the title. Most titles are published
in paperback and as an ebook. Paperbacks are available in
traditional bookshops. Both print and ebook formats are
available online.

Find more titles and sign up to our readers' newsletter at
http://www.johnhuntpublishing.com/fiction

Follow us on Facebook at https://www.facebook.com/
JHPfiction and Twitter at https://twitter.com/JHPFiction